The Man Who Could Fly
and Other Stories

CHICANA & CHICANO VISIONS OF THE AMÉRICAS

CHICANA & CHICANO VISIONS OF THE AMÉRICAS

The Man Who Could Fly
and Other Stories

Rudolfo Anaya

UNIVERSITY OF OKLAHOMA PRESS : NORMAN

Publication of this book was made possible by the assistance of *World Literature Today*, the critically acclaimed international magazine published at the University of Oklahoma since 1927.

Library of Congress Cataloging-in-Publication Data

Anaya, Rudolfo A.
  The man who could fly and other stories / Rudolfo Anaya.
      p.   cm.—(Chicana & Chicano Visions of the Américas ; v. 5)
  ISBN 0–8061–3738–X (alk. paper)
    1. Southwestern States—Social life and customs—Fiction. 2. Mexico—Social
life and customs—Fiction. 3. Mexican Americans—Fiction. I. Title. II. Series.

PS3551.N27M36 2006
813'.54—dc22

                                                                    2005051426

The Man Who Could Fly and Other Stories is Volume 5 in the Chicana & Chicano Visions of the Américas series.

This is a work of fiction. Names, characters, places, and incidents are either a product of the author's imagination or are used fictitiously, and any resemblance to actual events, locales, or persons, living or dead, is entirely coincidental.

The paper in this book meets the guidelines for permanence and durability of the Committee on Production Guidelines for Book Longevity of the Council on Library Resources. ∞

1 2 3 4 5 6 7 8 9 10

ALSO BY RUDOLFO ANAYA

Bless Me, Ultima
Heart of Aztlan
Tortuga
Alburquerque
Zia Summer
Rio Grande Fall
Shaman Winter
Jemez Spring
Jalamanta
Serafina's Stories
Elegy on the Death of César Chávez

CHILDREN'S BOOKS

The Farolitos of Christmas
Road Runner's Dance
The Santero's Miracle

For Patricia, my wife

*She is always my first reader, and when she gives a thumbs up
I know I'm on the right track.*

Contents

Preface

How does a short story begin? For me it starts with an image. The image, which is the heart of the short story, usually comes full blown. Suddenly it's there, and instinct tells me the image should not be developed into a novel, a play, or a poem. It is a short story.

What I call the "sudden image" can be a character who appears, or a word, a scene, a face, a smell, a sound, a dream, a landscape, a history, a thought. The image urges me to write the story. There is instant illumination in the subconscious, as characters leap into consciousness, and I cannot rest until I start writing.

I am continually *thinking* stories. Even when I am working on a novel, the images for short stories keep coming. When the image is very forceful, I have to put aside what I am doing and write the story. Sometimes the images of stories become part of a novel, but most often the short story has its own organic unity. In between drafts of a novel is a good time to write short stories. At such times I also write plays or poems.

Ah, so you toss off a short story to fill in the time, the reader might say. No way! One thing I have learned about writing short stories: They are difficult to capture. Short stories are special. They take patience. The image is the heart of the story, but the story is about a person. The characters who appear are persistent. I cannot just "toss them off."

Characters insist their story be told. They each have a purpose for being. I am the medium through which they come alive. Each character lives in a particular landscape and in a unique and critical time. A world of rhythm, cadence, and dialogue has to be developed around the character. Thus the story creates its own world, a universe that lasts a particular length of time. This is why it takes patience to get a story right. And practice.

The story becomes not only a fiction but a myth, as do all stories from the oral traditions of the past. From Homer on down, the stories create myths to live by. And to love by.

I am intensely interested in the role of the storyteller as myth-maker. "A Story" and "B. Traven Is Alive and Well in Cuernavaca" deal with the process of writing. This theme of the writer in search of a story and what it means to him are ingredients in several of my stories.

Landscape often has the force of character in my stories. I was born and raised in eastern New Mexico, and so the llano—that Spanish word that describes the plains of that area—haunts me. The landscape is as important as the people, and it too demands that its story be told. One day the face of a sad young woman suddenly appeared to me. She was staring out the window of one of those old, lonely adobe homes on the llano. That is all I saw, her face and the parted curtain, but the image was so intriguing that it forced me to write "The Silence of the Llano." Around the woman swirled the landscape I knew as a boy.

My wife and I have traveled widely in Mexico. The myths of Mexico are among the most interesting in the world. We spent many summers in Cuernavaca at the lovely quinta of Ana Rosinski. Mexico was not only magical, it was revolutionary. What a mine of inspiration for a writer! I met people like Jerónimo, the gardener in "Jerónimo's Journey." Well, the real gardener was only the inspiration; the composition of the story was up to me. Those flashes of insight we call epiphanies are sparks that constantly fill my days. But the writer must bring the passion of the psyche to the writing process.

One summer in Cuernavaca, B. Traven's past (his ghost) came alive through a series of events, and thus the story of what a writer seeks was born. That is why I say Mexico is magical, because the spirit of the past fuses with the present. Perhaps like Rosario in "The Village That the Gods Painted Yellow," I went looking for my lost faith in Mexico, and I found it. One of the many ancient places I visited was Uxmal. There I was led by a guide—a dwarf—through the ruins, and thus the story came to be.

I lectured in Israel, and from that brief visit came "Absalom." The story evolved from the place names, the men, especially the women, the desert. I visited Machu Picchu, and from that history and landscape was born "Message from the Inca."

The storyteller needs a guide into the hell and heaven of creativity, the subconscious. My characters become my guides. I have learned to trust my characters. They have been in that dark underworld. Writing their stories, I bring them into the realm of light.

The reader's response to the stories is most important. The stories now belong to the reader. They have served me as I wrote and rewrote them, crafting them to my personal cadences as best I could. Now I hope they serve the reader, in life and in love.

In the end the story has to speak for itself. In each story is a voice that is not the author's. The story becomes its own entity. Its purpose can be studied but never fully known. All artistic endeavors are like that: understandable, enjoyable, puzzling, challenging, but always partly shrouded in mystery. The mystery of life and good stories moves us forward.

That is the secret of stories. Like prisms they reflect parts of the eternal mystery, they lend a light in the darkness, and we hope that when the reading is done, we will sigh and say, "Yes, that's the way it is."

I published some of my early short stories in *The Silence of the Llano*, a book long out of print. I am grateful to everyone who worked on this collection, including the University of Oklahoma Press staff and Melanie Mallon, for her careful editing. Thanks to Robert Con-Davis Undiano, the executive director of *World Literature Today*, this collection is possible. Without his insistence and assistance, the stories would not be bound in this volume. Gracias, Roberto!

The Man Who Could Fly
and Other Stories

The Road to Platero

Everyone in the village knows that a ghost rides the road to Platero. Everyone watches, everyone waits, and at night we can hear the hoofbeats of the caballero's horse as he rides on that lonely road. During the long, hot days, my mother sings sad lullabies while she sits by the window and stares down the deserted road. She sighs when she sings, and she holds me on her lap and draws me close. I can feel the gentle pounding of her heart when she tells me that the caballero who haunts the road to Platero is the ghost of her father.

"Oh, he was a handsome man," she sings to me and tells me stories of the past, tales of her youth, times when Platero was the most thriving and beautiful village on the entire llano. "Then death came," she sighs. "Love came, death came, then you were born, my little son."

The wind dies at dusk. My mother's hands dart like nervous birds as she moves around the kitchen, touching things absent-mindedly. Her breath quickens, and from time to time she stops to listen. The vaqueros of Platero are returning from the llano. In the distance we can hear the thunder of their hot and tired horses. The other women of the village go to their windows and look out into the desolate llano. They know their men are coming, hungry from a long day's work, riding hard so that they will not see the ghost horseman who haunts the road.

My father rides with the vaqueros. For him the road is haunted, and every day I hear him curse God and torment his horse with whip and spur. He must drink for courage to ride that stretch of road where, my mother says, he killed her father.

Once it was a well-traveled road, my mother says, and everyone came to her father's ranch. There were good times and fiestas for every occasion. Now only these wild and brawling man-creatures ride the road to Platero.

"My father was a gentle man," she tells me, "a real caballero. All the people loved him. Oh, someday you will know the truth, my little one. He was a man of honor, a proud man. He rode so tall and noble. The women of Platero pretended to sweep their doorsteps when he rode by, but they really came out to admire him. And he would smile and tip his sombrero, then he would ride home to me. I was his jewel, his angel, his only daughter."

She tells me stories I have heard many times before, and I see how the memories make her heart pound. Purple veins rise on her temples, and I can almost see the images of violence and love that stir in her blood. Sometimes terrible dreams trouble my sleep, and I, too, am filled with fear.

"This man, this beast, destroyed the dreams of my father!" she cries, and her anguish and fury make my blood run cold. I see her reach for the knife on the table. She raises it high. "I will keep this near my heart, my father, and I will do your will. There is no pride nor honor left in Platero." Then she turns to me and whispers, "I submitted to that beast only to protect you, my son, but you are a man like any other man. Will you, too, raise your spurs and rake your mother's flanks when you are grown?" She laughs bitterly. "Yes, we are the slaves of our fathers, our husbands, our sons. And you, my little one, my life, you will grow to be a man."

The vaqueros of Platero arrive like a whirlwind. In the corral the mares paw the ground nervously as the stallions enter, the men laugh and call out, then there is silence. We wait; his footsteps sound on the porch, his spurs jingle, my mother makes the sign of the cross on her forehead. Her eyes stare with cold determination, then a strange smile curls her lips. "I loved him once," she whispers, and her trembling hands hide the knife. He enters and stands looking at her. He only looks at me to curse me. Then he sits, unbuckles his spurs, raises them, and runs them slowly across his stubbled cheek.

"What evil have you been up to, my Carmelita?" He grins and taunts her. "What lies have you been telling your son?"

"I tell him of the man who rides a red stallion to Platero," she answers calmly.

He stands and shouts. "It is not a man! It is a devil!"

"He will return to Platero," she insists. I crawl into a corner, where I watch and make no noise. I am afraid of his wrath, and now I fear her will.

"You evil woman," he accuses. "Can you tell him the truth? I will tell him who mounted his mother!"

"No!" she cries. "No! He is innocent. He knows nothing. Can't we forget the past?" She beckons him with her lovely hands. Of all the women in Platero, my mother is the youngest. She is thin, her hair is long and black, her skin is smooth. From the porch I have seen the vaqueros admire the sleek, beautiful mares, and I have seen them look at my mother.

He laughs and picks up his bottle. "So you want to play the game," he sneers. "Come and pull off my boots."

My mother hurries to help him with his boots. Outside, the stallions circle the mares; I hear them cry in the corral.

The moon hangs pallid in the dark sky. It bathes the black mesa, and shadows move like witches. My mother rises, sweat covering her body. She shivers as she parts the curtains and looks into the darkness. In the small adobe homes around us other women also rise from their labors and peer into the night. They watch the pale moonlight cast its spell while their men sleep. My mother comes to me and covers me with a quilt. She holds me, and we listen in silence for the sound of the caballero who rides toward Platero.

"Father," my mother whispers. "I swear to you, you will have your peace and rest. I will avenge."

In the morning the vaqueros leave. It has been this way since I can remember. It is cool inside our adobe home before the strong sun comes to bake the land. My mother sweeps the floor; beads of perspiration wet her face. She hums a lullaby for me while she works. She opens the door to let in the cool morning breeze. "To air our home of the evil of the night," she says. She gazes at the houses scattered along the dusty road and yearns to visit with the other women, but she cannot. They know the secret she keeps from me. They nod in greeting, that is all, and watch her in silence. Only one woman does not work. She sits by her door in the shade of a purple-plumed tamarisk and smokes cigarettes. She laughs softly when she sees my mother.

In the afternoon the wind rises, whipping the whirlwinds across the bare earth. My mother says they are the work of the devil. Sometimes huge sandstorms envelop the land, our house shudders, the day turns into night. Then my mother holds me close and whispers many things, but never the secret that causes so much anguish in her heart.

Every day the women wait in the oppressive heat, waiting for their men to return. Sometimes I see the faces of other children at the dark windows, pale, drawn faces, and sad eyes, which seem to bear the curse that revolves around me and my mother. There is no hope in Platero, there is only the waiting for the vaqueros as they come stinging their horses with their cruel whips and spurring blood from the creatures' soft flanks.

Long before my mother whispers to me, I know my father is coming. She moves nervously, and the cup she is holding falls and shatters on the floor. She stoops and gathers the broken pieces. "Fragments of the past," she murmurs as she stares at them. She sobs gently. The cup was a gift from her father, and every year on her birthday he would take it from the cupboard, fill it with wine, and drink to her health and beauty. He was never displeased that he had no sons; his dream was that she would be a great lady, the woman who would inherit all the lands of Platero.

"He thought time was his ally and he would live forever," she cries, "but he was wrong. Now there is only you, my son."

She dries her eyes with her apron and moves to the window to look into the gathering, somber dusk. "The nighthawks are flying low," she says. "It will rain tonight." The ground reverberates with hoofbeats. We hear shouts and the sharp crack of whips, then the whistle of the vaqueros as they unsaddle their horses and turn them loose in the corral. My mother shudders, and I know her resolution wavers when she catches sight of him.

On the portal I hear his sharp spurs jingle; then the door opens, and he fills the house like a howling wind, his harsh laughter echoing in the room.

"Ah, my Carmelita," he says, "have you been doing penance for your sins?"

My mother lights the farol; in its light the shadows rise and move like ghosts. Outside, the dark rumbles with the approaching storm. My father eats and drinks while we wait, and when he is done, he grabs her arm as she passes. He pulls her into the room beyond the kitchen, and I hear her cries and groans. I turn to see the lightning flash at the window; the rain falls in torrents, and I feel the dread that fills the night.

"There is still time," I hear her say. "Forgiveness will wash away all these years of torture, the ghost that haunts you."

His laughter is as savage as the thunder.

"We can forget the past," she prays, and I know that she has closed her eyes to imagine him as she saw him the first time he rode into the village.

"No, my Carmelita," he says with hate in his voice, "your father made sure that we could never forget the past."

"Forgive," my mother pleads.

"Forgive? Oh no, your sin is too dark to be forgiven," he taunts her. "Your sin is the sin of hell, and you will do penance by serving me forever. Only your penance can keep away that devil that rides the road at night."

He goes to the window to smoke and drink. The lightning flashes, and I see his face. For the first time I see that he is afraid of the ghostly caballero who nightly circles Platero. He curses the coyotes that cry fearfully in the hills, calling them witches of the devil. In her bed my mother rocks back and forth, her vacant eyes staring into the past. She knows what she must do.

When he is finished drinking, he throws the bottle aside and goes to stand over her. He is never done with his tormenting. He twists his hand into her hair and pulls her to her feet.

"I killed your father for this worthless land!" he shouts. "But I made the mistake of not killing him sooner." He looks at me, then savagely flings her across the room. "Whore!" he spits, then opens the door and moves into the night. "Ghost of Platero!" he shouts at the darkness. "Take your daughter!" We hear him laughing as he goes to the woman of the tamarisk tree.

The storm has passed. Now only gentle drops of rain drum on the roof. My mother wraps a blanket around her shoulders and clasps me to her side. "Platero is hell, my little one," she says as we go to the window. The night is silver with moonlight. Somewhere a woman laughs in the dark. I lie quietly and try to sleep, but not even my mother's gentle caress can keep away the monsters that ride into my dreams.

"Sleep, my little angel," she sings, "my father returns to avenge us." And she sings of the caballero who was her father, he who rode proud and tall on a red stallion.

Late in the night my father returns, his face ashen with fear. "I saw him," he cries, "I swear I saw him! Always before, it was only a shadow, but tonight I saw him!"

"He is dead," my mother moans.

"Damn you! You were not worth the killing!" he curses her.

She screams as if in pain. "Oh let me rest! Torment me no more!"

"He is out there!" my father shouts as he glances out the window, a ring of fear in his voice. "He haunts the road!"

"He comes to avenge us," my mother says coldly. I see her hands clutch the dagger near her heart.

"Let him come," my father cries, "I killed him once; I will kill him again."

"Murderer!" my mother screams, and instantly he is on her, striking hard, sending her crashing to the floor. He unwinds his whip and cracks it over her.

"Whore! Witch!" He fouls the air with curses. "It is you whose sin brings the ghost of hell to our doorstep. You will be happy with that devil! Come! Go with him!"

He grabs her hair and jerks her to her feet. "Go!" He laughs as he pushes her across the room to the door. Outside the door, the horseman has arrived. My mother smiles; her eyes light up. "He has come," she cries, and without hesitation she takes the dagger and strikes. My father gasps as the steel cuts through his chest; terror contorts his face.

"Now for you, my son!" my mother cries and strikes again.

"Witch!" he groans and lifts his sharp spurs and slashes at her. My mother cries out as the spurs cut a deep gash along her throat. Her blood gushes out, mixing with his as he stumbles forward. "Rest in hell!" he hisses and slashes again, and together they fall to the floor, still striking at each other until there is no strength left and their bodies lie still.

It is done, the torment is done. I feel death enter the room. Strangely, a peace seems to settle over them as they lie in each other's arms. Outside, the wind dies, and the streets of the village are quiet. The women of Platero sleep, a restless sleep. In the corral the mares shift uneasily and cry in the dark. The horseman who haunted the road is gone, and only the gentle moonlight shimmers on the road to Platero.

Children of the Desert

He had worked the oil fields of south Texas for as long as he could remember. Abandoned as a child, he was passed from family to family until he was old enough to work. He grew up living and breathing the desert, but never trusting it. He sometimes drove into the desert alone, not looking for anything in particular, perhaps testing some inner fear he felt of the vast landscape. Sometimes he would find sun-bleached bones, and he would feel compelled to take one back to his trailer.

Once he had seen the bodies of two Mexicans the sheriff had brought in. They had died of heat exposure in the desert. Their mouths were stuffed with sand, sand that in their last feverish moments they must have thought was water.

He could not forget the image of the two men, and after that he developed the habit of hiding plastic milk containers full of water along the desert trails he knew. The desert was merciless; without water, a man would die of thirst.

He kept to himself, but once a year at Christmastime he went to Juárez. He took the long drive across the desert to drink and to visit the brothels. It was a week in which he went crazy, drinking to excess and spending his money on the prostitutes.

When his money was gone, he would head back to the oil town, his physical yearning satisfied, but the deeper communion he had sought in the women remained unfulfilled.

One Christmas he stopped to clean up and eat at a trucker's cafe on the outskirts of El Paso. The waitress at his table was a young woman, not especially pretty, but flirtatious. She wore bright red lipstick, which contrasted with her white skin. She drew him into conversation.

He was self-conscious, but he smiled and told her he was going home. He talked about the oil town, the aluminum trailers clustered together in the desert. He had a job, he had a truck, and he lived alone.

"A man without water will die in that desert," he said and held his breath. Would she understand?

"The desert's all we got." She nodded, looking out the window, beyond the trucks and cars of the gas station to the desert, which stretched into Mexico. "It's both mother and father. Lover and brother." She was like him, an abandoned child of the desert. He looked at her and felt troubled. Why did she pay attention to him? What did she want?

She wanted to go with him. Would he take her? He had never shared his space with anyone. Only during the week in Juárez, and then he went crazy and could not remember what he had done. The women he slept with were a blur. After that week of debauchery, he would feel empty, like the unsatisfied desert.

Now a new emotion crept into his loneliness. He thought the feeling came with the sweet smell of her perfume, with her red lips and blue eyes. Her skin was white, and he saw the rise and fall of her breasts beneath her blouse. He wanted to touch her.

"I can't take you," he mumbled. He walked out and she followed.

"Why not?" she asked. She squinted in the bright sun as she looked at him. "I can take care of your place, wash your clothes, sew, cook. You said you ain't got a woman."

No, he didn't have a woman. Did he need one? He needed something, someone.

"Get in." He nodded.

"You won't be sorry," she said. She ran back into the cafe and returned with a small, worn suitcase. "All I got's in here," she whispered and smiled.

He had never been able to say much more than a few words to any woman, but as they drove across the desert, he opened up to her. He told her about his work on the oil rigs and about the small aluminum trailer he had in the oil town. He told her how once a year he went to Juárez and became a different person, but he would give that up for her.

She had no family, so they guessed they belonged together. She was happy with the trailer, happy to belong.

He was happy too; now he whistled on the way to work. He gave up the old habit of hiding the containers full of water, and he began to forget where the precious water lay hidden.

The other workers joked about him. The older men said they had never seen him so happy, and it must be because he was getting it regular now. Get your young wife pregnant, they said, otherwise she might start running around. They knew the women of the oil town were lonely. There was nothing for the women to do in the desert, and they spent a lot of time alone. Sometimes three or four of them gathered to talk or exchange recipes or to play cards. Usually they drank, and then they cursed their lives in the lonely and merciless desert.

The men didn't want their wives to form these groups. On those days when dinner wasn't ready, the men argued with their wives, and sometimes they fought. It was better to have the women stay at home, alone, not getting fancy ideas from the neighbor ladies, each man thought. In preserving that false peace, each woman was driven deeper into loneliness.

He thought about a baby, but he didn't mention it to her. The child would be an extension of something that happened when they made love. That was what he felt, and it provided a small measure of contentment.

He wondered if she thought of a child. She said nothing; she seemed happy. There was no sign of pregnancy, and he grew more intense, driving deeper into her flesh to deposit his fluid of life, water he hid in her desert. But she, like the desert, was never satisfied. She took pleasure from his emptying in her, but he had nothing to show for his possession. She lay in bed when he was done, glowing with the sweat of their love.

She is the desert, he thought. She thrives on the heat and sweat.

"I love the heat," she had told him once, and what she said mystified him. The heat of the desert was death. The men with sand stuffed in their mouths, the bleached bones of those who had died there.

One day, after making love, he remembered the earrings he had found in the sand. The glitter of gold and the red rubies had caught his attention. Someone had lost her way, a woman. The sheriff found dead people out there all the time. Mexicans coming across to look for work, looking for a better life. The Promised Land.

He had not told her of the earrings. He felt them in his pocket. Would he give them to her someday?

"Come here," she whispered and drew him to bed to make love, her words like the cry of the doves when they came to drink water. Her movements beneath him were urgent, searching for her relief. He was still thinking of the earrings when he tasted sand in his mouth.

He felt the hair rise along his back, and he drew away. She moaned and smiled, awash in the convulsion that swept over her. Sweat glistened on her breasts and stomach. She kept her eyes closed as she caressed herself, slowly running her hands between her breasts, along her flat stomach.

"Hotter than hell," he said and lit a cigarette.

She was still out there, in the space the orgasm created. The soft sounds she made irritated him.

"You sound like a cat," he said.

"It's just 'cause you make me feel so good," she answered. "When you're on me, a bubble forms right here, between us. I can feel it. I hold you tight so the bubble won't escape. Here. Feel."

He felt sand.

She held on to him even after he was spent. She held tight even when he was choking for air. The desert swept over him and covered his mouth with sand. At that moment he always cried out. Why did fear and pleasure come together?

"You're crazy," he said.

"I can feel it," she murmured.

He looked out the window at the hot, burning land. Mirages formed in the distance, green trees and the blue shimmer of water. An oasis. Hell, he knew there wasn't water out there. A mirage. Nothing. Death. Like the bubble, sucking you in.

"Crazy woman," he repeated. There she was, covered with sweat and rubbing herself, in dreamland, and the trailer was hot as an oven.

"It's hotter than hell!" he shouted, got up, and flipped on the air conditioner.

"I like it hot," she said.

He looked at her. She was caressing the spot where she said the bubble formed. Her nails were red against her white skin. Her breasts were full, round, crowned with pink nipples.

Sweat dripped from his armpits, trickled down his ribs. He thought of the pile of bones around the side of the trailer, bones he had collected over the years.

"What do you think about when you feel that bubble?" he asked.

"It's a secret," she answered.

A secret, he thought. A fucking secret. The men were right—a young wife shouldn't be running around with the other women. Getting ideas. He knew she went into town with them, drove the seventy miles just to sit in the cool movie house. Hell, they probably went drinking.

"I don't want you hanging around with the women. Damn floozies."

She looked at him. "They're not floozies."

"You do what I say!" he shouted, and kicked the small table near him. The red plastic flowers crashed to the floor.

"Get rid of your crazy ideas," he said and fell down on her, to crush away the secret of the bubble. But he couldn't do it. The irritation he felt made him impotent.

"You're hurting me," she said and struggled away.

He stood over her, trying to catch his breath, trying to understand what was happening. Her toenails were painted red. Red like the fruit of the cactus. Her lips were red, the curtains were red, the dress was red, even the plastic flowers were red. And the earrings were red. He stumbled to the sink to splash water on his face.

"You okay?" she asked.

The water was gritty. His hands trembled.

"You like it here, because of the bubble," he said.

"We both like it here," she answered. "Didn't I tell you, we're children of the desert."

He looked out the window over the sink. There was nothing. Nothing. Only heat and sand. He had forgotten where he had hidden the water, or where he had found the earrings. Now he had nothing. He was at the mercy of the desert.

"There is no bubble!" he shouted at her and struck out. The slap caught her flush across the mouth. Blood oozed from her lips.

"There is," she insisted, fighting back the pain. "It's here, between us. It's the most beautiful feeling on earth. There's no harm in it!"

Her cry rang in his ears long after he left the trailer. In the desert he could hear the sound of her voice, see the red of her lips. He drove deep into the desert, away from her. But now being alone frightened him. He lost his way, panic sweeping over him like a suffocating sandstorm.

He had never before been lost. He stopped at an arroyo he thought he knew and tore into the sand until his hands bled, but he couldn't find any of his water containers. He remembered the men with their mouths full of sand, their eyes eaten out by the vultures. In that moment of fear, his mother spoke to him, her red lips taunting him. He saw her clearly, the gold earrings dangling.

Finally, he found his way back, exhausted and trembling. A terrible fear made him shiver. He drank all night and the following day.

He used her roughly in a brutal attempt to destroy the images that haunted him. "No more bubble!" he insisted when he was done. "It's gone!" he shouted triumphantly.

But what was that pocket of air he had killed? The child he had wished for? The secret she hid from him? His failure to understand? And why had he seen his mother in the desert? The questions haunted him.

She withdrew, cowering in fear. He had become a man she did not know. He used her, but now there was only the suffering. The more frantic his need, the more silent and withdrawn she became.

He went across the border to Agua Arenosa, to the whore house. He drank and went to the prostitutes until he was exhausted. When his money was gone he argued and fought, and the cantinero threw him out in the street.

He sat in the dirt, a bitter taste in his mouth. Around him the town was deserted. A whirlwind swirled down the street, crying like a mourning woman.

He was lost in that wailing wind. Dust stung his eyes; he tasted it in his mouth.

He turned to an old woman who sat by the door of the cantina. Old and wrinkled and dirty, she was called into the cantina only to test the men before they went to the whores. He reached out and grabbed her.

"Demonio!" she cried and struggled to pull away. "Deja me ir, Diablo!"

"No! No! I won't hurt you!" he cried. "I won't hurt you. I only want to know! Inside! Aquí!" he shouted and pointed to his chest, the place where emptiness gnawed at his heart.

His cry was one of torment. The old woman grew calm. She had seen eyes like his before. The devil of the desert was in the man. He had seen death, or he was about to die.

"Aquí," she said. "Corazon."

Heart? His heart was dry. He had opened his heart, and the desert had swept in.

"Mira, hijo," the woman said kindly. She drew a line on the dirt. She spit to one side and a ball of mud formed from the dirt and the spittle. "Hombre," she said.

She spit to the other side. "Mujer," she said.

Then she spit on the line, and a perfect ball of wet earth formed. "Semilla." She smiled.

She pushed the two balls toward the one in the middle, and the three dissolved into one.

"Amor," she said and moved away.

The seed was love. It lay between the man and the woman. It belonged to both. It was like a child growing in the belly, or like the bubble his lover caressed.

Even in the sand the seed of love could grow. He reached into his pocket and found the gold earrings with the red rubies. He looked at them, feeling the great burden of the past. Whatever was out there in the desert would haunt him no more, and he threw the earrings as far as he could. For a moment they glistened in the sun, then disappeared into the sand.

He drove home, careening down the road, a speck in the vast bowl of desert and sky. He drove fast, full of a new urgency to see her. Near the trailer he crossed an arroyo, the front tires caught in the sand, the truck flipped over, and he was thrown out.

For some time he lay unconscious, then awoke to a sharp pain in his lungs. When he spit he saw the red stain of blood. But he could not rest until he saw her and told her what he had discovered.

Holding his side, he ran to the trailer, calling her name. She was not there when he arrived. The trailer was empty.

He slumped to the ground by the door. The pain was sharp in his chest, he could not breathe, but he felt a calmness. Around him the desert was a space opening and receding. Her bubble. A space to hold a seed. He looked across the silent sand and understood.

The Village That
the Gods Painted Yellow

It is there, the Natives whispered, just south of Uxmal, the village that the gods painted yellow. He heard the legend in the villages, in the cantinas, in the mercados; the stories were told wherever the Indians gathered, and the longer he stayed in Yucatán the more often he heard of the village. When the Indians spoke about the village, their dark eyes lit up and they nodded in acknowledgment, then, because he was a stranger in their midst, they would avert their eyes, and a heavy silence would fall over the group.

"It is only one more legend in a land of legends," he said to himself, as he boarded the bus at Mérida to go to Uxmal, and the stories are as countless as the Maya ruins that dot all of Guatemala and Yucatán. He found a seat by a window, huddled into himself, and closed his eyes. I have grown tired of following the legends, he thought. I have grown cynical in my quest.

Why, then, was he going to Uxmal? It was late December, the day of the winter solstice. All over Mexico and Central America there were a hundred more interesting places, villages where old ceremonies in honor of the dying sun would be reenacted, clothed by the thin veneer of Christianity to be sure, but he knew that at the core of every ceremony lay the same values and thought that were inherent in the original ancient ritual. That is what did not change, the purpose of the ceremony. The surfaces changed as the culture changed, but he always sensed wrapped within the ritual a moment so pregnant with meaning and power that he trembled, as if he were a witness to an act of great mystery. But the true revelation he sought in those moments, the miraculous epiphanies the Natives experienced, had never come to him. He had attended many of the ceremonies, but always he had been only the observer, never feeling the spiritual elation or revelation the ceremony intended to induce.

As the bus chugged up the small, unimpressive hills near Uxmal, he dozed and dreamed again of the ancient ruins he had haunted in search of a clue to the mystery of time and life in the new world. His first trip had been to the desert ruins at Casas Grandes in northern Mexico; a year later he was at Teotihuacán where he scrambled up the Pyramid of the Sun just like all the other tourists who came from Mexico City. But it was not really until he went to Tula that he first felt a little of the aura and mystery of an ancient, sacred place. Gradually he worked his way south into the land of the Maya, to Copán, Quiriguá, Palenque, Tikal, Tulum, Chichén Itzá, and today, on the day of the solstice, Uxmal. "Ooshmal," the very sound was like a dying breath. He gasped for air in the hot, stifling bus, sat up in the seat, and peered out the window. The green jungle stretched as far as he could see. Soon they would arrive.

Uxmal of the ancient Maya, temples of exquisite beauty and haunting power, built by a people who had developed superior astronomy and mathematics. The Maya had clocked the precise movements of the Sun and Moon and planets at a time when Europe was just awakening from its dark age. Here, on the peninsula of Yucatán, one of those mysterious upsurges in the cycle of time had suddenly and brilliantly illuminated the history of humanity, and then the Spaniards had arrived and destroyed nearly everything. Now there were only legends and whispers about that ancient civilization and its secrets.

The stela at Quiriguá computes time four hundred million years into the past, a feat modern mathematicians could only achieve recently with computers and atomic clocks. He thought about this as he looked at the cultivated fields of sisal, the yuccalike agaves cultivated for twine throughout the peninsula. Time was a god to those people, no, not a god, an element of life. They scanned the heavens at night, plotted their lunar calendars, knew the exact moment of the solstices and the equinoxes, computed astronomical charts, which finally meshed the movement of the planets and stars into the movement of the birth and life of the universe itself, a spiritual possession that drove them to plot the exact moment when life first throbbed on the planet Earth. Was that what they had learned? Was that year zero, moment zero, the first spark of life coming into consciousness on a foreboding Earth? If so, at that moment and in that place lay a power far beyond the understanding of any man—there at that ceremony lies the power of the gods.

"Rosario, it is time for you to go to Uxmal," the bartender at the Hotel Isabela had said, he whose face bore a faint resemblance to the Chinese visages carved into the stela of Copán. "Here, you are wasting your time." He nodded toward the European women, the pale Swedes and Germans who had fled their frigid winter for a week at Cancún or Cozumel. They came to Mérida as an afterthought, to tour Uxmal before returning to their own cold countries.

In the afternoons Rosario went to the bar of the hotel to escape the dust and heat of the streets, to drink cold Leon Negra, and to watch the European women who came in from their tours, hot and lonely and ready for company. He went there because the bartender was Mayan, a young, handsome fellow who attracted the European women, and together they kept the women of the pale legs happy.

But the bartender had been serious, and that had surprised Rosario. "Go to Uxmal," the bartender said, "and when you go, look for Gonzalo. He knows more than any of the other guides. He will show you the greatness of the Maya. He is muy Maya."

He was right. Rosario had been wasting his time drinking beer and playing around with women. He had felt trepidation, a reluctance, but that morning he had boarded the bus, seeking neither the village nor Gonzalo, seeking only, with what little faith he had left, what he had sought everywhere else, a clue that might reveal the source of the knowledge of the ancients.

He skirted the gate and the tourists who were lined up at the refreshment stand, and he climbed the rise near the Turtle House to get a clear view of the site. It was impressive. The Pyramid of the Magician was well preserved, white limestone framed against the flat expanse of jungle and the clear blue December sky. The colors reminded him of Monte Albán. Below him he could see the ball court, beyond the Temple of the Nuns. As impressive, yes, he thought, as Chichén Itzá or Monte Albán, but there is little magic left here. He stood for a long time, hoping he would feel some vibration from the place, praying it would be more than just an impressive reconstructed Maya site, desiring to feel the same power from the earth or the heavens that the ancient builders had felt when they constructed the magnificent temple. The hot sun moved overhead, and the tourists, who had come to see Uxmal, scurried over the site like ants, pausing only to take pictures or to listen to the guides who had come with the buses and who led them around. Then, seeking shade, he moved down toward the trees near the Pyramid of the Magician. That's where he met Gonzalo.

"A'ra! A'ra!" the impish man shouted, and people gathered around him. "Here we begin the best tour of Uxmal! Come with Gonzalo and learn all the history and ancient secrets of this glorious city of the Maya!" A few tourists clustered around the guide, a gnome with a crippled leg and a hunched back. He was immaculately dressed in the white pants and shirt of the peon. His white hair floated about his dark face, and his eyes were black and piercing. The women flocked around him, and he smiled and clicked his tongue and paid them compliments. In another country and time he would have been a Pan luring shepherd maidens into hidden bowers; here, he was a dwarf who led them into the secret, shady spots of Uxmal.

"You, too," he said. "Come." He beckoned to Rosario, drawing the young man forward with his hypnotic eyes, speaking in a Mayan dialect that Rosario understood. Rosario followed the impish guide of Uxmal, who shouted, "A'ra! A'ra! Follow me, and I will disclose the secrets of Uxmal!"

And Gonzalo was good, very good in his presentation. Standing at the foot of the Pyramid of the Magician, he enthralled the women in the group by telling the old story about the pyramid being built in one night, built by a dwarf who in ancient times was a magician who had great powers.

"But why was it built?" a big-bosomed, red-haired woman asked. Gonzalo smiled and answered, "To honor the gods. All this was built to honor the gods. And the people still say that the magician is not dead, he will come again to raise new pyramids to the gods!" The women oohed and aahed while Gonzalo grinned and moved closer to one woman, a Swede, middle aged, obviously traveling alone. "You see, my friend," Gonzalo whispered, "we know very little about the ancient Maya. We can only speculate about their ways. But I am a descendant of the Maya people, and I know in my blood that the story of the old magician is true. Anthropologists and archeologists have suggested that the ruins abound with symbols for the phallus, and some have gone as far as to say the Pyramid of the Magician is a phallic symbol. And is there not some truth in this? Don't all mythologies of mankind speak of the gods who have come down to Earth to visit woman and create a new race of man? And isn't man himself filled with a need to thrust his power beyond Earth, an urge to call down the gods and do honor to them, their fathers?"

He grinned. The Swede smiled but moved away.

Rosario felt tired. He wiped the sweat from his forehead. Our friend Gonzalo is a charlatan, he thought, and wondered if it would not have been better to stay in the cantina of the hotel until the fervor and tension of the solstice and the Christmas celebration in its wake were over and done with.

"A'ra!" Gonzalo shouted to keep the group together. "Come, I will show you more secrets. Look here," he cried as he pointed at a half-circle keystone that locked an arch into place. "Other guides will tell you the ancient Maya did not know the circle. But they did. See? There is a keystone built in a half circle!"

"But why didn't they build the wheel?" asked a thin American schoolteacher. She pushed up her glasses, which kept sliding down her nose.

"The circle is holy," Gonzalo intoned, "it is a sacred symbol of the gods. The Maya were wise not to profane the circle by using its shape in a common wheel!" The teacher nodded and took notes. Others moved away to the refreshment stand. Rosario remained unmoved. He had traveled too far and seen too much to be impressed. True, the old man was a dramatic, charismatic person, and one could not help being spellbound by his strength and gestures and tone of voice, but his anecdotes were trite. As Rosario turned away, he felt the old man's hand on his arm.

"We are brothers under the sun," Gonzalo whispered, then grinned and glanced at the women. "They are poor, pale chickens coming to their brown roosters, eh?"

"I didn't come to chase after women," Rosario answered, somewhat contemptuously, but instantly felt ashamed. Hadn't he spent the past few weeks doing exactly that?

"Why did you come to Uxmal?" Gonzalo asked, his dark eyes piercing Rosario.

"I . . . I've been searching" was all Rosario could stammer in response. Gonzalo's eyes held him.

"Yes, I can see you have come to learn the magic." Gonzalo nodded. "Then follow me, and I will reveal some secrets." He turned and called the group together again. Shouting "A'ra! A'ra!" he led them to the ball court of Uxmal. Huge numbered stones and lintels lay on the ground, ready to be lifted into their original positions.

"Long before your baseball or your football was invented, the Maya played a ball game in this court. The nobles came to watch, for the game was played in honor of the sun, the Lord of Light," Gonzalo said. "When the game was done, those who had won were judged to be close to the gods, so they were made priests." He waited a moment, and when no one in the now-weary group asked about the losers, he said, "And those who lost the game were judged not to be in close contact with the gods, so their hearts were cut out and offered as sacrifices to the Sun God. That way they were really close to the gods, eh?" Gonzalo smiled.

The women nodded, but Rosario shook his head. He had heard many variations of the story. Gonzalo looked at him and scowled as he removed his straw hat and wiped his brow with a white kerchief. So, you're not impressed, his eyes seemed to say, then he nervously replaced his hat and looked up as if to judge the place of the sun in the sky. A slight twitch showed under his left eye as he turned to the group.

"We are near the end of our tour," he said, a note of anxiety in his voice, the sharp sense of control gone. "From here you can go into the Temple of the Nuns, to see the faces of those ancient rulers who were really gods who came from—" He stopped, shook his head as if in pain. "Those rulers, who because of their dress are now called nuns, they were nobles of Uxmal—but here!" He whirled suddenly and leaped onto one of the huge blocks of stone, one of the massive pieces of the huge serpentine body that had once graced the lintel of the ball court.

"See here!" he cried. "I will tell you one more story. A story the other guides do not know. Only I, Gonzalo de las Serpientes, know it, and I will tell it to you. This snake you see decorating the lintel of the ball court. Who carved this masterpiece? And why? Is it enough to know that the snake is the predominant symbol of Mesoamerica? The snake copulates like men and women, and the female gives birth to its young like a woman. It is a symbol of fertility—" His voice cracked.

Rosario shook his head and wished he had not come to Uxmal. The old man told nothing new.

"But I have my own theory," Gonzalo continued, "and I will share this secret with you." The women of the group drew closer. "No one has ever dared to say this, but I say it. The artisans of the Maya society were women! Yes, women carved the figures in the Temple of the Nuns! And the serpent of the ball court, that too was carved by women! And do you want to know why they carved so many snakes?" He grinned fiendishly, drew closer as he whispered, "It's because the old Maya were insatiable lovers!" He tossed his head back and chuckled.

The women shook their heads and moved away, some walking the trail toward the Temple of the Nuns, others back to the air-conditioned bus for a break from the mounting heat of the day. Only Rosario and the old man were left in the ball court, and Rosario was not quite sure why he had remained this long. The sun had started its descent into the afternoon, a descent that would complete the shortest day of the year, in ancient times one of the most crucial days in the solar calendar and in the religious life of the Maya.

"Come!" Gonzalo said suddenly, serious again. "We are rid of the tourists. Now is time to do our work." His eyes burned with a deep, intense power. Rosario didn't understand what he meant by "our work," but he followed the old man as he scrambled like a goat up the steep steps of the Pyramid of the Magician. "A'ra!" he shouted, "A'ra!" Rosario followed as if hypnotized. There were no people at the top. Most had returned to the buses below. The tourists who came from Mérida liked to tour in the morning, when it was cool; the afternoons, as every civilized person knew, were to be spent in the cool cantina or by the swimming pool.

"Look," Gonzalo said, "Look around you. What do you see?" Beneath them the jungle and fields of sisal on the flat peninsula spread as far as the eye could see. Flat expanse and scorching blue sky, that was all there was.

"Look, see the roads?" Gonzalo pointed at the barely discernible straight lines that were like the spokes of a large wheel, with Uxmal at the hub. Now covered by jungle and leveled by fields, they were barely visible, straight lines that showed only because at one time they had been slightly elevated from the low-lying land. Rosario remembered the infrared prints he had seen, photos taken from the air that showed the old roads of the Maya.

"There, that road, you see?" Gonzalo pointed. "That leads to the village. At that village there is a large cenote, a natural reservoir of fresh water. . . . You see, that's why they came! The gods needed the fresh water of the cenotes; they came in great ships to the village—fresh water for their ships."

His eyes held Rosario spellbound. It was true: From the air, the peninsula of Yucatán was flat and dark green in the blue water of the gulf. There was space to maneuver, no mountains. Yes, he thought, the straight roads are like an airstrip; Uxmal was the center of the civilization that communicated with the gods! The outlying villages were near the cenotes, the fresh water. Fresh water to cool God-knows-what awesome power source. His heart pounded and his temples throbbed. Yes, he nodded and imagined the bright ships hovering in the night sky, giant beacons lighting up the jungle, the prayers of the winter solstice chanted by thousands of Natives, the offerings that had been raised to the gods—and then he shook his head, held his hands to his ears to shut away the humming sound. Off to his left, two vultures flying high over the jungle had broken his hypnotic gaze.

"No," he said vehemently, "I've heard that story, travelers from outer space. I don't believe it!" He pulled away from the old man, who stood dangerously close to the edge of the pyramid.

"I've heard all the stories you told the group, including the one about the gods who came from outer space to establish the ancient civilization of the Maya. Perhaps your European women believe you, but I don't! I've searched for too long to believe simple stories. For years I have searched for the clue, the secret of the Maya power, and I'll tell you right now, whatever power the ancient Maya had is dead! The land is dead! There is no power left!"

Rosario trembled, realizing the outburst was aimed not only at the old man, but also at himself. It was what he really felt, a realization that came welling from within, a truth he had not wanted to face as long as there had been some hope to his quest. Gonzalo's face grew dark and serious, and Rosario was reminded again of the stela of Copán where the visages suggested pale, yellow Chinese faces of a dark past.

Gonzalo drew close to Rosario, clutched his arm, and asked, "Have you been to Pacal's tomb?"

"Yes." Rosario nodded.

"Have you been to Palenque?"

"Yes."

"Do you know of the astronomers of Copán?"

"Yes."

"Do you believe the Pyramid of the Magician, this sacred place we stand on, was built to honor the gods, built in one night by the dwarf magician of Uxmal?"

Gonzalo's voice rose in strange incantation. Rosario shook his head and pulled free. The old man was crazy; he actually believed the legend.

"No!" Rosario said, "Impossible! The damned thing was built by slaves! So were all the other temples and pyramids—built by the sweat of slaves!"

It was as if he had slapped the old man in the face. He cringed, and Rosario reached out to grab him because he was so near the edge. "You fool," Gonzalo cursed, "you came to look for the source of power of the ancient Mayas and you can't see it."

"Show it to me!"

"I will show you," Gonzalo said softly. "I will show you how a magician can raise pyramids for the gods." He looked into the jungle, and for a long time he did not speak. He stood like a statue, a small, brown man peering into the jungle, an ancient Maya feeling the flow of power between Earth and Sun and the planets, listening intently as if to a whispered message.

"Where?" Rosario finally asked and broke the spell.

"There," Gonzalo said and pointed, "South of Uxmal, beyond the hacienda Iman, in that jungle is the village that the gods painted yellow. Come, they are waiting for us!" He scampered down the steep steps of the pyramid, and Rosario followed him. They left the ruins and followed a dusty path to the hacienda.

"I will show you a pyramid can still be raised," he mumbled as they walked. "The power of the dwarf is alive tonight," he said, but now the mutterings were in a different dialect, and Rosario couldn't understand all that he said.

At the hacienda Gonzalo sought out a hut near the edge of the field of sisal. There they found a man and a woman who appeared to be waiting for them. Two saddled horses stood beneath the shade of a roble tree. Gonzalo signaled with a flick of his hand, and the man brought the horses. When Gonzalo and Rosario had mounted, the woman stepped forward and handed each of them a small bundle of provisions; then the man and woman quickly disappeared into the hut.

"A'ra!" Gonzalo shouted, and the horse reared up as he spurred it forward. They turned south and rode across the fields of sisal.

Where are we going? Rosario thought. Why am I following this madman? The strange circumstances of the morning, Gonzalo's mad belief, the man and the woman with the horses, the day of the solstice, everything suggested an event of strange, mysterious importance. Something inexplicable had come alive, and Rosario wanted to believe, so he would ride with Gonzalo and see where the old man would lead.

In the fields a farmer and his workers burned brush. Huge, spiraling columns of greasy smoke rose in the air. They worked to clear the fields, chopping slowly at the dark jungle, which returned by night to reclaim the cultivated earth. Crumbling stone fences formed the barrier between cultivated land and wild jungle. The horses moved quietly, and Rosario closed his eyes to preserve his energy. From time to time Gonzalo called out, "A'ra! A'ra!" And he sang in Mayan: "Oh, lost island of Atlantis, floating island of the gods."

The oppressive, humid air was heavy and still. Nothing seemed to exist except the burning sun, which seared the land and the two lonely horsemen. Gonzalo seemed to be unaffected by the heat, but Rosario, parched with thirst, dug into the bundle the woman had given him and found a gutskin bag, but instead of water, it was full of balche, a fermented drink made of honey. He had tasted balche once before, at a ceremony for Chac, the rain god. The offerings had been bowlfuls of balche, which the participants drank after the ritual. It had been a pleasant experience, but here in the middle of the hot afternoon, Rosario yearned for water, not this sour drink, which fell like warm vinegar into his stomach. Its dizzying effect was immediate. He felt numbness in his arms and legs.

"Hurry! We don't want to be late!" Gonzalo shouted.

Late for what? Rosario wondered. "Do you really believe the gods will come?" he shouted back.

Gonzalo laughed. "They will come!"

Overhead, vultures dotted the clear blue sky, giant birds that rode on the heat waves rising upward from the torrid, decomposing jungle.

"The village that the gods painted yellow!" Rosario shouted, wondering if he understood the phrase correctly, because he had only heard it spoken in Mayan. "Could the translation be, 'the village painted yellow for the gods'?"

The old man didn't answer. The sun dropped into the western horizon as the two urged their horses over a break in the stone wall. They moved along the edge of the jungle until Gonzalo spotted a tree marked with a slash of yellow paint. There they found a deer path and entered the jungle. They were immediately swallowed up by the semidarkness and the sweltering, humid heat. Rosario thought briefly of Dante entering hell, the door beyond which there was no hope, then he shrugged and slumped in the saddle. Perhaps Gonzalo does know something, he thought, and the journey will reveal something new.

They moved down the narrow path, which was canopied by trees, bushes, and vines. The brambling vines scratched his face and arms, and when Rosario pushed at the overhanging leaves, clumps of stinging red ants fell on him. They swarmed over both man and beast, raising red welts wherever they stung. Gonzalo seemed unaffected. He led the way into the dark labyrinth. On the path snakes slithered out of the way as the two men rode deeper and deeper into the sunless maze.

"A'ra! A'ra!" Gonzalo shouted from time to time, and he laughed like a man possessed.

"Let's rest!" Rosario called. "Do you know where we are?"

"We go to greet the gods!" Gonzalo answered. "Soon we rest. We burn copal, drink balche. The gods are there already, in the sky. They wait for us to raise a temple in their honor!"

Overhead a low, eerie sound rose and fell, as if a giant creature were breathing in the darkness. The sound became a drone, growing louder as they penetrated the dark jungle.

Rosario rode as if in a trance. Images appeared in the phosphorescent light of the green night. He thought about the cool cantina, cold beer, the pale and lonely women. He heard their voices and thought how simple and full of pleasure their offering of love would be in his cool room, and he cursed himself for having left. And for what? To follow the dwarf into this hell in search of ancient secrets.

The path grew narrower and branched out into other deer trails, but Gonzalo led unerringly. Soaked with sweat, they continued their nightmarish journey. Rosario thought of the time he had run with the Tarahumaras in their deep canyons to the north, of the jump from the pole of the voladores when he had broken two ribs and sprained both ankles, and of the hunt in the desert with the Yaquis—all were ceremonies that tested the endurance of the body, but there was an unexplainable joy of the spirit in that rigorous punishment. Now there was only a deep, brutal pain that made no sense.

"The gods will find dead men tonight!" he laughed in the dark, but Gonzalo did not answer. And so with a fever working its way through his tortured body, Rosario slept, or thought he slept. He imagined the ruins of Uxmal; he dreamed of the astronomers who kept their vigil there, a vigil for the gods; and he heard again the story of the dwarf, the enano who had raised the Pyramid of the Magician in one night.

All of these images were linked to Gonzalo and to the trek through the jungle, but Rosario's feverish mind couldn't make a meaningful connection. Finally, they came to a small clearing in the path. A small altar stood beneath a large ceiba tree, a sacred tree to the Maya. Gonzalo dismounted and walked to the altar. He placed copal in the incense burner and placed it over the small glowing fire. Instantly the air was filled with the sweet smell of copal. The resinous smoke hung in the still air like a thin, blue veil.

"Come, drink balche, eat machaca," he commanded.

Rosario slipped off his horse and fell to the ground. His cramped legs wouldn't support him. He massaged them, then he rose and walked slowly and unsteadily to the altar. He bit savagely into the dry venison, the first food he had eaten all day, and he drank the bowl of balche.

"The spirit of the deer is offered to the gods," the old man said. "You may eat the flesh." Then he turned and gazed across the clearing. Before Rosario was finished with his meal, the bush parted and three Indians appeared. They wore only loincloths, and in the dim light of the altar fire, Rosario saw their bodies were completely covered with a paint or a chalk that glowed a pale yellow. He looked closely as the three approached and again remembered the faces on the stela at Copán. They bowed in front of Gonzalo and greeted him in a formal manner. "It is the time for the gods," Rosario heard them say, "the time for lights."

"It is the time of Ixchel," Gonzalo answered, "the time of Yum Kin. It is time to raise new pyramids."

Then he turned, pointed at Rosario, and used the Mayan word for "assistant." The three bowed. What they did next was done very deftly and quickly. Sharp knives cut away Gonzalo's and Rosario's pants and shirts, a cloth was slipped around their loins, and they were covered with the same yellow dust that colored the Indians. It was all done very smoothly, as if they had done it many times before. Gonzalo stood quietly, a willing participant in the ceremony, and Rosario had no time to be surprised. The pieces of some mad design were falling into place: They had found the altar in the clearing, the copal smoke was sweet and thick, and the balche made him numb, dizzy, so when the Natives motioned for them to follow, he followed obediently. One of the Indians led the way, and the other two came behind with the horses; Rosario understood that the village was very near. Overhead the droning sound returned, as if helicopters were whirling in the night sky above the canopy of the jungle. The Natives called excitedly to each other, and the pace quickened.

Rosario gasped and stumbled forward when they entered the village. The bright lights hurt his eyes, and he squinted. The chanting of the naked, yellow Natives rose in the dark. Around them huge bonfires crackled and lit up the night, and because everything was painted yellow, the light of the fires gave off a bright, phosphorescent glow. Rosario was awed by the yellowish color that had suddenly turned the night into eerie day. The Indians, the huts, the stone fence around the perimeter of the village, even the trees radiated with the yellow substance.

"El enano! El enano!" the Natives cried as Gonzalo and Rosario were led through the village to a large field where the priests of the village waited at a crude thatched hut, the altar where candles and copal burned. It was full of statuary, old pieces gathered by the Indians from the ruins in the area. Rosario recognized an old and weathered Christ on the cross, the last remembrance of a foolish priest who had tried to convert the Natives of the village long ago. In the middle of the hut stood a beautifully preserved stela with the figure of Yum Kin carved on it, and all around it rested the food offerings. The clay incense burners glowed with copal, and the sweet smoke filled the night air. At the foot of the altar stood the head priest, and on the ground in front of him rested the sacrificial stone. It was a small square stone carved from black volcanic rock, worn smooth with use.

"You have returned, Magician of Uxmal," the priest greeted Gonzalo. All the attendants bowed. "It is the time of the gods, time to raise a pyramid in their honor."

Gonzalo nodded. He drew his twisted body to its full height. "I have come to practice the old magic, and I have brought my assistant to help me." He motioned with his hand, and two attendants pushed Rosario forward. Now, for the first time, the full impact of the old man's insanity hit Rosario. What they had come through was unbelievable, yet everything seemed inevitable. Now they were part of the incredible scene of the yellow village, with hundreds of Natives surrounding the thatched altar and waiting patiently for the drama to begin. There is a purpose in all of it, he thought, perhaps I have finally come to that first step by which I will learn the secrets of the ancient Maya. Perhaps all the secrets I have searched for are about to be revealed to me. He shuddered and bowed his head, and like the Natives, he gave himself over to the ceremony about to begin.

"It is time to sing!" Gonzalo shouted. "It is time to pray. We are the people of the gods. We pray and they hear us, even as they rest in the bowels of the earth, even as they rest in the heavens. Tonight I will raise a wondrous pyramid for them, and they will come and visit us as they did long ago."

There was a murmur of assent as the Natives fell to their knees. These were the words of the Magician of Uxmal. The priests drew back. Two young women moved forward, naked virgins offering the magician and his assistant bowls of the sacred balche. First Gonzalo raised his bowl upward and offered it to the gods. In ancient Mayan he told the gods how the people had gathered to prepare for this most holy of feasts. For three days they had fasted, tasting only small portions of machaca and drinking only the sacred balche. Then he drank, followed by the priests and Rosario. The young women took the empty bowls and withdrew.

"I am the Magician of Uxmal," Gonzalo sang, "I light the way for the gods. In the Jungle of the Jaguar I will raise a pyramid to Yum Kin, Lord of the Sun. Because you have granted me this magic, I also dare to sing to Itzamna, the Lord of Life himself." His voice and the chorus of the people filled the night.

Rosario also sang. He found himself swaying to the rhythmic beat of the chant, and the loneliness he had felt lifted. A sense of responsibility filled him as he glanced at Gonzalo and saw how entranced the old man was in his work. Gonzalo actually believed he was the Magician of Uxmal, that tonight he would raise a pyramid in the jungle, and the people believed—they sang fervently. When Rosario closed his eyes and allowed the words of the chant to come pouring out, he too believed it was possible to raise a pyramid in honor of the gods. It could all be done here, tonight, and so he raised his voice and sang.

Deep into the night the chanting continued, the young women returned with bowls of balche, the incense burners were refilled with copal, the fires refueled. Lost Mayan words Rosario had never known tumbled from his lips. A great strength filled him.

He felt restored with a faith he had never known before, and in his heart he believed that he and Gonzalo were priests, messengers of the gods, men endowed with a special purpose and extraordinary powers. They could raise pyramids to the gods! They could recreate the terrible and ancient mysteries of the past! This is why he had come to the village painted yellow for the gods. This is why he had been chosen, because he had sought, and now he of little faith was restored. He felt the power course through his blood, and he raised his voice, calling for the pyramid to rise from the empty jungle. At that moment a great wind swirled down and swept up sparks and ashes from the fire. The people cringed with fear, then fell prostrate on the ground. Even the priests drew back before the released power.

"There!" Gonzalo cried. "There the Pyramid of the Magician rises!"

A shrill, hovering sound came with the wind; the sparks rained on the people, and they fled screaming. Out of the swirling, blinding dust a shaft of light broke through, and for a moment the image of a golden pyramid shone before their eyes. The earth seemed to shake. Rosario cried in praise, then fell to the earth, exhausted. The tremendous pain and joy of the night had suddenly drained away and left him empty. Somewhere in the excitement of the moment, he heard himself laughing.

He didn't know how long he had lain there, but when he looked up, he saw the first light of dawn. The air was quiet. Birds called and sang in the jungle. In the southwest, the moon was setting over Palenque. He turned and looked at Gonzalo. The old man stood with head bowed, his arms hung limply at his sides. Rosario tried to speak, but no words came.

"You have failed," he heard the priest murmur, but Rosario didn't believe they had failed.

"Next year," Gonzalo whispered, "next year." He looked at Rosario, and his eyes were brilliant and burning. Rosario nodded. He took a step forward to touch his master, but already the attendants had pulled Gonzalo back and bent him over the sacrificial stone. His heaving rib cage stood exposed to the priest, who raised the knife.

A glint of the rising sun caught in the sharp obsidian knife as the priest bent over Gonzalo. There was a short gasp for air, a gurgle, and when the priest raised his arms, he held Gonzalo's still-beating heart in his hands. He held it toward the rising sun, then he dropped the throbbing heart into the altar fire. The people murmured a prayer of thanksgiving.

Gonzalo had not cried out. It was something he seemed to expect. Like a ballplayer in the ball court of Uxmal, he had lost a game, and now he was closer to the gods. But Rosario did scream and struggle when the attendants turned on him. It wasn't his heart they wanted. They held him tightly while the priest cut. The cut was swift and sharp, he hardly felt the pain, but when they released him and he tried to stand, he fell forward. They had cut his Achilles tendon; they had made him a cripple. He stumbled forward, and they parted to let him pass. The searing pain ran up his leg, and he was barely able to crawl to the horses. No one moved to stop him. When he reached the staked horses, he pulled himself up and mounted while the people only watched. He turned and looked at them, and for a moment he saw the truth of ancient expectations written in their eyes. They had made him their new dwarf, the new magician. A year hence, when the day of the solstice came again to the Yucatán Peninsula, he would return, he would be here. This was the time of the Maya, the time of cycles, which not even the momentous earth changes nor the cultural changes of centuries could destroy. There was yet some power left to do the work of the gods. He looked across the gathered people, dazzling gold in the bright rays of the morning sun. Yes, now he understood his destiny.

He raised his arm in salute and shouted, "A'ra! Splendor to the Maya!" Then he spurred his horse and rode into the jungle.

A Story

Cast of Characters

The Writer, *myself*
My Wife, *herself*
Sabrina, *Grandpa's daughter*
Sabrina's Husband, *a foreigner*
Federico, *Grandpa's son*
Federico's Wife
Grandpa, *don Francisco Gómez*
Alfredo, *Grandpa's nephew*
Don Cosme del Rincón, *my dead uncle who wants to be a character*
Others, *characters on the periphery who also want to get into the story*

Time: Late New Year's morning.

Place: My writing room.

Situation: *I am trying to cure a hangover with a dose of New Year's football games and leftover, stale beer that tastes like sudsy water. I belch. Dandy Don smiles at me and reminds me the eyes of Texas are upon me. I remember a hangover remedy my uncle Cosme used to concoct when he was alive.*

"Poke a hole in an egg, pour some salt and Tabasco sauce in it, and stir it with a toothpick," he says from somewhere over my shoulder.

"It's not your story, Uncle," I remind him and frown. He's been trying to get into a story since last week, when I remembered the story my father told me about my uncle Cosme's death. But my head is too full of cobwebs to remember the details.

"Who are you talking to?" my wife calls from upstairs.

"The TV," I answer.

"I can't write today," I mumble to myself as I drag into the kitchen. "I need another situation. Real characters." I find a nice lopsided, speckled egg in the fridge, poke a hole in it, pour in salt and Tabasco sauce, and mix. The phone rings.

"Phone's ringing," I call to my wife, then suck at the egg. Only the hot sauce keeps me from emptying my queasy stomach.

"Damn, Uncle, I don't know what's worse, the hangover or the cure." I shudder and return to my room to sit at my typewriter. My uncle smiles. The paper stares at me.

Menudo, the Breakfast of Champions, I write, is a sure cure for a hangover.

"It's Sabrina!" my wife calls. "She wants us to come over for menudo!"

Great, I think, the situation is improving. It's just what I need, a new situation for a story. Then I remember last night's party. Slinky Sabrina kept throwing herself all over me, swearing I was the best writer she ever knew. The situation became, uh, sticky, uncomfortable. I erase quickly with Liquid Paper Correction Fluid, and I shout "No!" but it's too late. MENUDO, THE BREAKFAST OF CHAMPIONS has already become A STORY.

"We'll be right over, Sabrina," my wife says into the phone, "as soon as we can get ready."

"I don't want to go!" I shout. Sabrina and her husband live across the street in an old, rambling adobe house. He's a foreigner, a German, I think. He's the quiet type; he likes to pierce you with his cold, analytic eyes. Sabrina grew up in my hometown, left, some say because she got pregnant, wandered around the world, and found the German. They're both okay, but what I can't stand is her family. They are the greatest liars in the world. They love to make up stories. Awful stories! I can never think when I'm around people who tell stories.

"Ready?" my wife asks.

"What happened at the party last night?"

"You should know; you were there."

Perhaps it wasn't as bad as I thought, I reassure myself. I drank one too many, I remember. We lean into the cold January wind. It comes down like, like, a wolf on the fold—

"That's awful!" my wife says.

"It's cold," I answer lamely and stumble across the road to Sabrina's house. It's a large house, and it's always full of relatives. Everyone who comes from the llano, that vast grassy plain that haunts me, stops to visit. There's already a whiff on the llano that I'm a writer, so people poke around to see where they fit into my stories. Sabrina has many visitors because her family is large. And each one of them is an obsessive storyteller. Gaunt people with dark eyes set in deep sockets, they brood with their dark secrets. But they're lousy storytellers, I think, a bunch of liars.

"Don't talk nasty about people," my wife says over her shoulder.

I have to in order to write stories, I think. Who wants to read about saints? I remember my uncle Cosme del Rincón. What's the story he's trying to tell me? The wind moans and swirls dust. Suddenly Sabrina's house looms before us. The curtains are pulled, and eyes stare at me from the windows. I have the feeling that I shouldn't have come. Perhaps I should go back and start all over.

"No," my wife says and knocks. Sabrina opens the door. She's dressed in a dark, revealing morning gown. "I'm so glad you came!" She smiles and throws her arms around me. "Happy New Year! Happy New Year!" I glance at my wife. What a character, she's thinking.

"We're glad we came, too," my wife replies. There's a hug for her.

"Yes, so glad—come in, come in. Everything's fine. Oh, that was a great party last night!"

"Yes, it was nice—"

"Come in."

"Yes."

We enter, and Sabrina leads us to the den. It's a dark, subterranean room. Sabrina stumbles in the dark. She's already been nipping, I think. I take off my sheepskin jacket and look around. Good place for a scene. Shadows wander around the dark corners of the room, lurking at the story's edge. Sabrina reaches for two and brings them into the light.

"This is my brother, Federico, and his wife—they just came in from Tucumcari last night—well, you know, they were at the party!"

There are greetings and abrazos for everyone as we're introduced. I remember somewhere I wrote, "there's something rotten in Tucumcari." I look closely at Federico, but I can't remember him from anywhere. Federico looks closely at me. Sabrina's husband serves us sherry. "Want to play a game of billiards?" he asks and stares at me.

"No, thanks." I pick a chair where I can observe all the action. A writer always sits where he can observe the action. "Want to arm wrestle?" he asks, and I refuse. He draws back into the shadows; I know he'll keep his eyes on me, though. I look at Federico.

"Good party last night," he nods, "but I think this neighborhood is going to the dogs."

"Someone threw a rock at him last night," his wife explains.

"It's my story!" he growls at her. "I'll tell it!" He moves dramatically to the middle of the room. Center stage. Even the shadows that circle us turn to listen. I nod and Federico begins his story.

"I was driving home from the party last night," he begins. I don't remember him from the party.

"Alone?" I ask.

"That's what I'd like to know!" He glares at me and sips his beer. His drooping mustache glistens with droplets of beer. The dim overhead light makes his eyes look menacing. "That rock hit my window like an explosion!" he shouts. "There was flying glass all over!"

"Did you call the police?" Sabrina asks. She sips her sherry and swings a long, sleek leg for attention. I think she wants to get into the storytelling. Her husband clears his throat and leans over to whisper in my ear, "Federico thinks his wife was out with someone last night. He came from the party and didn't find her home."

"There were two cops just down the street!" Federico struggles to retain my interest in his story. "They were waiting for me! But I was drunk, so—"

"Was it a real rock?" I ask.

"You should know!" he answers sharply. "It was thrown so hard it shattered the entire window! There was glass all over! It could've killed me," he whispers sotto voce, for dramatic emphasis, but I'm not interested. It's a dull story. I know Sabrina's kin: They're all exaggerators, liars, storytellers.

"He could've been killed!" Sabrina gasps.

"He's too mean to kill," Federico's wife snickers.

"She's got a big insurance policy on him," Sabrina whispers to my wife. "He drinks a lot."

Sabrina's husband serves more sherry. Federico stalks off for a beer. Sabrina looks at me; she wants to begin her story.

"I wrecked my car before the party." She laughs. "I was at the beauty shop, getting all dolled up for that wild party last night, when who do you suppose called me and wanted a ride?" Her legs swing with mean intent. She looks at me. Don't look at me, I think.

Federico returns and fights to keep his position at the center of the stage. "I jumped out of the truck and looked around, but it was too dark. I couldn't see anything except the two cops down the street, drinking coffee while innocent drunk people are getting their windows smashed! Oh, I got madder than hell! I'm going to go home and get my guns and kill this sonofabeech that's throwing rocks, I said to myself!" He looks at me.

"He's got a lot of guns." His wife nods at me.

"I jumped out of my chair at the beauty shop and ran to my car to pick up whoever called me," Sabrina says. They're both working with a mystery element that keeps us listening, but the stories aren't very interesting. Soap opera, I think. Who threw the rock that bopped Federico? Who called Sabrina for a ride just before the party started? For these and more answers, tune in tomorrow for another exciting episode of AS THE SPIRIT MOVES US! Organ music. Fade out.

"I'm going home," I say. My wife agrees.

"Stay for menudo," Sabrina insists. "Grandpa's coming soon. Stay and meet him. I know he wants to meet you. He's a great storyteller! I swear, you won't believe a word he says."

"Is Grandpa coming?" Federico asks. He peers into the shadows.

Grandpa, don Francisco Gómez, was in the story we began at the party last night, I remember. That's where all this started.

"Yes," Grandpa speaks from the shadows, "and I have a story to tell."

I feel his presence and goose pimples spread along my back. "Not yet, Grandpa," I say and turn to Federico. "Did you save the rock for fingerprints?" I ask.

"Yes, I saved the rock." Federico nods and juts his face in front of mine. "I'm not dumb!" He spews beer breath all over me. "I saved that rock, and I'm goin' to find out who threw it, an', an' in case you don't know it," he said threateningly, "there's a dead cat on the street!" He nods for emphasis and staggers a little.

"Federico ran over a cat last week," his wife explains.

"Maybe that's why someone is throwing rocks at you!" Sabrina laughs. We all laugh.

"Yeah, dead pussy!" Federico exclaims.

"There's a lot of stories been told about dead pussy," Grandpa adds as he enters. "But jours is by far dee worse one I eber hear!" he says with his fake accent.

Grandpa is a small, wiry man. He wears boots, a leather jacket, and a cowboy hat. There's a twinkle in his eyes that can suddenly turn into a threatening flash. I feel uncomfortable with him, but it's too late to do anything about it; he's pushed his way in. Alfredo, his nephew, follows him.

"Grandpa!" Sabrina jumps up to greet her father. "When did you get here? Never mind, we're glad you're here." She hugs him. "You're just in time for a drink, then we're going to eat menudo. . . ."

I remember that it was menudo that got me into this situation. Everyone rises to greet Grandpa. Sabrina introduces me as a writer.

"Don Francisco Gómez, a sus ordenes," Grandpa says and shakes my hand. I wince in the grip of a man who has chopped a lot of wood in his time. I feel the bones in my hand cracking. Grandpa looks into my eyes; he recognizes me from somewhere.

"My writing hand." I smile weakly and withdraw it from his grip.

"So ju are a writer, huh?" He smiles. He has yellow teeth stained from tobacco. He wears a red kerchief tied around his neck. When he greets my wife, he bows low and says, "Enchanted, Miss." He kisses her hand. A real ham, I think. But then I've met enough of Sabrina's family to know they're all like that. Now I know they got it from the old man.

"I'm glad to meet you," my wife says. Grandpa winks.

Federico continues with his story. He's desperate now. "I ran ober dat cat a week ago," he slurs his words. "So last night they were waiting for me, right? I killed their pussy so they wanted to get even—"

"Federico, ju neber deed know how to tell a story. Dat dead pussy story, eet stink!" Grandpa says and moves toward center stage, threatening Federico; it's obvious Grandpa came to tell a story.

It's then that I remember Federico from the party. He came late. Stayed in a corner and drank by himself. But did he come before or after the rock-throwing incident? And was he looking for me? I look at his wife. She smiles.

"Let me tell ju a real story," Grandpa smiles, a cold glint in his eyes. He looks at me for approval. He sips his bourbon.

"Grandpa, we were talking about you last night, at the party!" Sabrina exclaims. "About the time you saw don Cosme del Rincón murdered! Don Cosme was—" She points at me, but Federico interrupts.

"I know the pussy was dead. I ran over it. I whammed it myself!" he shouts. "But I don't know who that pussy belongs to. I was too drunk," he admits and looks at his wife. "Maybe I was just thinking about dead pussy—but I could smell it." He shakes his head sadly. "But why did the rock hit my window at that exact spot? At that exact time?"

"It always happens like that," Sabrina insists. "The right situation requires the right time; that's what Grandpa always said." Grandpa nods. He's still looking at me. "Look what happened to me when I'm driving to meet my friend!" She emphasizes "my friend" and swings her legs. "I'm driving down Central, and I know it's very crowded at five o'clock, so I decide to take Lomas, and it's exactly at the moment that I decide to change streets that the other car hits me! Wham, just like that! Has that ever happened to you?" she asks.

"No," I answer. "So you never got to your friend, the one who called for a ride?"

"No," she pouts and downs the remainder of her sherry. I feel easier.

"So I decided to take the law into my own hands!" Federico continues. "I went home to get my guns."

"He's got a closet full of guns," his wife adds.

Sabrina whispers to my wife, "Federico shot a man once. He's very jealous. He came home late from work one night and found a man leaving his house, so he shot him. Turned out to be a poor delivery boy just delivering a pizza." She laughs. My wife looks at me as if to say "be careful with these characters." I shrug.

"I know who murder don Cosme del Rincón." Grandpa nods and begins his story. "I hab dee gun dat kill heem."

Cut the cheap theatrics, I think. Grandpa grins and drops his accent. "The first gun I ever owned was an old Smith and Wesson .38. I was just a kid, 1914, and I was herding sheep on the Rincón llano when three men who had just escaped from the Santa Fe Prison rode into our camp—"

Sabrina claps her hands. "But he's from that llano, from the Rincón!" She points at me. "He's a writer! He writes stories! And don Cosme was his uncle!"

"Ah, I thought so." Grandpa nods. The twinkle in his eyes has changed to a cold, piercing stare. "I thought I recognized you," he says, "the chin, the nose."

"Ju write books, huh?" Federico asks. He has acquired Grandpa's accent; he thinks I'm interested in the accent instead of the story.

"Yes," I say and stand to leave. "But I'm tired. I think we should leave." I look at my wife. She nods. It's hard to observe a potential story if the characters know the writer is present; it causes too many interferences. The characters start acting and hamming it up, looking for a part.

"You can't go until I show you the pistol," Grandpa says sternly. "Go get the pistol, Alfredo." Alfredo disappears into the shadows. "You know, they're writing a book about me, too," he says. His eyes bore into mine. "All those years I spent working on the llano, I saw a lot; there's a lot of stories I can tell." He turns and walks to center stage. His presence holds our attention. The room grows silent. This is the silence before the story begins, the most challenging part of the story. The silence is ominous. From it will come the words that will affect all of us. I shiver, lean forward, and wait. Alfredo returns with the pistol. The small Smith and Wesson curls like a black snake into Grandpa's hand.

"Three men escaped from prison," Grandpa begins. His words hypnotize us, rivet us to our spots. I have to give Grandpa credit: When he drops the cheap theatrics, he's a real storyteller. There's an aura around him, as if he's infused with the spirit of the past. "One of the escaped prisoners was a Mexican nationalist, and he was shot and killed by a deputy sheriff from Pastura. That man's family later sent many sons across the border to avenge the death, and for years the llano was filled with bloodshed—but that's another story. The other man was a dirt farmer who didn't know his way in the llano, so there's no need to speak of him. The third man—"

"The third man was the man who killed my uncle Cosme," I interrupt. I feel a cold sweat on my forehead. So this is what my uncle Cosme was trying to warn me about! That's why he keeps appearing at the edges of the story! But what were the details of that story? Why am I on dangerous ground with Grandpa?

"Uncle?" I say.

My uncle Cosme struggles forward. He is a terrible sight. He has been dead for half a century. He is moldy from the grave, but I can still make out the bullet hole in his forehead. He wants to speak, he wants to warn me, but there is only a dry, raspy rattle as Grandpa pushes him back into the shadows.

"It's my story," Grandpa insists, "and I haven't finished it yet!" He has grown very strong. His knuckles are white around the pistol as he points it my way. He grins. "The third man was my brother," he says, "and he returned to kill your uncle, who had stolen his woman. I was herding sheep for your uncle when they rode in. At first I didn't recognize my older brother. Then he shot don Cosme del Rincón, and he gave me the pistol, and he told me to hide it. I've kept it ever since. I needed to keep it because after that killing, a war broke out on the llano. There was no mercy when the family honor was violated. Blood called for blood—"

"So, you deserve what you get," Federico mumbles drunkenly.

I know, I had been told that story a hundred times, but I had forgotten it. I thought I had left the past behind. I thought I had left the family feuds of the llano behind me, and now they have returned to trap me, perhaps to kill me. My legs feel weak. I look at Grandpa pointing the pistol at me.

"It must have been you who called," Sabrina says. "You're the only one I could tell my story to."

Over my shoulder, I hear Sabrina's husband whisper, "You would have been better off playing cards with me, a simple game to pass the time. Now look at the situation you've gotten yourself into."

It was a situation I was looking for, I think. I needed a story, I needed to create a situation. I see the typewriter paper in front of me and secretly yearn to recreate the past. I wish I could undo what I have done. I look at Grandpa. I know I've created my own destruction. He's an old man, and he's still avenging the old feud. I can see blood in his narrow eyes.

"Grandpa, don't point the gun!" Federico's wife cries nervously.

"Don't, Grandpa!" Sabrina gasps.

"No!" my wife shouts and jumps between Grandpa and me.

There is a profound silence; the cold wind whistles around the edges of the house. The shadows shrink back into the dark corners. Then Grandpa smiles. He tosses the small pistol at me and I catch it. "It's not loaded," he says. "I just wanted you to see it. It's a beauty, isn't it? And it did so much killing in its time. But that's over now."

Yes, I nod and look at the small black pistol nestled in my hand, that's over now. My wife slips her arm around my waist. Her presence is reassuring. I think she's the only one who understands what I go through with my crazy characters.

"Oh, Grandpa, you're such a joker!" Federico's wife exclaims.

"It's not fair to use stuff like that when you tell a story," Federico says lamely.

"Okay, enough of this nonsense, enough of this storytelling!" Sabrina announces. "It's time to eat menudo! That's why all of you were invited, for a good meal of spicy menudo! And I've got hot chile and beans." She takes her husband's arm and leads us into the kitchen.

I feel my wife take my hand. "You ready to eat?" she asks.

"Yeah." I nod.

"How's the situation?"

"I think I've got it under control," I say. I look at Grandpa. "That was a good story," I tell him.

His eyes twinkle. "There's a lot of stories that happened on the llano," he says. "I never told too many of them, but now one of my granddaughters has gotten her college degree, and she wants to write down my stories. So why not?" He chuckles.

"Hey," Federico says as we enter the kitchen, "maybe someday you'll want to write down my story, huh? I could tell you about the time we went hunting up in the Pecos. . . ."

The Silence of the Llano

His name was Rafael, and he lived on a ranch in the lonely and desolate llano. He had no close neighbors; the nearest home was many miles away. The dirt road to the small village of Las Animas was overgrown with mesquite bushes and the sparse grasses of the flat country. The dry plain was a cruel expanse broken only by gullies and mesas, spotted with juniper and piñon trees. Rafael went to the village only once a month for provisions, quickly buying what he needed, never stopping to talk with the other rancheros who came to the general store to buy what they needed and to swap stories.

Long ago, the friends his parents had known stopped visiting Rafael. The people whispered that the silence of the llano had taken Rafael's soul, and they respected his right to live alone. They knew the hurt he suffered.

The people of this country knew the loneliness of the llano; they realized that sometimes the silence of the endless plain grew so heavy and oppressive that it became unbearable. When men heard voices in the wind of the llano, they knew it was time to ride to the village, just to listen to the voices of other men. They knew that after many days of riding alone under the burning sun and listening only to the moaning wind, a man could begin to talk to himself. When a man heard the sound of his voice in the silence, he sensed the danger in his lonely existence. Then he would ride to his ranch, saddle a fresh horse, explain to his wife that he needed something in the village, a plug of tobacco, perhaps a new knife, or a jar of salve for deworming the cattle. It was a pretense;

in his heart each man knew he went to break the hold of the silence.

Las Animas was only a mud cluster of homes, a general store, a small church, a sparse gathering of life on the wide plain. The old men of the village gathered in front of the store, shaded by the portal in summer, warmed by the southern sun in winter. They talked about the weather, the dry spells they had known as rancheros on the llano, the bad winters, the price of cattle and sheep. They sniffed the air and predicted the coming of the summer rains, and they discussed the news of the latest politics at the county seat.

The ranchers who rode in listened attentively, nodding as they listened to the soft, full words of the old men, rocking back and forth on their boots, taking pleasure in the sounds they heard. Sometimes one of them would buy a bottle, and they would drink and laugh and slap each other on the back as friends will do. Then, fortified by this simple act, each man returned home to share with his family what he had heard. Each would lie with his wife in the warm bed of night, the wind moaning softly outside, and he would tell the stories he had heard: So and so had died, someone they knew had married and moved away, the price of wool and yearlings had risen. The news of a world so far away was like a dream. The wife listened and was also fortified for the long days of loneliness. In adjoining rooms the children heard the muffled sounds of the words and laughter of the father and mother. Later they would speak the words they heard as they cared for the ranch animals or helped the mother in the house, and in this way their own world grew and expanded.

Rafael knew well the silence of the llano. He had been only fifteen when his father and mother died in a sudden, deadly blizzard, which caught them on the road to Las Animas. Days later, when finally Rafael could break the snowdrifts for the horse, he had found them. There at La Angostura, where the road followed the edge of a deep arroyo, the horses had bolted or the wagon had slipped in the snow and ice. The wagon had overturned, pinning his father beneath its massive weight. His mother had lain beside him, holding him in her arms. His father had been a strong man; he could have made a shelter, burned the wagon to survive the night, but pinned as he was, he had been helpless, and his wife could not lift the weight of the huge wagon. She had held him in her arms, covered both of them with her coat and blankets, but that night they had frozen. It took Rafael all day to dig graves in the cold ground; then he buried them there, high on the slope of La Angostura, where the summer rains would not wash away the graves.

That winter was cruel in other ways. Blizzards swept in from the north and piled the snowdrifts around the house. Snow and wind drove the cattle against the fences, where they huddled together and suffocated as the drifts grew. Rafael worked night and day to try to save his animals, and still he lost half the herd to the punishing storms. Only the constant work and simple words and phrases he remembered his father and mother speaking kept Rafael alive that winter.

Spring came, the land thawed, the calves were born, and the work of a new season began. But first Rafael rode to the place where he had buried his parents. He placed a cross over their common grave, then he rode to the village of Las Animas and told the priest what had happened. The people gathered, and a Mass for the Dead was prayed. The women cried, and the men slapped Rafael on the back and offered their condolences. All grieved; they had lost good friends, but they knew that was the way of death on the llano, swift and sudden. Now the work of spring was on them. The herds had to be rebuilt after the terrible winter, and fences needed mending. As the people returned to their work, they forgot about Rafael.

But one woman in the village did not forget. She saw the loneliness in his face and sensed the pain he felt at the loss of his parents. At first she felt pity when she saw him standing in the church alone; then she felt love. She knew about loneliness; she had lost her parents when she was very young, and she had lived most of her life in a room at the back of the small adobe church. Her work was to keep the church clean and to take care of the old priest. It was this young woman who reached out and spoke to Rafael, and when he heard her voice, he remembered the danger of the silence of the llano. He smiled and spoke to her. Thereafter, on Sundays he rode in to visit her. They would sit together during the Mass, and after that they would walk together to the general store, where he would buy a small bag of hard sugar candy, and they would sit on the bench in front of the store, eat their candy, and talk. The old people of the village as well as those who rode in from distant ranches knew Rafael was courting her, and knew it was good for both of them. The men tipped their hats as they passed by, because Rafael was now a man.

Love grew between the young woman and Rafael. One day she said, "You need someone to take care of you." Her voice filled his heart with joy. They talked to the priest, and he married them, and after Mass there was a feast. The women set up tables in front of the church, covering them with their brightest oilcloths, and they brought food, which they served to everyone who had come to the celebration. The men drank whiskey and talked about the good grass growing high on the llano, and about the herds, which would grow and multiply. One of the old men of the village brought his violin, followed by his friend with an accordion. The two men played the old polkas and waltzes, and the people danced on the hard-packed dirt in front of the church. The fiesta brought together the people of the big and lonely llano.

The violin and accordion music was accompanied by the clapping of hands and the stamping of feet. The dancing was lively, and the people were happy. They laughed and congratulated the young couple. They brought gifts, kitchen utensils for the young bride, ranch tools for Rafael, whiskey for everyone who would drink, real whiskey bought in the general store, not the mula some of the men made in their stills. Even Rafael took a drink, his first drink with the men, and he grew flushed and happy. He danced every dance with his young wife, and everyone could see that his love was deep and devoted. He laughed with the men when they slapped his back and whispered advice for the wedding night. Then the wind began to rise, and it started to rain; the first huge drops mixed with the blowing dust. People sought cover, others hitched their wagons and headed home, all calling their goodbyes and buena suerte in the gathering wind. And so Rafael lifted his young bride onto his horse and they waved goodbye to the remaining villagers, who also rode away, south, deep into the empty llano, deep into the storm that came rumbling across the sky, with thunder and lightning flashes, pushing the cool wind before it.

And that is how the immense silence of the land and the heavy burden of loneliness came to be lifted from Rafael's heart. His young bride had come to share his life and give it meaning and form. Sometimes late at night, when the owl called from its perch on the windmill and the coyotes sang in the hills, he would lie awake and feel the presence of her young, thin body next to his. On such nights the stillness of the spring air and her fragrance intoxicated him and made him drunk with happiness; then he would feel compelled to rise and walk out into the night, which was bright with the moon amid the million stars that swirled overhead. He breathed the cool air of the llano night, and it was like a liquor that made his head swirl and his heart pound. He was a happy man.

In the morning she arose before him, fixed his coffee, and brought it to him, and at first he insisted that it was he who should get up to start the fire in the wood stove, because he was used to rising long before the sun and riding in the range while the dawn was alive with its bright colors, but she laughed and told him she would spoil him in the summer, and in the winter, when it was cold, he would be the one to rise and start the fire and bring her coffee in bed. They laughed and talked during those still-dark, early hours of the morning. He told her where he would ride that day and about the work that needed to be done. She, in turn, told him about the curtains she was sewing and the cabinet she was painting and how she would cover each drawer with oilcloth.

He whitewashed the inside of the small adobe home for her, then plastered the outside walls with mud to keep out the dust that came with the spring winds and the cold that would come with winter. He fixed the roof and patched the leaks, and one night when it rained, they didn't have to rise to catch the leaking water in pots and pans. They laughed and were happy. Just as the spring rains made the land green, so his love made her grow, and one morning she quietly whispered in his ear that by Christmas they would have a child.

Her words brought great joy to him. "A child," she had said, and excitement tightened in his throat. That day he didn't work on the range. He had promised her a garden, so he hitched up one of the old horses to his father's plow, and he spent all day plowing the soft, sandy earth by the windmill. He spread manure from the corral on the soil and turned it into the earth. He fixed an old pipe leading to the windmill and showed her how to turn it to water the garden. She was pleased. She spent days planting flowers and vegetables. She watered the old, gnarled peach trees near the garden, and they burst into a late bloom. She worked the earth with care, and by midsummer she was already picking green vegetables to cook with the meat and potatoes. It became a part of his life to stop on the rise above the ranch when he rode in from the range, to pause and watch her working in the garden in the cool of the afternoon. There was something in that image, something that made a mark of permanence on the otherwise empty llano.

Her slender body began to grow heavier. Sometimes he heard her singing, and he knew it was not only to herself she sang or hummed. Sometimes he glanced at her when her gaze was fixed on some distant object, and he realized it was not a distant mesa or cloud she was seeing, but a distant future that was growing in her.

Time flowed past them. He thinned his herds, prepared for the approaching winter, and she gathered the last of the fruits and vegetables. But something was not right. Her excitement of the summer was gone. She began to grow pale and weak. She would rise in the mornings and fix breakfast, then she would have to return to bed and rest. By late December, as the first clouds of winter appeared and the winds from the west blew sharp and cold, she could no longer rise in the mornings. He tried to help, but there was little he could do except sit by her side and keep her silent company while she slept her troubled sleep. A few weeks later a small flow of blood began, as pains and cramps wracked her body. Something was pulling at the child she carried, but it was not the natural rhythm she had expected.

"Go for doña Rufina," she said. "Go for help."

He hitched the wagon and made the long drive into the village, arriving at the break of light to rouse the old partera from her sleep. For many years the old woman had delivered the babies born in the village or in the nearby ranches, and now, as he explained what had happened and the need to hurry, she nodded solemnly. She packed the things she would need, then kneeled at her altar and made the sign of the cross. She prayed to el Santo Niño for help and whispered to the Virgin Mary that she would return when her work was done. Then she turned the small statues to face the wall. Rafael helped her on the wagon, loaded her bags, then used the reins as a whip to drive the horses at a fast trot on their long journey back. They arrived at the ranch as the sun was setting. That night a child was born, a girl, pulled from the womb by the old woman's practiced hands. The old woman placed her mouth to the baby's and blew in air. The baby gasped, sucked in air, and came alive. Doña Rufina smiled as she cleaned the small squirming body. The sound was good. The cry filled the night, shattering the silence in the room.

"A daughter," the old woman said. "A hard birth." She cleaned away the sheets, made the bed, washed the young wife who lay so pale and quiet on the bed, and when there was nothing more she could do, she rolled a cigarette and sat back to smoke and wait. The baby lay quietly at her mother's side, while the breathing of the young mother grew weaker and weaker, and the blood, which the old woman was powerless to stop, continued to flow. By morning Rafael's young wife was dead. She had opened her eyes and looked at the small white bundle that lay at her side. She had smiled and tried to speak, but there was no strength left. She sighed and closed her eyes.

"She is dead," Doña Rufina said.

"No, no," Rafael moaned. He held his wife in his arms and shook his head. "She cannot die, she cannot die," he whispered over and over. Her body, once so warm and full of joy, was now cold and lifeless, and he cursed the forces he didn't understand that had drawn her into that eternal silence. He would never again hear her voice, never hear her singing in her garden, never see her waving as he came over the rise from the llano. A long time later he allowed doña Rufina's hands to draw him away. Slowly he took the shovel she handed him and dug the grave beneath the peach trees by the garden, that place of shade she had loved so much in the summer and that now appeared so deserted in the December cold. He buried her, then quickly saddled his horse and rode into the llano. He was gone for days.

When he returned, he was pale and haggard from the great emptiness that filled him. Doña Rufina was there, caring for the child, nursing her as best she could with the little milk she could draw from the milk cow they kept in the corral. Although the baby was thin and sick with colic, she was alive. Rafael looked only once at the child, then he turned his back to her. In his mind the child had taken his wife's life, and he didn't care if the baby lived or died. He didn't care if he lived or died. The joy he had known was gone; his wife's soul had been pulled into the silence he felt around him, and his only wish was to be with her. She was out there somewhere, alone and lost on the cold and desolate plain. If he could only hear her voice, he was sure he could find her. That was his only thought as he rode out every day across the llano. He rode and listened for her voice in the wind, which moaned across the cold landscape, but there was no sound, only the silence. His tortured body was always cold and shivering from the snow and wind, and when the dim sun sank in the west, it was his horse that trembled and turned homeward, not he. He would have been content to ride forever, to ride until the cold numbed his body and he could join her in the silence.

When he returned late in the evenings, he would eat alone and in silence. He did not speak to the old woman who sat huddled near the stove, holding the baby on her lap, rocking softly back and forth and singing wisps of the old songs. The baby listened, as if she, too, already realized the strangeness of the silent world she had entered. Over them the storms of winter howled and tore at the small home where the three waited for spring in silence. But there was no promise in the spring. When the days grew longer and the earth began to thaw, Rafael threw himself into his work. He separated his herd, branded the new calves, then drove a few yearlings into the village, where he sold them for the provisions he needed. But even the silence of the llano carries whispers. People asked about the child and doña Rufina, and only once did he look at them and say, "My wife is dead." Then he turned away and spoke no more. The people understood his silence and his need to live in it, alone. No more questions were ever asked. He came into the village only when the need for provisions brought him, moving like a ghost, a haunted man, a man the silence of the llano had conquered and claimed. The old people of the village crossed their foreheads and whispered silent prayers when he rode by.

Seven years passed, unheeded in time, unmarked time, change felt only because the seasons changed. Doña Rufina died. During those years she and Rafael had not exchanged a dozen words. She had done what she could for the child, and she had come to love her as her own. Leaving the child behind was the only regret she felt the day she looked out the window and heard the creaking sound in the silence of the day. In the distance, as if in a whirlwind that swirled slowly across the llano, she saw the figure of death riding a creaking cart, which moved slowly toward the ranch house.

So, she thought, my comadre la muerte comes for me. It is time to leave this earth. She fed the child and put her to bed; then she wrapped herself in a warm quilt and sat by the stove, smoking her last cigarette, quietly rocking back and forth, listening to the creaking of the rocking chair, listening to the moan of the wind that swept across the land. She felt at peace. The chills she had felt the past month left her. She felt light and airy, as if she were entering a pleasant dream. She heard voices, the voices of old friends she had known on the llano, and she saw the faces of the many babies she had delivered during her lifetime. Then she heard a knock on the door. Rafael, who sat at his bed repairing his bridle and oiling the leather, heard her say, "Enter," but he did not look up. He did not hear her last gasp for air. He did not see the dark figure of the old woman who stood at the door, beckoning to doña Rufina.

When Rafael looked up, he saw her head slump forward. He arose and filled a glass with water. He held her head up and touched the water to her lips, but it was no use. He knew she was dead. The wind had forced the door open, and it banged against the wall, filling the room with a cold gust, awakening the child. He moved quickly to shut the door, and the room again became dark and silent. One more death, one more burial, and again he returned to his work. Only out there, in the vast space of the llano, could he find something in which he could lose himself.

Only the weather and the seasons marked time for Rafael as he watched over his land and his herd. Summer nights he slept outside, and the galaxies swirling overhead reminded him he was alone. Out there, in that strange darkness, the soul of his wife rested. In the day, when the wind shifted direction, he sometimes thought he heard the whisper of her voice. Other times he thought he saw the outline of her face in the huge clouds that billowed up in the summer. And always he had to drive away the dream and put away the voice or the image, because the memory only increased his sadness. He learned to live alone, completely alone. The seasons changed, the rains came in July and the llano was green, then the summer sun burned it dry, later the cold of winter came with its fury. And all these seasons he survived, moving across the desolate land, hunched over his horse. He was a man who could not allow himself to dream. He rode alone.

II

And the daughter? What of the daughter? The seasons brought growth to her, and she grew into young womanhood. She learned to watch the man who came and went and did not speak, and so she, too, learned to live in her own world. She learned to prepare the food and to sit aside in silence while he ate, to sweep the floor and keep the small house clean, to keep alive the fire in the iron stove, and to wash the clothes with the scrubboard at the water tank by the windmill. In the summer her greatest pleasure was the cool place by the windmill where the water flowed. The spring she was sixteen, she stood and bathed in the cool water, which came clean and cold out of the pipe, and as she stood under the water, the numbing sensation reminded her of the first time the blood had come. She had not known what it was: It had come without warning, without her knowledge. She had felt a fever in the night, and cramps in her stomach; then in the restlessness of sleep, she had awakened and felt the warm flow between her legs. She was not frightened, but she did remember that for the first time she became aware of her father snoring in his sleep on the bed at the other side of the room. She arose quietly, without disturbing him, and walked out into the summer night, going to the water tank, where she washed herself. The water splashed and ran red into the garden.

That same summer she felt her breasts mature, her hips widen, and when she ran to gather her chickens into the coop for the night, she felt a difference in her movement. She did not think or dwell on it; a dark part of her intuition told her that this was a natural element that belonged to the greater mystery of birth she had seen take place on the llano around her. She had seen her hens seek secret nests to hatch their eggs, and she knew the proud, clucking noises the hens made when they appeared with the small yellow chicks trailing. There was life in the eggs. Once when the herd was being moved and they had come to the water tank to drink, she had seen the great bull mount one of the cows, and she remembered the whirling of dust and the bellowing that filled the air. Later, the cow would seek a nest and there would be a calf. These things she knew.

Now she was a young woman. When she went to the water tank to bathe, she sometimes paused and looked at her reflection in the water. Her face was smooth and oval, dark from the summer sun, as beautiful as that of the mother she had not known. When she slipped off her blouse and saw how full and firm her breasts had grown and how rosy the nipples appeared, she smiled and touched them and felt a pleasure she couldn't explain. There was no one to ask about the changes that came into her life. Once a woman and her daughters had come. The girl had seen the wagon coming up on the road, but instead of going out to greet them, she ran and hid in the house, watching through parted curtains as the woman and her daughters came and knocked at the door. She could hear them calling in strange words, words she did not know. She huddled in the corner and kept very still until the knocking at the door ceased; then she edged closer to the window and watched as they climbed back on the wagon, laughing and talking in a strange, exciting way. Long after they were gone, she could still smell the foreign, sweet odors they had brought to her doorstep.

After that, no one came. She remembered the words of doña Rufina and often spoke them aloud just to hear the sound they made as they exploded from her lips. "Lumbre," she said in the morning when she put kindling on the banked ashes in the stove, whispering the word so the man who slept would not hear her. "Agua," she said when she drew water at the well. "Viento de diablo," she hissed to let her chickens know a swirling dust storm was on its way, and when they did not respond, she reverted to the language she had learned from them, and with a clucking sound she drove them where she wanted. "Tote! Tote!" she called and made the clicking sound for danger when she saw the gray figure of the coyote stalking close to the ranch house. The chickens understood and hurried into the safety of the coop. She learned to imitate the call of the wild doves. In the evening when they came to drink at the water tank, she called to them, and they sang back. The roadrunner that came to chase lizards near the wind-mill learned to coo for her, and the wild sparrows and other birds also heard her call and grew to know her presence. They fed at her feet like chickens. When the milk cow wandered away from the corral, she learned to whistle to bring it back. She invented other sounds, other words, words for the seasons and the weather they brought, words for the birds she loved, words for the juniper and piñon and yucca and wild grass that grew on the llano, words for the light of the sun and the dark of the night, words that when uttered broke the silence of the long days she spent alone, never words to be shared with the man who came to eat late in the evenings, who came enveloped in silence, his eyes cast down in a bitterness she did not understand. He ate the meals she served in silence, then he smoked a cigarette, then he slept. Their lives were unencumbered by each other's presence; they did not exist for each other; both had learned to live in their own silent worlds.

But other presences began to appear on the llano, even at this isolated edge of the plain, which lay so far beyond the village of Las Animas. Men came during the season of the yellow moon, and they carried the long sticks that made thunder. In that season when the antelope were rutting they came, and she could hear the sound of thunder they made, even feel the panic of the antelope that ran across the llano. "Hunters!" her father said, and he spat the word like a curse. He did not want them to enter his world, but still they came, not in the silent horse-drawn wagons, but in an iron wagon that made noise and smoke.

The sound of these men frightened her, and life on the llano grew tense when they came near. One day, five of the hunters drove up to the ranch house in one of their iron wagons. She moved quickly to lock the door, to hide, for she had seen the antelope they had killed hung over the front of their wagon, a beautiful tan-colored buck, splattered with blood. It was tied with rope and wire, its dry tongue hanging from its mouth, its large eyes still open. The men pounded on the door and called her father's name. She held her breath and peered through the window. She saw them drink from a bottle they passed to each other. They pounded on the door again and fired their rifles into the air, filling the llano with explosive thunder. The acrid smell of burned powder filled the air. The house seemed to shake as they called words she did not understand. "Rafael!" they called. "A virgin daughter!" They roared with laughter as they climbed in their wagon, and the motor shrieked and roared as they drove away.

All day the vibration of the noise and the awful presence of the men lay over the house, and in nightmares she saw the faces of the men, heard their laughter and the sound of the rifle's penetrating roar as it shattered the silence of the llano. Two of them had been young men, broad-shouldered boys who had looked at the buck they had killed and smiled. The faces of these strange men drifted through her dreams, and she was at once afraid of and attracted to them.

One night in her dreams she saw the face of the man who lived there, the man doña Rufina had told her was to be called father, and she could not understand why he should appear in her dream. When she awoke she heard the owl cry a warning from its perch on the windmill. She hurried outside, saw the dark form of the coyote slinking toward the chicken coop. A snarl hissed in her throat as she threw a rock, and instantly the coyote faded into the night. She waited in the dark, troubled by her dream and by the appearance of the coyote, then she slipped quietly back into the house. She did not want to awaken the man, but he was awake. He, too, had heard the coyote and had heard her slip out, but he said nothing. In the warm summer night, both lay awake, encased in their solitary silence, saying nothing, expecting no words, but aware of each other as animals are aware when another is close by, as she had been aware even in her sleep that the coyote was drawing near.

III

One afternoon Rafael returned home early. He had seen a cloud of dust on the road to his ranch house. It was not the movement of cattle, and it wasn't the dust of the summer dust devils. The rising dust could only mean there was a car on the road. He cursed under his breath, remembering the signs he had posted on his fence and the chain and lock he had bought in the village to secure his gate. He did not want to be bothered, so he would keep everyone away. For a time he continued to repair the fence, using his horse to draw the wire taut, nailing the barbed wire to the cedar posts he had set that morning. The day was warm; he sweated as he worked, but again he paused—something made him restless, uneasy. He wiped his brow and looked toward the ranch house. Perhaps it is only my imagination, he thought. Perhaps the whirlwind was only a mirage, a reflection of the strange uneasiness he felt. He looked to the west, where two buzzards circled over the coyote he had shot that morning. Soon they would drop to feed. Around him the ants scurried through the dry grass, working their hills as he worked his land. There was the buzz of grasshoppers, the occasional call of prairie dogs, each sound in its turn absorbed into the hum that was the silence of the land. He returned to his work, but the image of the cloud of dust returned, and the thought of strangers on his land filled him with anger and apprehension. The bad feeling grew until he couldn't work. He packed his tools, swung onto his horse, and rode homeward.

Later, as he sat on his horse at the top of the rise, where he had a view of his house, the uneasy feeling grew more intense. Something was wrong, someone had come. Around him a strange dark cloud gathered, shutting off the sun, stirring the wind into frenzy. He urged his horse down the slope and rode up to the front door. All was quiet. The girl usually came out to take his horse to the corral, where she unsaddled and fed it, but today there was no sight of her. He turned and looked toward the windmill and the plot of ground where he had buried his wife. The pile of rocks that marked her grave was almost covered by windswept sand. The peach trees were almost dead. The girl had watered them from time to time, as she had watered the garden, but no one had helped or taught her, and so her efforts were poorly rewarded. Only a few flowers survived in the garden, spots of color in the otherwise dry, tawny landscape.

His horse moved uneasily beneath him; he dismounted slowly. The door of the house was ajar; he pushed it open and entered. The room was dark and cool, the curtains at the window were drawn, and the fire for the evening meal was not yet started. Outside the first drops of rain fell on the tin roof as the cloud darkened the land. In the room a fly buzzed. Perhaps the girl is not here, he thought. Maybe it is just that I am tired and I have come early to rest. He turned toward the bed and saw her. She sat huddled on the bed, her knees drawn up, her arms wrapped around them. She looked at him, her eyes terrified and wild in the dark. He started to turn away, but he heard her make a sound, the soft cry of an injured animal.

"Rafael," she moaned as she reached out for him. "Rafael . . ."

He felt his knees grow weak. She had never used his name before.

At the same time, she flung back the crumpled sheet and pointed to the stain of blood. He shook his head, gasped. Her blouse was torn off, red scratch marks scarred her white shoulders, tears glistened in her eyes as she reached out again and whispered his name. "Rafael . . . Rafael . . ."

Someone had come in that cloud of dust, perhaps a stray vaquero looking for work, perhaps one of the men from the village who knew she was here alone. A man had come in the whirlwind and forced himself into the house. "Oh God," he groaned as he stepped back, felt the door behind him, saw her rise from the bed, her arms outstretched, the curves of her breasts rising and falling as she gasped for breath and called his name, "Rafael . . . Rafael . . ." She held out her arms, and he heard his scream echo in the small adobe room, which had suddenly become a prison, suffocating him. Still the girl came toward him, her eyes dark and piercing, her dark hair falling over her shoulders and throat. With a great effort he found the strength to turn and flee. Outside, he grabbed the reins of his frightened horse, mounted, and dug his spurs into the sides of the poor creature. Whipping it hard he rode away from the ranch and from what he had seen.

He had fled once before, on the day he buried his wife. He had seen her face then, as he now saw the image of the girl, saw her eyes burning into him, saw the torn blouse, the bed, and most frightening of all, heard her call his name, "Rafael . . . Rafael . . ." The image opened and broke the shell of his silence; it was a wound that brought back the ghost of his wife, the beauty of her features, which he now saw again and which blurred into the image of the girl. He spurred the horse until it buckled with fatigue and sent him crashing into the earth. The impact brought a searing pain and the peace of darkness.

He didn't know how long he lay unconscious. When he awoke, he touched his throbbing forehead and felt the clotted blood. The pain in his head was intense, but he could walk. Without direction he stumbled across the llano and found his horse. Late in the afternoon he came to his ranch house. He approached the water tank to wash the clotted blood from his face, then he stumbled into the tool shed by the corral and tried to sleep. Dusk came, the bats and nighthawks flew over the quiet llano. Night fell and still he could not sleep. Through the chinks of the weathered boards, he could see the house and the light that burned at the window. The girl was awake. All night he stared at the light burning at the window, and in his fever he saw her face again, her pleading eyes, the curve of her young breasts, her arms as she reached out and called his name. Why had she called his name? Why? Was it the devil who rode the whirlwind? Was it the devil who had come to break the silence of the llano? He groaned and shivered as the call of the owl sounded in the night. He looked into the darkness and thought he saw the figure of the girl walking to the water tank. She bathed her shoulders in the cold water, bathed her body in the moonlight. Then the owl grew still, and the figure in the flowing gown disappeared as the first sign of dawn appeared in the clouds of the east.

He rose and entered the house, tremulously, unsure of what he would find. There was food on the table and hot coffee on the stove. She had prepared his breakfast as she had all those years, and now she sat by the window, withdrawn, her face pale and thin. She looked up at him, but he turned away and sat at the table with his back to her. He tried to eat, but the food choked him. He drank the strong coffee, then he rose and hurried outside. He cursed as he reeled toward the corral like a drunken man, then he stopped suddenly and shuddered with a fear he had never known before. He shook his head in disbelief and raised his hand as if to ward away the figure sitting on the huge cedar block at the woodpile. It was the figure of a woman, a woman who called his name and beckoned him. And for the first time in sixteen years, he called out his wife's name.

"Rita," he whispered, "Rita."

Yes, it is she, he thought, sitting there as she used to, laughing and teasing while he chopped firewood. He could see her eyes, her smile, hear her voice. He remembered how he would show off his strength with the axe, and she would compliment him in a teasing way as she gathered the chips of piñon and cedar for kindling. "Rita," he whispered and moved toward her, but now the figure sitting at the woodblock was the girl; she sat there, calling his name, smiling and coaxing him as a demon from hell would entice the sinner into the center of the whirlwind. "No!" he screamed and grabbed the axe, lifted it, and summoning his remaining strength, brought it down on the dark heart of the swirling vortex. The blow split the block in half and splintered the axe handle. The pain of the vibration numbed his arms. The devil is dead, he thought, opened his eyes, and saw only the split block and the splintered axe in front of him. He shook his head and backed away, crying to God to exorcize the possession in his tormented soul. And even as he prayed for respite, he looked up and saw the window. Behind the parted curtains was her face, his wife, the girl, the pale face of the woman who haunted him.

Without saddling the horse, he mounted and spurred it south. He had to leave this place; he would ride south until he could ride no more, until he disappeared into the desert. He would ride into oblivion, and when he was dead, the tightness and pain in his chest and the torturous thoughts would be gone; then there would be peace. He would die and give himself to the silence, and in that element he would find rest. But without warning, a dark whirlwind rose before him, and in the midst of the storm, he saw a woman. She did not smile, she did not call his name. Her horse was the dark cloud that towered over him, the cracking of her whip a fire that filled the sky. Her laughter rumbled across the sky and shook the earth, and her shadow swirled around him, blocking out the sun, filling the air with choking dust, driving fear into both man and animal until they turned in a wide circle back toward the ranch house. And when he found himself once again on the small rise by his home, the whirlwind lifted and the woman disappeared. The thunder rumbled in the distance, then was gone, and the air grew quiet around him. He could hear himself breathe, could hear the pounding of his heart. Around him the sun was bright and warm.

He didn't know how long he sat there remembering other times when he had paused at that place to look down at his home. He was startled from his reverie by the slamming of a screen door. The girl walked toward the water tank. He watched her as she pulled the pipe clear of the tank, then removed her dress and began her bath. Her white skin glistened in the sunlight as the spray of water splashed over her body. Her long black hair, shining from the water, fell over her shoulders to her waist. He could hear her humming. He remembered his wife bathing there, covering herself with soap foam, and he remembered how he would sit and smoke while she bathed, his life full of peace and contentment. She would wrap a towel around her body and come running to sit by his side in the sun, and as she dried her hair, they would talk. Her words had filled the silence of the llano. Her words were an extension of the love she had brought him.

And now? He touched his legs to the horse's sides and the horse moved, making its way down the slope toward the water tank. She turned, saw him coming, and stepped out of the cascading water to gather a towel around her naked body. She waited quietly. He rode up to her, looked at her, looked for a long time at her face and into her eyes. Then slowly he dismounted and walked to her. She waited in silence. He moved toward her, and with a trembling hand, he reached out and touched her wet hair.

"Rita," he said. "Your name is Rita."

She smiled at the sound. She remembered the name from long ago. It was a sound she remembered from doña Rufina. It was the sound the axe made when it rang against hard cedar wood, and now he, the man who had lived in silence all those years, he had spoken the name.

It was a good sound, which brought joy to her heart. This man had come to speak this sound she remembered. He turned and pointed at the peach trees at the edge of the garden.

"Your mother is buried over there," he said. "This was her garden. The spring is the time for the garden. I will turn the earth for you. The seeds will grow."

The Place of the Swallows

Again our tribe of boys is at the river, stumbling in the dense green darkness, cutting a trail through the thick undergrowth that engulfs us.

It seems we are always at the river, gathering by the bank before the first rays of the sun have cut away the damp mist, breathing the night air, which clings like veils of lace to the spongy earth, moving in a thin line toward the dark recesses we can never conquer, emerging only at the end of day. We move like shadows in the darkness, struggling to keep up with the leader. Why? I ask myself with each swing of the long knife I use to clear the trail. Behind me I can hear the breathing of the boy who follows me; ahead, I catch only glimpses of a sweating brown back and the swinging knife that hacks away at the thick brush. The trail can never end if it follows the river, I think. Startled birds fly up around us and utter fearful cries; the only other sound is the swishing of the machetes we use—machetes? Knives stolen from our mothers' kitchens and carried secretly to the camp, where in the ritual of the campfire, they become our hunting instruments; or slabs of steel scavenged from the old man's refuse heap and honed sharp on his grinding stone, the one he keeps for his axes. The fire in the stone puts an edge on the common steel, changes what is simple and honest in the light of day into a weapon that can draw blood. I know how the tribe uses fire.

Even now, as we are gathered around the campfire, the dancing light and shadows play on our faces and create a circle of changing masks. I glance at the others, searching for a clue in their eyes. I want to know how they feel about the day's adventure.

Everyone is relaxed; some are mending their equipment, others sharpening their knives. I look at the leader and wonder if he will ask me to tell the story tonight; I have an uneasy feeling in my stomach. All day I have known that someone will have to tell the story of today's exploration; someone will be chosen to give form to our exploits. It is always like this. Before we leave the camp for the night, the talk will turn to our adventure, and someone will pick up the thread of our story and tell it. Some are very good at it—I am not. I know the moment for telling the story comes as unexpectedly as the force of night when one is not quite ready for it. Suddenly all the members of the tribe are silent; only the cries of the birds from the river and the hissing of the fire can be heard, that and the sound of the wind moaning across the empty flats. Then everyone looks at the chosen one, and the silence can be broken only by the words that begin the story. The storyteller must begin; he can leave nothing out; he must tell the story of the tribe's wanderings; and he must tell the truth.

Tonight their eyes focus on me. I feel their stares, and the only way I can relieve the tension is to begin.

I ask to speak in the name of the tribe, and the leader nods. In the flickering light of the fire, I look for a clue in his face. What does he feel about the day's adventure, what does he want the tribe to hear, what did he learn at the Place of the Swallows? Long ago he used to work the line near me; we were friends then. But now he has moved to the front of the long line that relentlessly moves along the river valley. We used to talk when we paused to rest. One day we joked when a bird dropped shit on his head. Now he is the leader, and we are no longer friends. I wonder how he became the leader. I don't remember, but he must have performed an extraordinary feat to allow him to move to the head of our small wandering tribe. I look at him, and when our eyes meet, another dread fills my heart. Suddenly I realize that someday I may be the leader. Someday it will be my turn to meet an unknown enemy, perhaps one of the many shadows that stalk the river. Then my courage will be tested, and if I am victorious, the tribe will cheer me, raise me on their shoulders, and that night by the campfire, I will be their new leader. I shiver. As my lungs draw breath to begin the story. I think of home. I sense the warmth of my mother's kitchen and the strong presence of my father. There is light in our home, and there is protection from the cold air that comes swiftly across the flats as soon as the sun sets. Here there is only the meager light of the small fire, barely warming my hands and face, while the cold air that creeps up from the river chills my back.

I stutter and begin, but it's the wrong story! I start the story of the killing of the giant river turtle, and I realize that happened in a different time and at another place along the river. That story has already been told! I glance at the others, and the look in their eyes makes me shiver. I curse myself for thinking of that incident tonight. Why did it suddenly flood my thoughts? Is it because the killer of the river turtle is gone, and I know he is doomed to tell his story wherever he goes? I look at the empty place in the circle where he used to sit. I begin again.

"Today," I hear myself say, "a story was created as we hunted along the river. Our explorations took us into unknown territory. There are no stories that tell of anyone ever crossing the great swamp that lies to the south, but today, with the urging of our leader, we crossed that dangerous place."

I hear murmurs of approval. The leader nods. The tribe is happy tonight. One boy has brought tobacco, stolen from his father's store, I'm sure. Now it is rolled, lit, and passed around so that we can all smoke as the story unfolds. When it is my turn, I take a deep breath and fill my lungs with smoke. As I breathe out, I feel dizzy. My muscles relax. I close my eyes and continue the story, this time at a slower pace and with more rhythm. I sway to the chant of the words that come pouring out to tell of the day's adventure. I grow bolder with my descriptions.

"Oh, it was a miserable place, thick with brush, which our trusty machetes cut away, treacherous with quicksand, which sucked at our legs, and crawling with poisonous snakes. Our brave leader killed one to clear the way for those of us who came behind."

Again there are murmurs and nods of approval. I see the leader smile in the dark. Tomorrow he may invite me to walk with him, to carry his machete and to learn how to lead the tribe along the river. He may want to teach me how to meet the sudden dangers that lie in wait in the dark—but that's not what this story is about.

I am ready to resume when suddenly there is a signal from our sentry, and the night air is chilled with the horrifying scream of an animal. Something is stalking our camp! We grab our weapons and freeze, ready to move at the next signal, but after long breathless moments we hear the hoot of an owl. All is clear; there is no cause for alarm. I feel the hackles on my back go down. My sweating hand clutches my soiled weapon. I curse myself and wonder how I dare to question the leader when I still rely on cold steel. I toss the knife aside and try to relax and return to the thread of the story. The interruption makes it clear that the telling of the story creates a special time, a time and place that become more important than the adventure lived. Why? I ask myself. What do the words create? In the story the small marsh becomes a swamp, slipping into mud becomes a near-fatal fall into the quagmire, and the stoning of a harmless garter snake becomes the killing of a poisonous viper. In the shadows of the river, I make them see giant monsters, unknown enemies that I know are only reflections of the words I use. I choose details carefully and weave them all into the image; they see themselves as heroes and nod their approval.

I laugh and remind them of the exploits of two new members of the tribe. "They whacked at a hanging vine and cried out that it was a snake," I say, "and when the wind blew in the trees, they said they heard monsters!" Laughter of ridicule floats in the air; the new boys wince; I feel the power of my words. But still I am uneasy. There is something I want to say; I want to get to the germ of the story in today's adventure. The night wears on; I know I must get to it.

"And when we had crossed that dismal swamp, the river valley narrowed into a gorge, and the walls of the canyon were so high and the growth so thick that the sun was shut out. There was only dim light to guide us. Surely, our courage and our steel were tested in that dark pit. The air was thick with sulfurous gases, and in the dark, strange animals cried for our blood! On one side the raging river rushed past us, and one false step would have sent us to our death. But our courage served us well, and the instinct of our leader was great. Never wavering, he cut a path for us to follow. When we finally carved our way out of that stinking and fearful jungle, we came upon the place where the river gorge widened— The Place Where the Swallows Died." I hear a murmur of dissension. I feel their bodies shift uneasily in the dark.

"In that canyon the river widened into a large, deep lake, and springs of clear, sweet water flowed from the earth, and we drank our fill. In the trees the birds sang sweetly, and berries grew in abundance in that quiet paradise. We found strange writings on the rock cliffs, the signs of another tribe that had visited that shelter long before we found it. The sides of the lake were lined with clean, sparkling sand, and in the waters swam the large, golden carp, which we caught and ate."

I pause and remember that in another story, it was forbidden to eat the golden fish. I am about to remind the tribe of their sin when a grunt from the leader cuts me short. I feel cold sweat wet my body. He does not want the mood of the tribe spoiled, and I have already gone too far.

"After we ate," I continue, "we went swimming in the lake, and then we lay naked on the clean sand. Above us the swallows flew, like dancers—they swirled and darted high above the cliffs of the gorge that imprisoned us. 'When they fly high, there will be no rain,' our leader said, 'and that is good because when the rains flood this canyon, there is no escape.' We marveled at his wisdom while looking at the high watermarks on the sides of the sandstone cliffs, and it was true, when the flash floods come, the paradise becomes a tomb of water. We were thankful that our leader could read the signs, and so we rested peacefully.

"The swallows darted and danced brilliantly in the clear blue sky while we played on the sandbars of the river. Glistening wet and naked, we wrestled with each other, and the leader oversaw our contests, awarding prizes to the winners. When we were tired we sat in the shade of the trees and talked. Some talked about women and the things they knew of women, and others whispered the vague dreams and desires that thoughts of women brought into their nights. Overhead the swallows danced—"

Suddenly something in the air is not pure. The fire is dying, and the clean scent of green juniper is gone. The story has already lasted too long, and it is missing its mark. The wind shifts, and a new smell curls at my nostrils; it is the smell of sweat and rotten eggs. In the fading light a golden speck on my arm catches my eye. I scratch and lift the flake of yellow dried egg, encrusted on my skin like spent semen. I rub the fleck of egg with my fingers and it crumbles into dust.

It is then that I remember how the leader called us away from our rest. "He pointed to the cliffs where the mud nests of the swallows clung like beehives to the bare stone. The nests covered the huge slabs of rock. 'We have been deceived,' our leader cried angrily. 'It is the season of the eggs! It's the male swallows that fly high! We have been deceived!' He picked up a stone and sent it crashing against the mud nests. The fragile mud and straw came falling down, and the female swallows darted into flight, cruelly awakened from their time of waiting."

The leader clears his throat, as if to stop me, but I continue, and the uneasiness I have felt all night leaves me.

"We were called into battle, and we obeyed; that peaceful gorge became our battleground. Our missiles found their marks as our barrage of rocks and sticks rained upon the nests. The startled cries of the swallows pierced the air, but we were without mercy! The dry nests exploded with dust and downy feathers, which fell earthward and covered us. The blood of the swallows dripped from the high cliffs, mixed with bits of eggshell and yellow mucous, which rained upon our heads and covered us, and still we did not stop until we were too tired to lift our arms! Oh God, only then did we look around and see what we had done. Some of us went to the river to wash away the stains; I stood and watched the juices of the shattered eggs drain into the once-clean sand. Overhead, the swallows cried."

I pause to catch my breath. I feel a tension in the cold night air. The silence erodes my story; there is nothing more to say. The fire licks at the wind and dies. One by one the members of the tribe stand and leave, without looking at me, without saying a word. The leader stands and looks at me; his icy stare cuts through me, but he cannot hurt me; and when I look at him, I know that I spoke the truth and that my power has been greater than his. We both know that I won't be here in the morning, but I don't care, I have made my choice. He turns and leaves, and for a long time I sit alone, staring into the glowing embers. An animal cries in the dark, a gust of wind makes the sparks fly, then all is quiet again. I stand and face the darkness of the river's shadows, and the night through which I must walk alone.

The Apple Orchard

It was the last week of school, and we were restless. Pico and Chueco ditched every chance they got, and when they came to school it was only to bother the girls and upset the teachers; otherwise they played hooky in Duran's apple orchard, the large orchard that lay between the school and our small neighborhood. They smoked cigarettes and looked at the *Playboy* magazines they had stolen from their older brothers.

I stayed with them once, but my father found out about it and was very angry. "It costs money to send you to school," he said. "So go! Go and learn everything there is to learn. That's the only way to get ahead in this world! Don't play hooky with those tontos. They will never amount to anything!"

I dragged myself to school, which, in spite of the warm spring weather, had one consolation: Miss Brighton. She was the young substitute teacher who had come to replace Mr. Portales after his nervous breakdown. She was my teacher for first-period English and last-period study hall. The day she arrived I helped her move her supplies and books, so we became friends. I think I fell in love with her—I looked forward to her class, and I was sad when she told me she would be with us only until the end of school. She had a regular job in Santa Fe for the following year. For a few weeks my fascination with Miss Brighton grew, and I was happy. During study hall I would pretend to read, but most often I would sit and stare over my book at her. When she happened to glance up, she would smile at me, and sometimes she came to my desk and asked me what I was reading. She loaned me a few books, and after I read them, I told her what I had found in them. Her lips curled in a smile, and her bright eyes shone with light. I began to memorize her features, and at night I began to dream of her.

On the next to the last day of school Pico and Chueco came up with their crazy idea. It didn't interest me at first, but I was also filled with curiosity. Reluctantly, I gave in.

"It's the only way to become a man," Pico said, as if he really knew what he was talking about.

"Yeah," Chueco agreed, "we've seen it in pictures, but you gotta see the real thing to know what it's like."

"Okay, okay," I said finally, "I'll do it."

That night I stole into my parents' bedroom. I had never done that before. Their bedroom was a place where they would go for privacy, and I was never to interrupt them there. My father had told me that only once. We were washing his car when unexpectedly he turned to me and said, "When your mother and me are in the bedroom, you should never disturb us, understand?" I nodded. I knew that part of their life was shut off to me, and it was to remain a mystery.

Now I felt like a thief as I stood in the dark and saw their dark forms on the bed. My father's arm rested over my mother's hip. I heard his low, peaceful snore, and I was relieved that he was asleep. I hurried to her bureau and opened her vanity case. The small mirror we needed for our purpose lay among the bottles of perfume and nail polish. My hands trembled when I found it. I slipped it into my pocket and left the room quickly.

"Did you get it?" Pico asked the next morning.

We met in the apple orchard, where we always met on the way to school. The flowering trees buzzed with honeybees, which swarmed over the thick clusters of white petals. The fragrance reminded me of my mother's vanity case, and for a moment I wondered if I should surrender the mirror to Pico. I had never stolen anything from her before. But it was too late to back out. I took the mirror from my pocket and held it out. For a moment it reflected the light that filtered through the canopy of apple blossoms, then Pico howled and we ran to school.

We decided to steal the glue from Miss Brighton's room. "She likes you," Pico said. "You keep her busy, I'll get the glue." So we pushed our way past the mob that filled the hallway and slipped into her room.

"Isador." She smiled when she saw me. "What are you doing at school so early?" She looked at Pico and Chueco and a slight frown crossed her face.

"I came for the book," I reminded her. She was dressed in bright spring yellow, and the light that shone through the windows glistened on her dress and her soft hair.

"Of course, . . . I have it ready." I walked with her to the desk and she handed me the book. I glanced at the title, *The Arabian Nights*. I shivered because out of the corner of my eye, I saw Pico grab a bottle of glue and stick it under his shirt.

"Thank you," I mumbled.

We turned and raced to the bathroom. A couple of eighth-graders stood by the windows, looking out and smoking cigarettes. They usually paid little attention to us seventh-graders, so we slipped unnoticed into one of the stalls. Pico closed the door. Even in the early morning, the stall was already warm and smelly.

"Okay, break the mirror," Pico whispered.

"Seven years' bad luck," Chueco reminded me.

"Don't pay attention to him, break it!" Pico commanded. I took the mirror from my pocket, recalled for a moment the warm, sweet fragrance that filled my parents' bedroom, the aroma of the vanity case, the sweet scent of the orchard, like Miss Brighton's cologne, and then I looked at Pico and Chueco's sweating faces and smelled the bad odor of the crowded stall. My hands broke out in a sweat.

"Break it!" Pico said sharply.

I looked at the mirror, briefly saw my face in it, saw my eyes, which I knew would give everything away if we were caught, and I thought of the disgrace I would bring my father if he knew what I was about to do.

I can't, I said, but there was no sound, there was only the rancid smell rising from the toilet stool. All our eyes were glued on the mirror as I opened my hand and let it fall. It fell slowly, as if in slow motion, reflecting us, changing our sense of time, which had moved so fast that morning, into a time that moved so slowly I thought the mirror would never hit the floor and break. But it did. The sound exploded, the mirror broke and splintered, and each piece seemed to bounce up to reflect our dark, sweating faces.

"Shhhhhhhh," Pico whispered, finger to lips.

We held our breath and waited. Nobody moved outside the stall. No one had heard the mirror breaking, which to me had sounded like thunder.

Then Pico reached down to pick up three well-shaped pieces, about the size of silver dollars. "Just right!" He grinned and handed each of us a piece. He put his right foot on the toilet seat, opened the bottle, and smeared the white, sticky glue on the tip of his shoe. He placed the piece of mirror on the glue, looked down and saw his sharp, weasel face reflected in it, and smiled. "Fits just right!"

We followed suit, first Chueco, then me.

"This is going to be fun!" Chueco giggled.

"Hot bloomers! Hot bloomers!" Pico slapped my back.

"Now what?"

"Wait for it to dry."

We stood with our feet on the toilet seat, pant legs up, waiting for the glue to dry.

"Whose panties are you going to see first?" Chueco asked Pico.

"Concha Panocha's," Pico leered. "She's got the biggest boobs!"

"If they have big boobs, does that mean they have it big downstairs?" Chueco asked.

"Damn right!"

"Zow-ee!" Chueco exclaimed and spit all over me.

"Shhhh!" Pico whispered. Some boys had come in. They talked while they used the urinals, then they left.

"Ninth-graders," I said.

"Those guys know everything," Chueco added.

"Sure, but after today we'll know too," Pico said and grinned.

"Yeah." Chueco smiled.

I turned away to escape another shower of his bad breath. The wall of the bathroom stall was covered with drawings of naked men and women. Old Placido, the janitor, worked hard to keep the walls clean, but the minute he finished scrubbing off the drawings in one stall, others appeared next door. The drawings were crude, hastily done outlines. The ninth-graders drew them because they knew everything. But after today, Pico had assured us, we would all know, and we would be real men.

Last year the girls didn't seem to matter to us, we played freely with them, but the summer seemed to change everything. When we came back to school, the girls had changed. They were bigger; some of them began to wear lipstick and nail polish. They carried their bodies differently, and I couldn't help but notice for the first time their small, swollen breasts. Pico explained about brassieres to me. An air of mystery began to surround the girls we had once known so well.

I began to listen closely to the stories ninth-grade boys told about girls. The boys gathered in the bathroom to smoke before class and during lunch break, and they talked about cars or sports or girls. Some of them were already dating girls, and a few bragged about girls they had seen naked. They always talked about the girls who were "easy" or girls they had "made," and they laughed at us, chasing us away when we asked questions.

Their stories were incomplete, half whispered, and the crude drawings only aroused more curiosity. The more I thought about the change coming over us, the more troubled I became, and at night my sweaty dreams were filled with images of women, phantasmal creatures who danced in a mist and removed their veils as they swirled around me. But always I awoke before the last veil was removed. I knew nothing. That's why I gave in to Pico's idea. I wanted to know.

He had said that if we glued a small piece of mirror to our shoes, we could push our feet between the girls' legs when they weren't watching; then we could see everything.

"And they don't wear panties in the spring," he said. "Everybody knows that. So you can see everything!"

"Hijola!" Chueco whistled.

"And sometimes there's a little cherry there—"

"Really?" Chueco exclaimed. "Like a cherry from a cherry tree?"

"Sure," Pico said, "watch for it. It's good luck." He reached down and tested the mirror on his shoe. "Hey, it's dry! Let's go!"

We piled out of the dirty stall and followed Pico toward the water fountain at the end of the hall. That's where the girls usually gathered because it was right outside their bathroom.

"Watch me," he said daringly, then he worked his way carefully behind Concha Panocha, who stood talking to her friends. She wore a very loose skirt, perfect for Pico's plan. She was a big girl, and she wasn't very pretty, but Pico liked her. Now we watched as he slowly worked his foot between her feet until the mirror was in position. Then he looked down and we saw his eyes light up. He turned and looked at us with a grin. He had seen everything!

"Perfect! Perfect!" he shouted when he came back to us. "I could see everything! Panties! Nalgas! The spot!"

"Eee-heee-heeee," Chueco laughed. "Now it's my turn!"

They ran off to try Concha again, and I followed them. I felt the blood pounding in my head, and a strange excitement ran through my body. If Pico could see everything, then I could too! I could solve the terrible mystery that had pulled me back and forth all year long. I slipped up behind a girl, not even knowing who she was, and with my heart pounding madly, I carefully pushed my foot between her feet. I worked cautiously, afraid to get caught, afraid of what I was about to see. Then I peered into the mirror, saw in a flash my guilty eyes, moved my foot to see more, but I could see nothing. I leaned closer to her, looked closely into the mirror, but there was nothing except the brief glimpse of her white panties and then the darkness.

I moved closer, accidentally bumped her, and she turned, looking puzzled. I said excuse me, pulled back, and ran away. There was nothing to see; Pico had lied. I was disappointed. So was Chueco when we met again at the bathroom.

"They all wear panties, you liar!" Chueco accused Pico. "I couldn't see anything. One girl caught me looking at her and she hit me with her purse," he complained. His left eye was red. "What do we do now?"

"Let's forget the whole thing," I suggested. The excitement was gone; there was nothing to discover. The mystery that was changing the girls into women would remain unexplained. And not being responsible for the answer was even a relief. I reached down to pull the mirror from my foot.

"No!" Pico exclaimed and grabbed my arm. "Let's try one more thing."

"What?"

He looked at me and grinned. "Let's look at one of the teachers."

"What? You're crazy!"

"No, I'm not! The teachers are more grown up than the girls. They're really women!"

"Bah, they're old hags." Chueco frowned.

"Not Miss Brighton," Pico said, smiling.

"Yeah." Chueco's eyes lit up, and he wiped the white spittle that gathered at the edges of his mouth. "She reminds me of Wonder Woman!" He laughed and made a big curve with his hands.

"And she doesn't wear a bra. I know, I've seen her," Pico added.

"No," I shook my head. No, it was crazy. It would be as bad as looking at my mother. Again I reached down to tear the mirror from my shoe, and again Pico stopped me.

"You can't back out now!" he hissed.

"Yeah," Chueco agreed, "we're in this together."

"If you back out now you're out of the gang," Pico warned. He held my arm tightly, hard enough for it to hurt. Chueco nodded. I looked from one to the other, and I knew they meant it. I had grown up with them, knew them even before we started school; we were a gang. Friends.

"This summer we'll be the kings of the apple orchard, and you won't be able to come in," Pico added to his threat.

"But I don't want to do it," I insisted.

"Who then?" Chueco asked and looked at Pico. "We can't all do it. She'd know."

"So let's draw," Pico said and drew three toothpicks out of his pocket. He always carried toothpicks and usually had one hanging from his lips. "Short man does it. Fair?"

Chueco nodded. "Fair." They looked at me. I nodded. Pico broke one toothpick in half, then he put one half with two whole ones in his hand, made a fist, and held it out for us to draw. I lost.

"Hijo, Isador, you're lucky," Chueco said.

"I, I can't," I mumbled.

"You have to!" Pico said. "That was the deal!"

"Yeah, and we never break our deals," Chueco reminded me, "as long as we've been playing together, we never broke a deal."

"If you back out now, that's the end—no more gang," Pico said seriously. Then he added, "Look, I'll help you. It's the last day of school, right? So there's going to be a lot of noise during last period. I'll call her to my desk, and when she bends over, it'll be easy! She won't know!" He slapped my back.

"Yeah, she won't know!" Chueco repeated. I finally nodded. Why argue with them, I thought. I'll just put my foot out and fake it, and later I'll make up a big story to tell them in the apple orchard. I'll tell them I saw everything. I'll say it was like the drawing in the bathroom. But it wasn't that easy. The rest of the day my thoughts crashed into each other like the goats Mr. Duran sometimes lets out in his orchard. Fake it, one side said; look and solve the mystery, the other whispered. Now's your chance!

By the time I got to last-period study hall, I was very nervous. I slipped into my seat across the aisle from Pico and buried my head in the book Miss Brighton had lent me. I sat with my feet drawn in beneath my desk so the mirror wouldn't show. After a while my foot grew numb in its cramped position. I flipped through the pages and tried to read, but it was no use, my thoughts were on Miss Brighton. Was she the woman who danced in my dreams? Why did I always blush when I looked in her clear blue eyes, those eyes that even now seemed to be daring me to learn their secret?

"Ready," Pico whispered and raised his hand. I felt my throat tighten and go dry. My hands broke out in a sweat. I slipped lower into my desk, trying to hide as I heard her walk toward Pico's desk.

"I want to know this word," Pico pointed.

"Contradictory," she said, "con-tra-dic-to-ry."

"Cunt-try-dick-tory," Pico repeated.

I turned and looked at her. Beyond her, through the window, I could see the apple orchard. The buzz of the bees swarming over the blossoms filled my ears.

"It means to contradict . . . like if one thing is true, then the other is false," I heard her say.

I would have to confess, I thought. Forgive me, Father, but I have contradicted you. I stole from my mother. I looked in the mirror and saw the secret of the woman. And why shouldn't you? something screamed in my head. You have to know! It's the only way to become a man! Look now! See! Learn everything you can!

I took a deep breath and slipped my foot from beneath my desk. I looked down, saw my eyes reflected in the small mirror. I slid it quietly between her feet. I could almost touch her skirt, smell her perfume. Behind her the light of the window and the glow from the orchard were blinding. I will pull back now, won't go all the way, I thought.

"Con-tra . . . " she repeated.

"Cunt-ra . . . " Pico stuttered.

Then I looked, saw in a flash her long, tanned legs, leaned to get a better image, saw the white frill, then nothing. Nothing. The swirl of darkness and the secret. The mystery remained hidden in darkness.

I gasped as she turned. She saw me pull my leg back, caught my eye before I could bury myself in the book again, and in that brief instant I knew she had seen me. A frown crossed her face. She started to say something, then she stood very straight

"Get your books ready, the bell's about to ring" was all she said. Then she walked quickly to her desk and sat down.

"Did you see?" Pico whispered. I said nothing, but stared at a page of the book, which was a blur. The last few minutes of the class passed very slowly. I thought I could even hear the clock ticking.

Then seconds before the bell rang, I heard her say, "Isador, I want you to stay after school."

My heart sank. She knew my crime. I felt sick in the pit of my stomach. I cursed Pico and Chueco for talking me into the awful thing. Better to have let everything remain as it was. Let women keep their secret, whatever it was; it wasn't worth the love I knew would end between me and Miss Brighton. She would tell my parents, and everyone would know. I wished that I could reach down and rip the cursed mirror from my shoe, undo everything and set it right again.

But I couldn't. The bell rang. The room was quickly emptied. I remained sitting at my desk. Long after the noise had cleared from the school grounds, she called me to her desk. I got up slowly, my legs weak and trembling, and I went to her. The room felt very big and empty, bigger than I could ever remember it. And it was very quiet.

She stood and came around her desk. Then she reached down, grabbed the small mirror on my shoe, and jerked it. It splintered when she pulled and cut her thumb, but she didn't cry out; she was trembling with anger. She let the pieces drop on the floor; I saw the blood as it smeared her skirt and formed red balls on the tip of her thumb.

"Why did you do it?" she asked. "I know that Pico and Chueco would do things like that, but not you, Isador, not you!"

I shook my head. "I wanted to know," I heard myself say, "I wanted to know—"

"To know what?" she asked.

"About women . . ."

"But what's there to know? You saw the film the coach showed you, and later we talked in class when the nurse came. She showed you the diagrams, pictures!"

I could only shake my head. "It's not the same. I wanted to know how women are—why different? How?"

She stopped trembling. Her breathing became regular. She took my chin in her hand and made me look at her. Her eyes were clear, not angry, and the frown had left her face. I felt her blood wet my chin.

I cried out, "There's stories . . . and drawings, everywhere . . . and at night I dream, but I still don't know, I don't know anything!"

She looked at me and sighed. Then she drew me close and put her arms around me and smoothed my hair. "I understand," she said. "I understand, but you don't need to hide and see through the mirror. That makes it dirty. There's no secret to hide . . . nothing to hide . . ."

She held me tight, I could feel her heart pounding, as if she too was troubled by the same questions that hounded me. Then she let me go and went to the windows where she pulled shut all the venetian blinds. Except for a ray of light streaming through the top of the blinds, the room grew dark. She went to the door and locked it, turned and looked at me, smiled with a look I had never seen before, then walked gracefully to the small elevated platform in the back of the room.

She stood in the center, and very slowly and carefully she unbuttoned her blouse. She let it drop to her feet, then she undid her bra and let it fall. I held my breath and felt my heart pounding wildly. Never had I seen such beauty as I saw then in the pale light that bathed her naked shoulders and her small breasts. She unfastened her skirt and let it drop; then she lowered her panties and stepped out of them. When she was completely naked, she called me.

"Come and see what a woman is like," she said.

I walked very slowly to the platform. My legs trembled, and I heard a buzzing sound, the kind bees make when they are swarming around the new blossoms of the apple trees. I stood looking at her for a long time, and she stood very still, like a statue. Then I began to walk around the platform, still looking at her, noting every feature and every curve of her long, firm legs, her flat stomach with its dot of a navel, the small round behind that curved down between her legs then rose along her spine to her hair, which fell over her shoulders. I walked around and began to feel a pleasant swirling sensation, as if I was getting drunk. I continued to hear the humming sound—perhaps she was singing, or it was the sound of the bees in the orchard, I didn't know. She was smiling, a distant, pleasant smile.

The glowing light of the afternoon slipped through the top of the blinds and rested on her hair. It was the color of honey, spun so fine I wanted to reach out and touch it, but I was content to look at her beauty. Once I had gone hunting with my uncles and I had seen a golden aspen forest that had entranced me, but even that was not as beautiful as she was. Not even the summer nights when I slept outside and watched the swirl of the Milky Way in the dark sky could compare with the soft curves of her body. Not even the brilliant sunsets of summer, when the light seemed painted on the glowing clouds, could be as full of wonder as the light that fell on her naked body. I looked until I thought I had memorized every curve, every nook, and every shadow of her body. I breathed in, deep, to inhale her aroma; then when I could no longer stand the beauty of the mystery unraveling itself before my eyes, I turned, unlocked the door, and ran into the bright setting sun. A cry of joy exploded from my lips. I ran as hard as I could, and I felt I was turning and leaping in the air like one of the goats in the apple orchard.

"Now I know!" I shouted. "Now I know the secret, and I'll keep it forever!"

I ran through the orchard, laughing with joy. All around me the bright white blossoms of the trees shimmered in the spring light. I heard music in the radiance that exploded around me; I felt like I was dreaming.

I ran around the trees and then stopped to caress them, the smooth trunks and branches reminding me of her body. Each curve developed a slope and shadow of its own; each twist was rich with the secret we now shared. The flowers smelled like her hair and reminded me of her smile. Gasping for breath and still trembling with excitement, I fell exhausted on the ground.

It's a dream, I thought, and I'll soon wake up. No, it had happened! For a few brief moments I had shared the secret of her body, her mystery. But even now, as I tried to remember how she looked, her image was fading as a dream fades. I sat up straight, looked toward the school, and tried to picture the room and the light that had fallen on her bare shoulders, but the image was fuzzy. Her smile, her golden hair, and the soft curves of her body were already fading into the sunset light, dissolving into the graceful curves of the trees. The image of her body, which just a short time ago had been so vivid, was working itself into the apple orchard, becoming the shape of trunks and branches, and her sweet fragrance blended into the damp-earth smell of the orchard, with its nettles and wild alfalfa.

For a moment I tried to keep her image from fading away. Then I realized that she would fade and grow softer in my memory, and that was the real beauty. That's why she told me to look! It was like the mystery of the apple orchard, changing before my eyes even as the sun set. All the curves and shadows, and the sounds and smells, were changing form! In a few days the flowers would wilt and drop; then I would have to wait until next spring to see them again, but the memory would linger. Parts of it would keep turning in my mind; then next spring I would come back to the apple orchard to see the blossoms again. I would always keep coming back, to rediscover, to feel the smoothness of flesh and bark, to smell hair and flower, to linger as I bathed in beauty. The mystery would always be there, and I would be exploring its form forever.

B. Traven Is Alive and Well
in Cuernavaca

I didn't go to Mexico to find B. Traven. Why should I? I have enough
to do writing my own fiction, so I go to Mexico to write, not to
search out writers. B. Traven? you ask. Don't you remember *The
Treasure of the Sierra Madre*? A real classic. They made a movie
from the novel. I remember seeing it when I was a kid. It was
set in Mexico, and it had all the elements of a real adventure
story. B. Traven was an adventurous man, traveled all over the
world, then disappeared into Mexico and cut himself off from
society. He gave no interviews and allowed few photographs.
While he lived he remained unapproachable, anonymous to his
public, a writer shrouded in mystery.

He's dead now, or they say he's dead. I think he's alive and
well. At any rate, he has become something of an institution in
Mexico, a man honored for his work. The cantineros and taxi
drivers in Mexico City know about him as well as the cantineros
of Spain knew Hemingway, or they claim to. When I'm in a cantina,
I never mention I'm a writer, because inevitably some aficionado
will ask, "Do you know the work of B. Traven?" And from some
dusty niche will appear a yellowed, thumb-worn novel by Traven.
Then if the cantinero knows his business, and they all do in Mexico, he is apt to say, "Did you know that B. Traven used to drink
here?" If you show the slightest interest, he will follow with "Sure,
he used to sit right over here. In this corner. . . ." And if you don't
leave right then, you will wind up hearing stories about the mysterious B. Traven while buying many drinks for the local patrons.

Everybody reads his novels, on the buses, on street corners.
One turned up for me, and that's how this story started. I was

sitting in the train station in Juárez, waiting for the train to Cuernavaca, which would be an exciting title for this story. I was drinking beer to kill time, the erotic and sensitive Mexican time that is so different from the clean-packaged, well-kept time of the Americanos. Time in Mexico can be cruel and punishing, but it is never indifferent. It permeates everything, it changes reality. Einstein would have loved Mexico because there, time and space are one. I stare into empty space more often when I'm in Mexico. The past seems to infuse the present, and in the brown, wrinkled faces of the old people, one sees the presence of the past. In Mexico I like to walk the narrow streets of the cities and the smaller pueblos, wandering aimlessly, feeling the distinctively Mexican sunlight, listening to voices call in the streets, peering into dark eyes so secretive and proud. The Mexican people guard a secret. But in the end, one is never really lost in Mexico. All streets lead to a good cantina. All good stories start in a cantina.

At the train station, after I let the kids who hustle the tourists know that I didn't want chewing gum or cigarettes, and I didn't want my shoes shined, and I didn't want a woman at the moment, I was left alone to drink my beer. Luke-cold Dos Equis. I don't remember how long I had been there or how many Dos Equis I had finished when I glanced at the seat next to me and saw a book, which turned out to be a B. Traven novel, old and used and obviously much read. What's so strange about finding a B. Traven novel in that dingy little corner of a bar in the Juárez train station? Nothing, unless you know that in Mexico, one never finds anything. It is a country that doesn't waste anything; everything is recycled. Chevrolets run with patched-up Ford engines and Chrysler transmissions; buses are kept together, and kept running, with baling wire and homemade parts; yesterday's Traven novel is the pulp on which tomorrow's Fuentes story will appear. Time recycles in Mexico. Time returns to the past, and Christians find themselves dreaming of ancient Aztec rituals. They who do not believe that Quetzalcoatl will return to save Mexico have little faith.

So the novel was the first clue. Later there was Justino. Who is Justino? you want to know. Justino was the jardinero who cared for the garden of my friend, the friend who had invited me to stay at his home in Cuernavaca while I continued to write. The day after I arrived, I was sitting in the sun, letting the fatigue of the long journey ooze away, thinking nothing, when Justino appeared on the scene. He had finished cleaning the swimming pool and was taking his morning break, so he sat in the shade of the orange tree and introduced himself. Right away I could tell that he would rather be a movie actor or an adventurer, a real free spirit. But things didn't work out for him. He got married, children appeared, he took a couple of mistresses, more children appeared, so he had to work to support his family. "A man is like a rooster," he said after we had talked awhile, "the more chickens he has, the happier he is." Then he asked me what I was going to do about a woman while I was there, and I told him I hadn't thought that far ahead, that I would be happy if I could just get a damned story going. This puzzled Justino, and I think for a few days it worried him. So on Saturday night he took me out for a few drinks, and we wound up in some of the bordellos of Cuernavaca in the company of some of the most beautiful women in the world. Justino knew them all. They loved him, and he loved them.

I learned something more of the nature of this jardinero a few nights later, when the heat and an irritating mosquito wouldn't let me sleep. I heard music from a radio, so I put on my pants and walked out into the Cuernavacan night, an oppressive, warm night heavy with the sweet perfume of the dama de noche bushes that lined the wall of my friend's villa. From time to time I heard a dog cry in the distance, and I remembered that in Mexico, many people die of rabies. Perhaps that is why the walls of the wealthy are always so high and the locks always secure. Or maybe it was because of the occasional gunshots that explode in the night. The news media tell us that Mexico is the most stable country in Latin America, and with the recent oil finds, the bankers and the oil men want to keep it that way. I sense, and many know, that in the dark the revolution does not sleep. It is a spirit kept at bay by the high fences and the locked gates, yet it prowls the heart of every man. "Oil will create a new revolution," Justino had told me, "but it's going to be for our people. Mexicans are tired of building gas stations for the Gringos from Gringolandia." I understood what he meant: There is much hunger in the country.

I lit a cigarette and walked toward my friend's car, which was parked in the driveway near the swimming pool. I approached quietly and peered in. On the back seat, with his legs propped on the front seatback, smoking a cigar, sat Justino. Two big, luscious women sat on either side of him, running their fingers through his hair and whispering in his ears. The doors were open to allow a breeze. He looked content. Sitting there, he was that famous artist on his way to an afternoon reception in Mexico City, or he was a movie star on his way to the premiere of his most recent movie. Or perhaps it was Sunday and he was taking a drive in the country, toward Tepoztlán. And why shouldn't his two friends accompany him? I had to smile. Unnoticed I backed away and returned to my room. So there was quite a bit more than met the eye to this short, dark Indian from Ocosingo.

In the morning I asked my friend, "What do you know about Justino?"

"Justino? You mean Vitorino."

"Is that his real name?"

"Sometimes he calls himself Trinidad."

"Maybe his name is Justino Vitorino Trinidad," I suggested.

"I don't know, don't care," my friend answered. "He told me he used to be a guide in the jungle. Who knows? The Mexican Indian has an incredible imagination. Really gifted people. He's a good jardinero, and that's what matters to me. It's difficult to get good jardineros, so I don't ask questions."

"Is he reliable?" I wondered aloud.

"As reliable as a ripe mango," my friend replied.

I wondered how much he knew, so I pushed a little further. "And the radio at night?"

"Oh, that. I hope it doesn't bother you. Robberies and break-ins are increasing here in the colonia. Something we never used to have. Vitorino said that if he keeps the radio on low, the sound keeps thieves away. A very good idea, don't you think?"

I nodded. A very good idea.

"And I sleep very soundly," my friend concluded, "so I never hear it."

The following night when I awakened and heard the soft sound of the music from the radio and heard the splashing of water, I had only to look from my window to see Justino and his friends in the pool, swimming nude in the moonlight. They were joking and laughing softly as they splashed each other, being quiet so as not to awaken my friend, the patrón who slept so soundly. The women were beautiful. Brown skinned and glistening with water in the moonlight, they reminded me of ancient Aztec maidens, swimming around Chac, their god of rain. They teased Justino, and he smiled as he floated on a rubber mattress in the middle of the pool, smoking his cigar, happy because they were happy. When he smiled, the gold fleck of a filling glinted in the moonlight.

"Que cabrón!" I laughed and closed my window.

Justino said a Mexican never lies. I believed him. If a Mexican says he will meet you at a certain time and place, he means he will meet you sometime at some place. Americans who retire in Mexico often complain of maids who swear they will come to work on a designated day, then don't show up. They did not lie. They knew they couldn't be at work, but to tell the señora otherwise would make her sad or displease her, so they agree on a date so that everyone will remain happy. What a beautiful aspect of character. It's a real virtue, which Norteamericanos interpret as a character fault, because we are used to asserting ourselves on time and people. We feel secure and comfortable only when everything is neatly packaged in its proper time and place. We don't like the disorder of a free-flowing life.

Someday, I thought, Justino will give a grand party in the sala of his patrón's home. His three wives, or his wife and two mistresses, and his dozens of children will be there. So will the women from the bordellos. He will preside over the feast, smoke his cigars, request his favorite beer-drinking songs from the mariachis, smile, tell stories, and make sure everyone has a grand time. He will be dressed in a tuxedo, borrowed from the patrón's closet of course, and he will act gallantly and show everyone that a man who has just come into sudden wealth should share it with his friends. And in the morning he will report to the patrón that something has to be done about the poor mice that are coming in from the streets and eating everything in the house.

"I'll buy some poison," the patrón will suggest.

"No, no." Justino will shake his head. "A little music from the radio and a candle burning in the sala will do."

And he will be right.

I liked Justino. He was a rogue with class. We talked about the weather, the lateness of the rainy season, women, the role of oil in Mexican politics. Like other workers, he believed nothing was going to filter down to the campesinos. "We could all be real Mexican greasers with all that oil," he said, "but the politicians will keep it all."

"What about the United States?" I asked.

"Oh, I have traveled in the Estados Unidos to the north. It's a country that's going to the dogs in a worse way than Mexico. The thing I liked the most was your cornflakes."

"Cornflakes?"

"Sí. You can make really good cornflakes."

"And women?"

"Ah, you better keep your eyes open, my friend. Those gringas are going to change the world just like the suecas changed Spain."

"For better or for worse?"

"Spain used to be a nice country." He winked.

We talked, we argued, we drifted from subject to subject. I learned from him. I had been there a week when he told me the story that eventually led me to B. Traven. One day I was sitting under the orange tree reading the B. Traven novel I had found in the Juárez train station, keeping one eye on the ripe oranges, which fell from time to time, my mind wandering as it worked to focus on a story so that I could begin to write. After all, that's why I had come to Cuernavaca, to get some writing done, but nothing was coming, nothing. Justino wandered by and asked what I was reading, and I replied that it was an adventure story, a story of a man's search for an illusive pot of gold at the end of a make-believe rainbow. He nodded, thought awhile, and gazed toward Popo, Popocatepetl, the towering volcano that lay to the south, shrouded in mist, waiting for the rains as we waited for the rains, sleeping, gazing at his female counterpart, Itzá, who lay sleeping and guarding the valley of Cholula, where over four hundred years ago, Cortés had shown his wrath and executed thousands of Cholulans.

"I am going on an adventure," he finally said and paused. "I think you might like to go with me."

I said nothing, but I put my book down and listened.

"I have been thinking about it for a long time, and now is the time to go. You see, it's like this. I grew up on the hacienda of don Francisco Jiménez—it's to the south, just a day's drive on the carretera. In my village nobody likes don Francisco; they fear and hate him. He has killed many men, and he has taken their fortunes and buried them. He is a very rich man, muy rico. Many men have tried to kill him, but don Francisco is like the devil—he kills them first."

I listened as I always listen, because one never knows when a word or a phrase or an idea will be the seed from which a story sprouts, but at first there was nothing interesting. It sounded like the typical patrón-peón story I had heard so many times before. A man, the patrón, keeps the workers enslaved in serfdom, and because he wields so much power, soon stories are told about him, and he begins to acquire superhuman powers. He acquires a mystique, just like the divine right of old. The patrón wields a mean machete, like old King Arthur swung Excalibur. He chops off heads of dissenters and sits on top of the bones-and-skulls pyramid, the king of the mountain, the top macho.

"One day I was sent to look for lost cattle," Justino continued. "I rode back into the hills where I had never been. At the foot of a hill, near a ravine, I saw something move in the bush. I dismounted and moved forward quietly. I was afraid it might be bandidos who steal cattle, and if they saw me, they would kill me. When I came near the place I heard a strange sound. Somebody was crying. My back shivered, just like a dog when he sniffs the devil at night. I thought I was going to see witches, brujas who like to go to those deserted places to dance for the devil, or la Llorona."

"La Llorona," I said aloud. My interest grew. I had been hearing Llorona stories since I was a kid, and I was always ready for one more. La Llorona is that archetypal woman of ancient legends who murdered her children, then repentant and demented, she spends the rest of eternity searching for them.

"Sí, la Llorona. You know that poor woman used to drink a lot. She played around with men, and when she had babies, she got rid of them by throwing them into la barranca. One day she realized what she had done and went crazy. She started crying and pulling her hair and running up and down the river looking for her children. It's a very sad story."

A new version, I thought, and yes, a sad story. And what of the man who made love to the woman who became la Llorona? I wondered. Did he ever cry for his children? It doesn't seem fair to have only her suffer, only her crying and doing penance. Perhaps a man should run with her, and in our legends we would call him "El Mero Chingón," he who screwed up everything. Then maybe the tale of love and passion and insanity will be complete. Yes, I think someday I will write that story.

"What did you see?" I asked Justino.

"Something worse than la Llorona," he whispered.

To the south a wind mourned and moved the clouds off Popo's crown. The bald, snow-covered mountain thrust its power into the blue Mexican sky. The light glowed like liquid gold around the god's head. Popo was a god, an ancient god. Somewhere at his feet Justino's story had taken place.

"I moved closer, and when I parted the bushes I saw don Francisco. He was sitting on a rock, and he was crying. From time to time he looked at the ravine in front of him; the hole seemed to slant into the earth. That pozo is called el Pozo de Mendoza. I had heard stories about it before, but I had never seen it. I looked into the pozo, and you wouldn't believe what I saw.

He waited, so I asked, "What?"

"Money! Huge piles of gold and silver coins! Necklaces and bracelets and crowns of gold, all loaded with all kinds of precious stones! Jewels! Diamonds! All sparkling in the sunlight that entered the hole. More money than I have ever seen! A fortune, my friend, a fortune that is still there, just waiting for two adventurers like us to take it!"

"Us? But what about don Francisco? It's his land, his fortune."

"Ah," Justino smiled, "that's the strange thing about this fortune. Don Francisco can't touch it—that's why he was crying. You see, I stayed there, and I watched him closely. Every time he stood up and started to walk into the pozo, the money disappeared. He stretched out his hand to grab the gold, and poof, it was gone! That's why he was crying! He murdered all those people and hid their wealth in the pozo, but now he can't touch it. He is cursed."

"El Pozo de Mendoza," I said aloud. Something began to click in my mind. I smelled a story.

"Who was Mendoza?" I asked.

"He was a very rich man. Don Francisco killed him in a quarrel they had over some cattle. But Mendoza must have put a curse on don Francisco before he died, because now don Francisco can't get to the money."

"So Mendoza's ghost haunts old don Francisco," I said.

"Many ghosts haunt him," Justino answered. "He has killed many men."

"And the fortune, the money?"

He looked at me, and his eyes were dark and piercing, "It's still there. Waiting for us!"

"But it disappears as one approaches it. You said so yourself. Perhaps it's only a hallucination."

Justino shook his head. "No, it's real gold and sliver, not hallucination money. It disappears for don Francisco because the curse is on him, but the curse is not on us." He smiled. He knew he had drawn me into his plot. "We didn't steal the money, so it won't disappear for us. And you are not connected with the place. You are innocent. I've thought very carefully about it, and now is the time to go. I can lower you into the pozo with a rope. In a few hours we can bring out the entire fortune. All we need is a car. You can borrow the patrón's car; he is your friend. But he must not know where we're going. We can be there and back in one day, one night." He nodded as if to assure me, then he turned and looked at the sky. "It will not rain today. It will not rain for a week. Now is the time to go."

He winked and returned to watering the grass and flowers of the jardín, a wild Pan among the bougainvillea and the roses, a man possessed by a dream. The gold was not for him, he told me the next day, it was for his women: He would buy them all gifts, bright dresses, and he would take them on a vacation to the United States; he would educate his children, send them to the best colleges. I listened, and the germ of the story cluttered my thoughts as I sat beneath the orange tree in the mornings. I couldn't write, nothing was coming, but I knew that there were elements for a good story in Justino's tale. In dreams I saw the lonely hacienda to the south. I saw the pathetic, tormented figure of don Francisco as he cried over the fortune he couldn't touch. I saw the ghosts of the men he had killed, and I saw the lonely women who mourned over them and cursed the evil don Francisco. In one dream I saw a man I took to be B. Traven, a gray-haired, distinguished-looking gentleman who looked at me and nodded approvingly. "Yes, there's a story there, follow it, follow it. . . ."

In the meantime, other small and seemingly insignificant details came my way. During a luncheon at the home of my friend, a woman I did not know leaned toward me and asked me if I would like to meet the widow of B. Traven. The woman's hair was tinged orange; her complexion was ashen gray. I didn't know who she was or why she would mention B. Traven to me. How did she know Traven had come to haunt my thoughts? Was she a clue that would help unravel the mystery? I didn't know, but I nodded.

Yes, I would like to meet her. I had heard that Traven's widow, Rosa Elena, lived in Mexico City. But what would I ask her? What did I want to know? Would she know Traven's secret? Somehow he had learned that to keep his magic intact, he had to keep away from the public. Like the fortune in the pozo, the magic feel for the story might disappear if unclean hands reached for it. I turned to look at the woman again, but she was gone. I wandered to the terrace to finish my beer. Justino sat beneath the orange tree. He yawned. I knew the literary talk bored him. He was eager to be on the way to el Pozo de Mendoza.

I was nervous, too, but I didn't know why. The tension for the story was there, but something was missing. Or perhaps it was just Justino's insistence that I decide whether I was going or not that drove me out of the house in the mornings. Time usually devoted to writing found me in a small cafe in the center of town. From there I could watch the shops open, watch the people cross the zócalo, the main square. I drank lots of coffee, I smoked a lot, I daydreamed, I wondered about the significance of the pozo, the fortune, Justino, the story I wanted to write, and B. Traven. In one of these moods I saw a friend I hadn't heard from in years. Suddenly he was there, trekking across the square, dressed like an old rabbi, moss and green algae for a beard, and followed by a troop of very dignified Lacandones, Mayan Indians from Chiapas.

"Victor," I gasped, unsure if he was real or a part of the shadows the sun created as it flooded the square with its light.

"I have no time to talk," he said as he stopped to munch on my pan dulce and sip my coffee. "I only want you to know, for the purposes of your story, that I was in a Lacandonian village last month, and a Hollywood film crew descended from the sky. They came in helicopters. They set up tents near the village, and big-bosomed, bikinied actresses emerged from them, tossed themselves on the cut trees that are the atrocity of the giant American lumber companies, and they cried while the director shot his film. Then they produced a gray-haired old man from one of the tents and took shots of him posing with the Indians. Herr Traven, the director called him."

He finished my coffee, nodded to his friends, and they began to walk away.

"B. Traven?" I asked.

He turned. "No, an imposter, an actor. Be careful for imposters. Remember, even Traven used many disguises, many names!"

"Then he's alive and well?" I shouted. People around me turned to stare.

"His spirit is with us" were the last words I heard as they moved across the zócalo, a strange troop of nearly naked Lacandon Maya and my friend the Guatemalan Jew, returning to the rain forest, returning to the primal, innocent land.

I slumped in my chair and looked at my empty cup. What did it mean? As their trees fall, the Lacandones die. Betrayed as B. Traven had been betrayed. Does each one of us also die as the trees fall in the dark depths of the Chiapas jungle? Far to the north, in Aztlán, it is the same: The earth is ripped open to expose and mine the yellow uranium. A few poets sing songs and stand in the way as the giant machines of the corporations rumble over the land and grind everything into dust. New holes are made in the earth, pozos full of curses, pozos with fortunes we cannot touch, should not touch. Oil, coal, uranium from holes through which we suck the blood of the earth.

There were other incidents. A telephone call late one night: A voice with a German accent called my name, but when I replied, the line went dead. A letter addressed to B. Traven came in the mail. It was dated March 26, 1969. My friend returned it to the post office. Justino grew more and more morose. He sat under the orange tree and stared into space, and my friend complained about the garden drying up. Justino looked at me and scowled. He did a little work, then went back to daydreaming. Without the rains the garden withered. His heart was set on the adventure that lay at el pozo. Finally I said yes, dammit, why not, let's go, neither one of us is getting anything done here, and Justino, cheering like a child, ran to prepare for the trip. But when I asked my friend for the weekend loan of the car, he reminded me that we were invited to a tertulia, an afternoon reception, at the home of Señora Ana

Rosinski. Many writers and artists would be there. It was in my honor so that I could meet the literati of Cuernavaca. I had to tell Justino I couldn't go to el pozo.

Now it was I who grew morose. The story growing within would not let me sleep. I awakened in the night and looked out the window, hoping to see Justino and women bathing in the pool, enjoying themselves. But all was quiet. No radio played. The still night was warm and heavy. From time to time gunshots sounded in the dark, dogs barked, and the presence of a Mexico that never sleeps closed in on me.

Saturday morning dawned with a strange overcast. Perhaps the rains will come, I thought. In the afternoon I reluctantly accompanied my friend to the reception. I had not seen Justino all day, but I saw him at the gate as we drove out. He looked tired, as if he, too, had not slept. He wore the white shirt and baggy pants of a campesino. His straw hat cast a shadow over his eyes. I wondered if he had decided to go to the pozo alone. He didn't speak as we drove through the gate; he only nodded. When I looked back, I saw him standing by the gate, looking after the car, and I had a vague, uneasy feeling that I had lost an opportunity.

The afternoon gathering was a pleasant affair, attended by a number of vociferous artists, critics, and writers who enjoyed the refreshing drinks and hors d'oeuvres.

But my mood drove me away from the crowd. I wandered around the terrace and found a foyer surrounded by green plants, huge fronds and ferns and flowering bougainvillea. I pushed the green aside and entered a quiet, very private alcove. The light was dim, the air was cool, a perfect place for contemplation. At first I thought I was alone, then I saw the man sitting in one of the wicker chairs next to a small wrought-iron table. He was an elderly white-haired gentleman. His face showed that he had lived a full life, yet he was still very distinguished in his manner and posture. His eyes shone brightly.

"Perdón," I apologized and turned to leave. I did not want to intrude.

"No, no, please." He motioned to the empty chair. "I've been waiting for you." He spoke English with a slight German accent. Or perhaps it was Norwegian, I couldn't tell the difference. "I can't take the literary gossip. I prefer the quiet."

I nodded and sat. He smiled and I felt at ease. I took the cigar he offered and we lit up. He began to talk and I listened. He was a writer also, but I had the good manners not to ask his titles. He talked about the changing Mexico, the change the new oil would bring, the lateness of the rains and how they affected the people and the land, and he talked about how important a woman was in a writer's life. He wanted to know about me, about the Chicanos of Aztlán, about our work. It was the workers, he said, who would change society. The artist learned from the worker. I talked, and sometime during the conversation, I told him the name of the friend with whom I was staying. He laughed and wanted to know if Vitorino was still working for him.

"Do you know Justino?" I asked.

"Oh, yes, I know that old guide. I met him many years ago, when I first came to Mexico," he answered. "Justino knows the campesino very well. He and I traveled many places together, he in search of adventure, I in search of stories."

I thought the coincidence strange, so I gathered courage and asked, "Did he ever tell you the story of the fortune at el Pozo de Mendoza?"

"Tell me?" the old man smiled. "I went there."

"With Justino?"

"Yes, I went with him. What a rogue he was in those days, but a good man. If I remember correctly I even wrote a story based on that adventure. Not a very good story. Never came to anything. But we had a grand time. People like Justino are the writer's source. We met interesting people and saw fabulous places, enough to last me a lifetime. We were supposed to be gone for one day, but we were gone nearly three years. You see, I wasn't interested in the pots of gold he kept saying were just over the next hill; I went because there was a story to write."

"Yes, that's what interested me," I agreed.

"A writer has to follow a story if it leads him to hell itself. That's our curse. Ay, and each one of us knows his own private hell."

I nodded. I felt relieved. I sat back to smoke the cigar and sip from my drink. Somewhere to the west the sun bronzed the evening sky. On a clear afternoon, Popo's crown would glow like fire.

"Yes," the old man continued, "a writer's job is to find and follow people like Justino. They're the source of life. The ones you have to keep away from are the dilettantes like the ones in there." He motioned in the general direction of the noise of the party. "I stay with people like Justino. They may be illiterate, but they understand our descent into the pozo of hell, and they understand us because they're willing to share the adventure with us. You seek fame and notoriety and you're dead as a writer."

I sat upright. I understood now what the pozo meant, why Justino had come into my life to tell me the story. It was clear. I rose quickly and shook the old man's hand. I turned and parted the palm leaves of the alcove. There, across the way, in one of the streets that led out of the maze of the town toward the south, I saw Justino. He was walking in the direction of Popocatepetl, and he was followed by women and children, a ragtag army of adventurers, all happy, all singing. He looked up to where I stood on the terrace, and he smiled as he waved. He paused to light the stub of a cigar. The women turned, and the children turned, and all waved to me. Then they continued their walk, south, toward the foot of the volcano. They were going to el Pozo de Mendoza, to the place where the story originated.

I wanted to run after them, to join them in the glorious light that bathed the Cuernavaca valley and the majestic snow-covered head of Popo. The light was everywhere, a magnetic element that flowed from the clouds. I waved as Justino and his followers disappeared in the light. Then I turned to say something to the old man, but he was gone. I was alone in the alcove. Somewhere in the background I heard the tinkling of glasses and the laughter from the party, but that was not for me. I left the terrace and crossed the lawn, found the gate and walked down the street. The sounds of Mexico filled the air. I felt light and happy. I wandered aimlessly through the curving, narrow streets, then I quickened my pace because suddenly the story was overflowing and I needed to write. I needed to get to my quiet room and write the story about B. Traven being alive and well in Cuernavaca.

Jerónimo's Journey

Jerónimo began his journey home to deliver his father's leg the day before el Día de los Muertos. The Cuernavaca bus station was crowded; the workers who had gotten a day off waited anxiously for the buses to arrive. When a bus did arrive, they rushed forward to get a good seat. All were going home to celebrate the feast of the Day of the Dead.

Jerónimo's patrona came with him to the bus station; she bought the ticket and handed him the package that contained the artificial leg she had bought for Jerónimo's father. He thanked her, boarded the bus, and found a seat by the window. The dusty, creaking bus was crowded, but Jerónimo knew that most of the passengers would be going farther south. Only he would be getting off at Pena Mayor.

The bus lurched forward, and Jerónimo waved at his patrona. "Hasta pasando mañana!" the patrona called.

"Sí," Jerónimo answered. He was going home for only one day, only for el Día de los Muertos; then he would return to take care of his patrona's garden. A fine garden it is, Jerónimo thought with satisfaction, as fine a garden as the patrona is a good woman. Not many of the jardineros of Cuernavaca got a day off during the dry season, and fewer had as thoughtful a patrona as Jerónimo had. Only a generous woman like his patrona would have gone to the trouble and expense to have the false leg built so that Jerónimo's crippled father could walk.

Jerónimo thought of home as the bus headed south, climbing into the high, dry mountains. A thin old woman dressed in black sat next to him. The fragrance around her reminded Jerónimo of the old women who burned votive candles at the church altar. He had moved to make room for her, holding the package with the false leg on his lap. The old woman spoke only once, to say, "Este loco nos va matar."

She meant the bus driver. He was driving very fast around the curves of the mountain. From time to time the driver took swigs from a bottle of tequila, then passed the bottle to his friend, who stood by the front door. The friend strummed on a guitar, and they sang.

They are just enjoying themselves, Jerónimo thought. Tomorrow was the Day of the Dead. Everybody was in a happy mood. Some were traveling home to be with their families; others were going to mercados they knew; some were planning special pilgrimages to the churches of the pueblos south of Pena Mayor. There they would visit the campo santos and make offerings to their dead; they would share the bread of the dead with those loved ones who rested in their graves.

Everyone was happy: The women talked, the men told stories of their villages, the bus driver and his friend sang, and the bus swayed from one side of the road to the other. Like a giant animal drunk with the passengers it carried, it swayed back and forth and tipped dangerously on the high cliffs, catching the gravel on the shoulder of the road and spitting the small rocks to the bottom of the steep barranca.

Except for the old woman, the other passengers did not appear to be apprehensive about the wild ride and the tipsy bus driver; they were used to reckless bus drivers. He drove and sang with passion; they appreciated that. Bottles of tequila and mescal were opened, the men relaxed, the women exchanged gossip; one woman with two children, a boy and a girl, opened her bundle of food and gave her children some of the cookies she had baked for the Day of the Dead. For the boy, a cookie shaped like a skull; for the girl, a cookie shaped like the skeleton of death. The other women followed suit. They, too, opened their bundles, and their children munched on the skeleton-shaped cookies.

Before they ate, the women and the children displayed their sweet wares; they compared the shapes and the decoration on the cookies, the red eyes of death, the sugar bones of the skeleton, the white candy teeth. They compared prices, talked about the best panaderías, and admired the work of the baker as art. The best-decorated cookies were passed around for all to see; the owners glowed with pride, and the others grew envious.

Only Jerónimo had nothing to show. He carried the artificial leg for his father, but he couldn't show that; the people would only laugh. For now, he was happy to see the children eating the cookies and candy shaped in the form of death; tomorrow he would be eating the cookies his mother baked for the feast day. Tomorrow he would be resting peacefully in Pena Mayor.

Jerónimo smiled and tried to relax. He looked out the window. Far below he could see fields of corn and patches of red where roses grew. Jerónimo sighed. Something he could not understand made him uneasy. Was it the old woman falling asleep and pressing against him, or was it the wooden leg he was delivering to his father? The leg seemed to grow heavier and heavier, and he was forced to clutch it to his chest. At times the leg seemed to move in the bag, and a dread filled Jerónimo. Was the leg alive? No, it could not be. It was made only of wood and steel and leather straps.

Life was only in man, in animals, in the green plants, but if the leg felt alive, maybe it had a power to help his father walk again. This is what Jerónimo was thinking when a brilliant light appeared outside the bus window. The flash was like lightning that lit up the sky. It was a blinding light, with the sound of a whirlwind around it. A woman screamed; others gasped as the celestial light filled the bus with its brilliance.

The light lit up Jerónimo's shirt, the black and white striped shirt that looked like a baseball shirt and that made him feel very self-conscious. When he had put it on that morning, he had been afraid his friends in the village would laugh at him. The shirt was a gift from la señora Ana Rosinski, his patrona, and to please her he had worn it. He had put the shirt on and looked in the mirror and nodded. So I will be the only person in Pena Mayor with such a shirt, he thought. Let them laugh.

The light subsided, leaving only the howling wind and the storm of dust covering the mountain.

The bus stopped. Jerónimo got off at the crossroads, where a plain stone marker indicated the name of his village, Pena Mayor. He stood swaying in the wind, trying to get his bearings. He trudged up the dirt road that led to his village, high on the mountain. The strong wind swept the chalky, blinding dust in great clouds, and Jerónimo felt lost. There was no one else on the road, no workers, no one going to or from the fields. The wind moaned and grew in force, and the dust obscured the mountain and the local landmarks that were familiar to Jerónimo. Clutching the wooden leg to his chest, he lowered his head against the wind and entered the village.

One of the village dogs greeted him, growling and snarling.

Don't you know me, dog? Jerónimo spoke. *This is my home. My father and mother live here, there in the house by the barranca. Don't you know me?*

The dog whimpered, then turned and slunk down the dusty road.

The village appeared deserted. Clouds of white dust swept down the road, and Jerónimo could see only the barest outline of the stone houses, which were shut tight against the wind. For a moment Jerónimo felt unsure. Had he left the bus at the right spot on the highway, had he come to the right place? Yes, he remembered the sign, Pena Mayor, the village of his birth. It was the dust that blinded him and made the surroundings unfamiliar. The white cloud blew from the dry mountain top, sifting down on the village where he had lived most of his life.

As a child he had tended goats on the mountain, following the herd, which he cared for from day to day, year to year, on the rocky cliffs. He looked up, to see if he could see the peaks where he had roamed for so many years with his goats, but the billowing dust covered everything. The wind mourned like a lost spirit through the streets of the small village, and it shrieked through the cliffs and barrancas of the mountain.

In Pena Mayor life was barren. Jerónimo had left to start a new life in Cuernavaca. There he had found work as a jardinero in the gardens of the wealthy. He had made a new life among the people who seemed to have life so easy. The friends of his patrona came from many foreign places: They spoke languages he did not understand, sat by the swimming pool, drank coffee in the morning and beer or refrescos in the afternoon; they lay in the sun, and they laughed. Jerónimo listened as he trimmed the grass and the bushes, as he watered during the dry spell. Compared to the dryness and the poverty of his village on the mountain, Jerónimo thought, the gardens of Cuernavaca were heaven.

And now Jerónimo was returning to his village to deliver the leg to his father, la pierna postiza, a leg made of wood, steel splints, and leather straps. The wood was smooth and painted a pale flesh color.

What are you carrying? a voice asked, startling Jerónimo.

The old woman had come out of the dust, suddenly appearing close to him. A rebozo covered her head and most of her face. She was bent and old, and on her arm she carried a tin bucket covered with a threadbare towel. Jerónimo recognized her. She was the old woman who sold nopales. She went up to the mountain daily and cut the palm-shaped leaves of the cactus, which she brought down to sell in the village.

Everyone said she was a witch, but they bought her nopales anyway. She was the only one who knew the crags and cliffs where the most succulent nopales grew. Once a man had died after eating the woman's cactus. The man had laughed at the old woman and ridiculed her; then that evening at his supper, he had eaten the nopal and died.

"The old witch poisoned me!" he shouted as he ran in agony through the village. Then he collapsed and died in the dust of the street. No one laughed at the old woman after that. They bought the nopales and prepared them with goat meat for their evening meal; they enjoyed the delicacy even as they thought of death.

Jerónimo stood bewildered, looking into the sharp eyes of the old woman. The wind whipped at her rebozo and ragged skirt.

I have brought a leg for my father, a new leg for him to stand on, he said. *As you know, years ago he lost his leg. Some say a rattlesnake bit him and caused the leg to rot; some say he stepped on a nail. I don't know, but he lost the leg. Now he will have a new leg.* Jerónimo opened the bag and showed her the false leg.

Is it hollow? the old woman asked.

No, solid, Jerónimo answered, raising his voice to be heard above the sound of the wind. *It is very heavy. Very heavy.*

He did not understand why the leg should be so heavy. "It is made of good wood," the patrona had explained. "It will last forever. Now your father can wear two boots," she had said, "and the boots will wear out before this leg. This leg will last forever."

Jerónimo was grateful to his patrona for having the leg built. She had heard Jerónimo speak of his father and how he could not get around on one leg, so she'd had the leg made in a shop in Mexico City. But when Jerónimo had taken the leg from his patrona, he had felt a wave of terror. The leg felt alive, and if it was alive, it could not last forever. Nothing can last forever; that is what Jerónimo had been thinking on the bus. Not even the gardens of Cuernavaca.

The furious wind swirling around him reminded Jerónimo that in Cuernavaca the wind did not blow. There it was always sunny, the gardens always green and in bloom.

You are a good son, the old woman said. *You will go to heaven.*

Then she hobbled away, disappearing into the cloud of dust. Jerónimo turned to resume his way to his father's house, but still he was unsure of his surroundings. He looked for landmarks but saw none in the thick dust. There was only the howling wind as it swept down the rocky mountain. On the mountainside, Jerónimo knew, were the milpas of corn, the fruit trees. In the good years, the people had corn and fruit, in dry years, only hunger. Then the men tightened their belts and grimly joked when they met each other. They were robbing death of some fat, they said.

Jerónimo shivered. Something in the cry of the wind reminded him of the coyote that had come to kill his goats. The coyote had come near the camp late in the evening, and Jerónimo had brought only a slingshot for protection. The coyote was big, so big it looked like a wolf. It came toward Jerónimo, looked into his eyes, and seemed to laugh. Then it seized a kid from the herd and disappeared up the mountain.

After that it came every evening, filling Jerónimo with terror. It cried and howled in the crags at night, and Jerónimo shivered by the fire. He could not eat; he could only watch as the coyote depleted his herd.

He went to the village, to the one man who owned a gun. Coyote skulls hung by the old man's front door, and in his hut, the pelts of coyotes lay on the floor. Once the man had come to Jerónimo's camp, and Jerónimo had invited him to share his evening meal and the campfire for the night. The old man had just killed a coyote, and he put the meat in the fire to cook. He gave Jerónimo a piece of the meat when it was done.

The meat was hard and greasy. Jerónimo found he could not swallow it. The old man ate the meat of the coyote and kept his eyes on the boy. Jerónimo chewed and chewed and could not swallow the meat. Finally, the old man turned his head, and Jerónimo spit the meat into the fire. It sizzled and sputtered, and strange forms rose in the smoke from the fire.

Now the evil coyote was killing his goats, so Jerónimo went to borrow the old man's rifle.

"Do not look straight at the coyote when you shoot it," the old man said. "An animal like that has the sign of the devil on its fore-head. A bullet will not enter there. Shoot it only from the side; that is the only way to kill this coyote."

Jerónimo returned to his camp and waited for the coyote. As darkness swept over the mountain peaks, the coyote appeared. It came straight at him, its eyes full of flame, the mark of the devil clear on its forehead. There in the dusk the young man and the coyote met, and Jerónimo was helpless. He had no strength in his arm, and his knees felt weak. His mouth became dry, then it ran with saliva as if the coyote had infected him with some strange illness. He could not kill the coyote; he was filled with terror.

When the last goat had been taken by the coyote, Jerónimo had stumbled down from the high peaks of the mountain and taken the bus to Cuernavaca. He had told his mother that he would never return. Now he was returning to deliver the false leg to his father.

There, Jerónimo thought, that must be the cantina. But why do I feel so disoriented? Why am I thinking of these things now? I must get out of this wind; a wind like this can only carry bad spirits. The old woman who sells nopales, I should not have let her touch the leg. She may have put a spell on it.

Yes, that is the cantina, he thought as he moved into the sobbing wind. There was a lighted window, a blue door. Perhaps the men of the village are in there. A long time ago, when he was still a child, he heard someone say that his father had been stabbed in the leg in the bar. It was in a fight over a woman. That was how his leg had been poisoned and why they had cut it off.

Jerónimo moved toward the light of the cantina, but he stopped short as he heard the song, an old children's song he himself had once sung; now it was sung by a group of children who gathered in front of the door of the bar. They were playing and dancing.

> La Siriaca está pegada
> con chicle y con caca. . . .

Jerónimo stepped back. The sight of the children dancing in the terrible sandstorm frightened him. The children were singing about death. Doña Siriaca, Siriaca, la muerte. The skeleton of death. The song said her bones were held together with chewing gum and shit. The sweet smell and the foul odor combined in death. Death was sweet, death was foul, is that what the song said? He had sung the song as a child, but he had never thought about the meaning of the words.

When one was young, one did not think of death. Nor had he thought of death that morning when he'd boarded the bus in Cuernavaca. No, on the contrary, he was happy to be going to visit his parents. He had not seen them in a long time. His father would be very pleased that his son returned home to deliver a new leg.

What did it mean? Jerónimo thought, as he heard the children singing and moving away into the dust storm. He could still hear the words in the wind:

> La Siriaca está pegada
> con chicle y con caca!

He turned away from the cantina. Perhaps the men of the village were inside; perhaps they had started celebrating a day early. He was sure tomorrow was el Día de los Muertos, not today. For the first time since he had begun his journey, Jerónimo wished he had not come. He should have remained in Cuernavaca where the wind did not blow, where the gardens were green and lush and cool, where there was no death.

He shook his head in frustration. Of course death is there, he thought, death is everywhere. It is just that in the gardens of the wealthy life is so pleasant that there seems to be no death. Time is held in check by the beautiful things of the rich. The women do not seem to age: They sit by the pool, their beautiful bodies covered with oil, their sweet perfumes competing with the fragrances of the flowers, their men plump and healthy. The large, well-polished cars came and went. Every weekend they arrived from Mexico City, cars laden with those who could afford the luxury of the Cuernavaca gardens, those who could flee to the land where there was no death, only pleasure, only the call of children as they played in the pool, only the conversation and the laughter of the sleek men and women who drank their cocktails and acted as if death were not a concern in their lives. Could money buy off death? Jerónimo had wondered.

"Hay que robarle tiempo al tiempo," his patrona had said. Steal time from time. But could one steal time from time? Even the smartest man could not stop the ticking of the clock. Time was stronger than death, or maybe death was but a germ hidden in time. It was time that got you, put the germs of death in you and made you die, like the germ that had gotten into his father's leg and killed it, so that it had to be cut off.

Jerónimo knew the same mystery came to nestle in the flowers. The blossoms of the flowers wilted, the fruit grew rotten, decayed, gave off a bad odor. Even in the beautiful gardens of Cuernavaca, the fruit decayed. Rats from the street came to eat at the trash pile. He set traps and killed the rats. He sprayed the red ants; he set poison for the mice. He crushed the caterpillars and the snails because they ate the tender leaves. Death was in the garden—he was death. He was the jardinero, the man who kept the garden lush and trim, the man who sustained the bushes and the trees and the grass, but to keep everything growing he had to kill some things. Was it that way in paradise?

He was thinking about those things now, and they frightened him. He did not like to think of such things. He was a jardinero, a worker; he did his work and did not think. That was what the patrona was for, to think. But once, a very smart man who was the guest of his patrona had told him there was a germ that could kill even the maggots of death. Everything was slowly dying.

"Look closely," the man said, "everything is dying."

When Jerónimo looked closely, he saw wrinkles under the eyes of the beautiful women who came from the city; he saw their breasts sag. He saw the paunches of the businessmen. He saw that they, too, were dying, and the thought made him sad. He tried not to think about what the man had said, but it stayed with him a long time, and now the thought returned. Why had he remembered that now?

Jerónimo grew fearful. Stop wind! Stop so I can see my village as I knew it before I left! Am I dreaming? Will I awaken in my room in Cuernavaca? If the patrona tells me it is time to deliver the leg to my father, I will say no. I do not want to go to Pena Mayor. He closed his eyes against the wind, but when he opened them, he was still there in the howling windstorm, standing in the dusty street. Far in the distance he could hear the last refrain of the children's song.

Again Jerónimo leaned into the wind, and clutching the leg tightly, he moved down the street, desperate now to find the home of his father. The day had been very long and he was tired. He only wanted to rest. He had seen many windstorms on the mountain, but never one as strong as this. He felt joy when he finally recognized the door of his father's house. He blinked and looked up and suddenly it was before him, the door he knew so well. A wreath of flowers hung on the door; someone had died in his father's home. The relief Jerónimo had felt drained away. Who had died? It had been a long time since he had communicated with his parents, and now he had come to find the wreath of death on his father's door. Jerónimo shivered, not from the gust of wind that swirled around him and battered the wreath's paper flowers, but from the thought of death. Perhaps it is only my father's way of celebrating the Day of the Dead, Jerónimo thought. He knocked and entered.

He closed the door quickly behind him, leaned against the door, and sighed in relief. How calm and peaceful the dark room felt. Here there was respite from the howling wind, which had battered him since he'd left the bus. He blinked to grow accustomed to the dark. Outside the dust had shut off the sun, and yet the strange opaque light hurt his eyes. He had been squinting from the dust and the light, now the darkness provided solace.

Papá, Jerónimo spoke into the dark, *soy yo, Jerónimo.*

He peered into the room and saw his father sitting at the table. Behind his father, the figure of his mother was a shadow at the stove. The sweet aroma of sugar cookies filled the room. It was as he had imagined; she was baking the cookies for the Day of the Dead.

Jerónimo moved to his father. *I have brought you a new leg,* he said proudly. *It was built in one of the finest shops in Mexico City. My patrona had it made for you. I came to bring it to you.*

Jerónimo moved to his mother. In the shadows he thought he saw tears in her eyes.

Why is the room so dark? Jerónimo asked.

"This is for my son," his mother whispered. She turned and looked at the cookies she had baked. She took one, a perfectly shaped skeleton of death, and placed it on the table.

When Jerónimo was a child, he had always liked to bite off the head first. The head of the skeleton of death. The perfectly shaped skeleton, brown from the oven and shimmering from the sugar sprinkled on it, reminded him of a pilgrimage his family had made to the cathedral in Mexico City. Every church had a wall or a niche where the people left their crutches or canes once they had been cured. It was customary to make a promise to a saint or to la Virgen, and if the saint helped the person get well, then the pilgrimage was made to church and a token of the sickness was left there. The ex votos, the votive offerings, marked the promises made, the return of good health.

But what Jerónimo remembered now was the zócalo. He had liked to watch the vendors, to wander along the back of the cathedral where people set up their stalls to sell their goods. It was there he had seen a young man selling skeletons no bigger than a man's hand that danced like puppets. The young man held no strings, but the skeletons danced. Jerónimo was fascinated, and for a long time he wondered what made the skeletons dance. After a short time the skeleton would fall lifeless on the sidewalk, as if the magic energy the vendor commanded had suddenly run out. Those who could afford the price bought the tiny skeletal dolls for their children.

"This is la muerte, the skeleton of death," the young salesman said. "Long ago, when the Aztecs ruled Mexico, at this very place two sorcerers came to do evil to the people. One was dressed as a vendor, the other as a mannequin, a skeleton of death. When the people came to see the dancing figure of death, the sorcerer turned on them and killed them."

The people laughed at the young man's story. Jerónimo begged his father to buy one of the dancing skeletons, but no, there was not enough money, and so he returned to his village without the skeleton of death.

He picked up the cookie his mother had placed on the table. When he went to bite the cookie, he found that he could not. He held the cookie to his mouth to bite off the head of the skeleton, but he could not. He turned away so that his mother would not see him.

I thought perhaps the men were in the cantina, he said to his father. *The village appears empty.*

"The men are coming," his father said. He picked up his crutches and stood. He was a giant figure rising from his chair. Jerónimo knew his father was a short man, thick and squat, surely no taller than Jerónimo. But now his father rose like a spectral shadow in the darkened room.

"It is time," his father said, and he walked slowly to the window. He parted the curtains and looked out the window.

Jerónimo stepped forward. A line of mourners came down the street. All were dressed in black; all were bent with the hard work and misery of life in the village, and, now, added to that was the burden of death. Four men carried the plain casket. The coffin was open, and Jerónimo found himself leaning forward to peer into the cajón as it passed outside the window. He wanted to look into the casket, and yet he felt afraid. Who had died? He heard the song of the children. That is what they had been waiting for, for the funeral procession that was now leaving the cantina, the largest building in the village.

Some of the men held bottles of tequila and mescal. They drank as they stepped into the wind. Then the mourners stopped in front of the window.

Who has died? Jerónimo wondered.

His father turned to face his mother, and when he spoke, there was sadness in his voice.

"Do you remember Cruz? I don't know why I remember his death now, it was so many years ago. He fell in love with a married woman. Later she turned against him and confessed everything to her husband. Then together they plotted to kill Cruz. We found him in his orchard, and there wasn't a mark on him. It was as if he had died in his sleep, but when we went to bathe his body for the wake, we saw that his testicles had been crushed. There was no other mark on him. Death itself is not evil, but evil uses the disguise of death."

Jerónimo's father shook his head, as if to say he did not understand death and how it came in such strange ways. He picked up his old worn jacket, which had been neatly pressed by his wife for the funeral. He put it on; again he took his crutches and walked slowly across the room to the door, where he waited for the woman. Her baking was done; the table was the bier on which the skeleton cookies lay.

Later the mourners would come to their home to eat the cookies of the feast of the dead and drink hot coffee. Some of the men would drink tequila. Perhaps one of the men would sing, a song for the dead. They would speak of the dead person, remember him for the things he had done in life. Some of the men would get drunk, and the feast of the wake would continue into the night, long after the deceased was buried, and in the morning the sun would shine and the wind would no longer be blowing in Pena Mayor. The Day of the Dead would arrive, and the people would celebrate. Those who had died would be remembered.

Jerónimo's mother covered the cookies with a white towel, then went to the door, where she took her rebozo from a hook. She drew it tightly around her shoulders, looked sadly once about the room, then followed her husband. The wind roared as they stepped outside, then died down as the door closed behind them.

Jerónimo looked out the window. He saw his father and mother join the mourners. The wail of the women became the cry of the wind. The men hugged his father, giving him their condolences. Then the line of mourners began to move toward the cemetery just outside the village. They passed under the window and disappeared into the sandstorm.

At the campo santo they would lower the plain casket into the grave with ropes. Then each person would toss paper flowers into the hole; there were no fresh flowers in Pena Mayor. The priest would pray, and each person would walk by the open grave and toss in a handful of dirt, the chalky earth of the mountain. The men would fill the grave, the wind would rise and sweep up the dust, and the women would cry and hold Jerónimo's mother.

They would huddle in their dark rebozos to ward off the cold wind. The men would stand stiffly, knowing each one owed death a visit. Life was only a handful of ashes, and the earth of Pena Mayor was so poor and miserable that it was worth next to nothing.

Jerónimo sighed, a deep sigh. It had been a long day, a strange journey home. Perhaps it was his destiny to return to Pena Mayor. After all, no one knows a man's destiny. No one knows where death comes from, how it is that each person carries it so lightly within the heart, how it turns in the simplest way to claim what is due.

Perhaps when his father returned from the burial, Jerónimo could ask him some of the strange questions that had plagued his day. Yes, he would wait for his parents to return, then he would speak to his father. Man to man they would speak, about the weather, the crops in the field, the gardens of Cuernavaca, the simple work of farmers and jardineros.

Jerónimo looked out the window again. He could see nothing but swirls of dust and the opaque light that hurt his eyes. He turned away from the window toward the darkness of the room. He looked at his hand and saw that he still held the cookie. He smiled. There was no better cook than his mother. He remembered that after a long day's work in the garden of his patrona, he would often lie in his room and remember his mother's cooking. That was one thing he missed in Cuernavaca.

As he thought of Cuernavaca, he thought of the garden of his patrona. He thought about which bushes he had to trim, and he remembered where the grass was dry and he would have to water. He knew which flowers would be in bloom, and he knew exactly how their aroma would fill the garden in the quiet of the night. He thought of all the gardens where he had worked and how beautiful his labor had left them. Thinking about this, he felt complete.

He looked at the cookie. Tomorrow was el Día de los Muertos, the feast Day of the Dead. Today it had been his day to return to

Iliana of the Pleasure Dreams

Iliana stirred in the summer night, then awakened from her dream. She moaned, a soft sigh, her soul returning from its dreams of pleasure. She opened her eyes; the night breeze stirred the curtains; the shadows created images on the bare adobe wall; a figure appeared then moved away.

In the darkness of the night, smelling the sweet fragrance of the garden that wafted through the open door, lying quietly so as not to awaken Onofre, her husband, she lay smiling and feeling the last wave of pleasure that had aroused her so pleasantly from her deep sleep. It was always like this, first the images, then the deep stirring that touched the depths in her, then the soft awakening, the coming to life.

In the summer Onofre liked to sleep with the doors and windows open, to feel the mountain coolness. Her aunts had never allowed Iliana to sleep in the moonlight. The light of the moon disturbs young girls, they had said.

Iliana smiled. Her aunts had given her a strict religious upbringing, and they had taught her how to care for a home, but they had never mentioned dreams of pleasure. Perhaps they did not know of the pleasure that came from the images in her dreams, the outlines that at first were vague, forms in a place she did not recognize, fragments of faces, whispers. The figure came closer, there was a quickening to her pulse, a faster tempo to her breathing, then the dream became clear, and she was running across a field of alfalfa to be held by the man who appeared in her dreams. The man pressed close to her, sought her lips, caressed her, whispered words of love, and she was carried away into a spinning dream of pleasure. She had never seen the man's face, but always when she awakened, she was sure he was standing in the garden, just outside the door, waiting for her.

Yes, the dream was so real, the flood of pleasure so deep and true, she knew the man in the dream was there, and the shadows of the garden were the shadows of her dreams.

She rose slowly, pushing away the damp sheet, which released the sweet odor of her body. Tonight the man had reached out, taken her in his arms, and kissed her lightly. The pleasure of his caress consumed her and carried her into a realm of exhilaration. When she awakened she felt she was falling gently back to earth, and her soul came together again.

She walked to the window quietly, so as not to awaken her husband. She had never told him of her private world of dreams, and even when she confessed her thoughts to the priest at Manzano, she could not tell him everything. The dreams were for her, a private message, a disturbing pleasure she did not know how to share. Perhaps with the man in the dream she could share her secret, share the terrible longing that filled her and that erupted in the world of sleep.

She leaned against the door and felt the cool breeze caress her perspiring body. Was he there, in the shadows of the garden, waiting for her? She peered into the dark. The shadows the moon created were as familiar as those she saw in her dreams. She wanted to cry out to understand the dream, to share the pleasure, but there was no one there. Only the soft shrill of the night crickets filled the garden. The cry of the grillos foretold rain: The clouds would rise over the mountain, the thunder would rumble in the distant sky, and the dry spell of early summer would be broken.

Iliana sighed. She thought of her aunts, Tía Amalia and Tía Andrea. Why had they not explained the dreams of pleasure? They were women who had never married, but they had said marriage would be good for her. All the girls in the village married by eighteen and settled down to take care of their families. Onofre was a good man, a farmer, a hard worker; he did not drink;

he was a devout Catholic. He would provide a home, they said, and she would raise his children.

The girls of the mountain valley had said Onofre was handsome but very shy. He would have to wait many years and marry a widow, they had whispered, and so they were surprised when Iliana married him. Iliana was the most beautiful girl in the valley. It was a marriage of convenience, the young women gossiped to explain the match, and Iliana went to her marriage bed with no conception of what was expected of her. Onofre was gentle, but he did not kiss the nape of her neck or whisper the words of pleasure she heard in her dreams. She vaguely understood that the love of Onofre could be a thread to her secret dreams, but Onofre was abrupt, the thread snapped, and the fire of her desire died.

She was unsure, hesitant; she grew timid. They ate in silence, and they lived in silence. Like an animal that is careful of its master, she settled around the rhythms of his workday, being near when it was time to be close, staying in her distant world the rest of the time. He too felt the distance; he tried to speak but was afraid of his feelings. Sitting across the table from her, he would see the beauty of her face, her hands, her throat and shoulders, and then he would look down, excuse himself, and return to his work, with which he tried to quench the desires he did not understand.

There is little pleasure on earth, the priest said. We were not put on earth to take pleasure in our bodies. And so Onofre believed in his heart that a man should take pride in providing a home, in watching his fields grow, in the blessing of the summer rains, which made the crops grow, in the increase of his flocks. Sex was the simple act of nature he knew as a farmer. The animals came together, they reproduced, and the priest was right—it was not for pleasure. At night he felt the body of Iliana, and desire came to engulf him for a moment, to overwhelm him and suffocate him. Then, as always, the thread severed, the flame died.

Iliana waited at the window until the breeze cooled her skin and she shivered. In the shadows of the garden she felt a presence, and for a moment she saw again the images of her dream, the contours of her body, the purple of alfalfa blossoms. A satisfaction in the night, a sensuous pleasure welled up from a depth of passion she knew only in her dreams. She sighed. This was her secret.

How long had it been in her soul, this secret of pleasure? She had felt it even in the church at Manzano, where she went to confession and to Mass. She had gone to confess to the priest, and the cool earth fragrance of the dark church and the sweetness of the votive candles had almost overwhelmed her. "Help me," she whispered to the priest, desiring to cleanse her soul of her secret even as the darkness of the confessional awakened the images of her dream. "I have sinned," she cried, but she could not tell him of the pleasures of her dreams. The priest, knowing the young girls of the village tended to be overdramatic in the stories of their love life, mumbled something about her innocence, made the sign of the cross absolving her, and sent her to her small penance.

Iliana walked home in deep despair. Along the irrigation ditch, the tall cottonwood trees reminded her of strong, virile men, the trees' roots digging into the heart of the earth, their branches creating images of arms and legs against the clear sky. She ran, away from the road, away from the neighboring fields; over the pine mountain she ran until, exhausted, she clutched at a tree, leaned against the huge trunk; trembling, she listened to the pounding of her heart. The vanilla smell of the pine was like the fragrance of the man in her dreams. She felt the rough bark, like the rough hands of Onofre at night. She closed her eyes and hugged the tree, holding tight to keep from flying into the images of her dream, which swept around her.

Iliana remembered her visit to the church as she returned to her bed, softly so as not to awaken Onofre. She lay quietly and pulled the sheet to her chin. She closed her eyes, but she couldn't sleep. She had been overcome with joy when she had pressed against the tree. It was the same tonight in her dream, the immense pleasure that filled her with a desire so pure that she felt she was dying and returning to God. Why?

She thought of her aunts, spinsters whose only occupation was to care for the church at Manzano. They swept, they sewed the cloths for the altar, they brought the flowers for Mass, they made sure the candles were ready. They had given their lives to God; they did not speak of pleasure. What would they think if they knew of the dreams that came to Iliana?

Release me, Iliana cried silently. Free me. Leave me to my work and to my husband. He is a good man, leave me to him. Iliana's tears wet the sheet, and it was not until the early morning that she could sleep again.

"We can go this afternoon," Onofre said as they ate.

"Oh, yes," Iliana nodded. She was eager to go to the church at Manzano. Just that morning her aunts had come to visit her. They had been filled with excitement.

"An apparition has appeared on the wall of the church," Tía Amalia said.

"The face of Christ," Tía Andrea said, and both bowed their heads and made the sign of the cross.

That is what the people of the mountain valleys were saying, that at sunset the dying light and the cracks in the mud painted the face of Jesus on the adobe wall of the church. A woman on the way to rosary had seen the image, and she had run to tell her comadre. Together they saw it, and then their story spread like fire up and down the mountain. The following afternoon all the people of the village came and gathered in the light of dusk to see the face of Christ appear on the wall. Many claimed they saw the face; some said a man crippled by arthritis was cured and could walk when he saw the image.

"I see! I see!" the old man had shouted, and he had stood and walked. The people believed they had experienced a miracle. "There!" each shouted in turn as the face of Jesus appeared. The crown of thorns was clear; blood streamed down the sad and anguished face. The women fell to their knees. A miracle had come to the village of Manzano.

The priest came and with holy water blessed the wall, and the old people understood that he had sanctified the miracle. Those who saw the face of the savior cried aloud or whispered a private prayer; the women on their knees in the dust prayed rosary after rosary.

People from the nearby villages came; families came in their cars and trucks. The women came to pray, eager to see the image of Jesus. Their men were more guarded; they stood away from the church wall and wondered if it was possible. The children played hide-and-seek as all waited for the precise moment of dusk when the image would appear.

The young men came in their customized cars and trucks, drinking beer, eager to look at the young women. Boys from the ranches around the village came on horseback, dressed in their Sunday shirts and just-pressed jeans; they came to show off their horsemanship to the delight of the girls. A fiesta atmosphere developed; the people were glad for the opportunity to gather.

The men met in clusters and talked politics and rain and cattle. Occasionally one would kick at the ground with his boot, then steal an uncomfortable glance at his wife. The women also gathered in groups, to talk about their children, school, marriages, and deaths, but mostly to talk about the miracle that had come to their village and to listen to the old women who remembered seeing an apparition when they were young. A young woman, they said, years ago, before cars came to the mountains, had seen the face of the Virgin Mary appear, on a wall, and the praying had lasted until the image disappeared.

"One never knows which is the work of the devil or the work of God," an old woman said. "One can only pray."

A strange tension developed between the men and the women who went to see the miracle. It was the women who organized the rosaries and the novenas. It was the women who prayed, kneeling on the bare ground for hours, the raw earth numbing their knees and legs. It was they who prayed for the image to appear, their gaze fixed on the church wall, their prayers rising into the evening sky, where the nighthawks flew as the sun set red in the west.

The priest grew concerned and tried to speak to the men, but they greeted him quietly, then looked down at the ground. They had no explanation to share. The priest turned to the women; they accepted him but did not need him. Finally, he shut himself up in the church, to pray alone, unsure of the miracle, afraid of the tension in the air, which had turned the people in a direction he did not understand. He could not share in the fervent prayers of the women, and he could not control them. The people of this valley in the Sangre de Cristo Mountains, he had been warned, were different. Now he understood the warning. The image had come to the wall of the church, and the people had devoutly accepted it as a miracle. Why had he been sent to the church at Manzano? He belonged in the city, where the politics of the church were clear and manageable. The transformation in his parishioners worried him. He opened the chest where he kept the altar wine and drank, wondering what it was he had seen in the lines and shadows when he looked at the wall. He wasn't sure, but he didn't look again.

In the afternoon Onofre and Iliana drove over the ridge of the mountain to the church at Manzano. Onofre drove in silence, wondering what the visitation of the image meant. Iliana rode filled with a sense of excitement. Perhaps the miracle was a sign for her. She would see her savior, and he would absolve the pleasure dreams; all would be well.

Iliana smiled, closed her eyes, and let herself drift as the rocking of the truck swayed her gently back and forth. Through the open window, the aroma of the damp earth reached her nostrils. She smelled the pregnant, rich scent of the soil and the pine trees. She remembered the dapple horse she used to ride across the meadow from her Tía Amalia's house to her Tía Andrea's.

When they arrived at Manzano, Iliana opened her eyes and saw the crowd of people around the church. Cars and trucks lined the dirt road. Together Onofre and Iliana walked toward the group by the church.

Onofre felt awkward when he walked in public with his wife. She was a young and beautiful woman. He did not often think of her beauty, except when they were with other people. Then he saw her as others might see her, and he marveled.

"It's the Spanish blood of her mother that gives her her beauty," her aunts were fond of saying.

Her oval face reminded Onofre of a saint he had seen once in a painting, perhaps at the cathedral in Santa Fe. Her face, the dark eyelashes, the dark line of the eyebrows, the green eyes—she was exquisite, a woman so beautifully formed that people paused to watch her. Onofre felt the eyes of the young men on his wife, and he tried to shake away the feeling of self-consciousness as he walked beside her. He knew the men admired the beauty of his wife, and he had been kidded about being married to an angel.

Iliana was aware of her beauty; it was something she felt in her soul. Everything she did was filled with a sensuous pleasure in which she took delight, and she took delight in feeling the gaze of the men on her. But she looked down and did not look at them, understanding that she should not bring shame to her husband.

Instead she looked at the children who played around the church; the gathering had become a fiesta. Someone had brought an ice machine to sell flavored ice. Another person had set up a stand to sell rosaries and other religious items, and a farmer was selling green chile and corn from the bed of his truck. There were people Iliana did not recognize, people from as far away as Taos and Española.

As Iliana and Onofre passed, friends and neighbors greeted them, but when the young bachelors of the village saw her, a slight tension filled the air. Her beauty was known in the mountain villages, and at eighteen she was more beguiling than ever. All of the young men had at one time or another dreamed of her; now they looked at her in awe, for underneath her angelic beauty lay a sensuality that almost frightened them.

"Onofre must be treating her right," one young man whispered to his friend. "She is blossoming."

How lucky Onofre is, they thought. He so plain and simple, and yet she is his. God is not fair, they dared to think as they tipped their cowboy hats when she passed. All were young and virile men of the mountains, handsome from their Spanish and Indian blood, and all were filled with desire when they saw Iliana.

They called Onofre a lucky man, but the truth was that each one of them could have courted Iliana. They had known her at school, they saw her at church on Sundays, and each year her beauty grew. They could not touch her; even in the games they had played as children, they had dared not touch her. When they grew into young manhood, a few of them had sought her out, but one glance from her told them that Iliana was a young woman filled with mystery. They had turned away and married the simple girls of the village, those in whom there was no challenge, no mystery to frighten and test them.

Now, as Iliana passed by, she felt the admiration of the young men of the mountains. She smiled and wondered, as she stole a glance at their handsome faces, if one of them was the man who appeared in her dreams.

Her aunts were there; indeed, they had been there all day, waiting for the setting of the sun, waiting for the image of Christ to appear. They saw Iliana and drew her forward.

"We're pleased you arrived," they said. "Come, hija, it's almost time." They pulled her away from Onofre, and he sighed with relief and stepped back into the crowd of men.

The women parted as the two aunts drew Iliana forward so that she could have a good view of the church wall. Already candles were lighted, and a rosary was being prayed. The singing of the Hail Marys sanctified the air, as did the sweet scent of paraffin. The women drew close together, prayed; the crowd grew quiet as the sun set. The cracks in the old plaster on the wall appeared thick and textured as the sun touched the horizon of the juniper-covered hills. If the image appeared, it would be for only a few minutes, then it would dissolve into the gray of the evening.

Iliana waited. She prayed. Pressed between her aunts and the other women, she smelled their fragrances mixed with the wax scent of the candles. So it had been at the church, the distinctive aroma of women commingling with the holiness of God. The hush of the crowd reminded her of the church, and she remembered images and scenes. She felt anew the pleasure that had come with her first blood, and with riding her dapple horse from the house of one aunt to that of the other. Her senses awakened to memories of the field of alfalfa with purple blossoms and the buzzing of the honeybees, the taste of the thick white paste at school, the tartness of the first bite of an apple, the fragrance of fresh bread baked in the horno behind her Tía Amalia's house. She remembered the day the enraged bull had broken loose and torn down the horno, leaving only a pile of dirt, and the frightened women had watched from their windows, cursing the bull, praying to God. She swayed on her knees, felt the roughness of the pebbles, heard the prayers of the women, felt a flood of disconnected images, which dissolved into the smell of the mountain earth after a summer rain, the welcome smell of piñon wood burning in the fireplace and flavoring the air, the feeling of pleasure these sights and sounds and memories wove into her soul.

She closed her eyes and pressed her hands to her bosom to still the pounding of her heart, to stop the rush of heat that moved up from the earth to her knees and thighs. Around her she heard the women praying. Beads of sweat wet her upper lip as the images came to tease her; she licked at the sweat and tasted it.

Then the crowd grew still; the magic hour had come. "Look," one of the aunts whispered. Iliana opened her eyes and looked up at the lines and shadows on the wall.

"You see!" the other aunt said.

Iliana, in reverie, nodded, smiled. Yes, I see, she wanted to say aloud, her gaze fastened on the scene on the wall. She saw a figure, then two. Arms and legs in an image of love. The figures from her dream. Iliana quivered with pleasure.

"Dear God," she cried, overwhelmed by the warm waves that rolled through her body. "Dear God," she cried again, then Iliana fainted.

In her dream she walked on purple blossoms whose sweet aroma rose and touched the clouds of summer. Red and mauve and the crimson of blood. In the darkness of the field, a man waited by the dapple horse. The waves of pleasure dissipated, and the thread broke before she reached the man.

Tía Amalia touched camphor to her nose, and Tía Andrea patted her hand vigorously. Iliana awoke and saw the shadows of the women around her. Beyond the women, Iliana caught a glimpse of the wall, dark now; the congealing of shadows and lines no longer held the secret she had seen.

"A miracle," her aunt whispered. "You saw the face of Christ! You are blessed!"

"Blessed be the Lord Jesus Christ," the chorus of women responded.

"When you fainted, you smiled like an angel," her aunt said. "We knew you had seen the miracle."

"Yes," Iliana whispered, "I have seen the face of God." She struggled to rise, to free herself from the press of the women. On their knees they prayed, in the darkness, and when she rose, they looked up at her in awe.

"Onofre!" she cried. She pulled away from the cluster of women, away from the ring of candles, whose flames danced in the rising wind of night. What had become of Onofre?

Onofre, who in his quiet way had gazed at the wall, now stood waiting in the dark. He stood alone, confused, unsure, not understanding the strange messages of his blood. He had looked at the wall, but he had not prayed to see the image of Christ; he had prayed that Iliana would understand his dreams of the warm earth he worked daily. He had seen the men leave, taking away the exhausted children, the limp bodies of the boys and girls who moaned in their dreams as they were carted home. Chairs and blankets were brought for the women; they would pray all night. The men would return to work the following day.

The wind rose in the dark night, moaned on the pines of the mountain, and cried as it swept around the church and snapped at the candles, creating shadows on the church wall. The women huddled in prayer. Iliana stumbled in the dark, wondering why she had seen the image of pleasure on the wall and not the face of

Christ. Was the devil tempting her? Or had the image on the wall been the answer she sought?

"Onofre!" she cried in the dark. The cold wind made her shiver. She found the truck, but Onofre was not there. In the dark she crossed the road, drawn by the dark, purple scent of alfalfa. She ran across the field, stumbling forward, feeling the weakness in the pit of her stomach give way to an inner resolution. "Onofre!" she cried, feeling as if she had awakened from a dream into another dream, but this one she could live in and understand.

In the middle of the field she saw the image of the man, the man who stood in the dark holding the neck of a horse, the dapple horse of her dreams. Heart pounding, she ran into the arms of Onofre. She felt his strong arms hold her, and she allowed herself to be held, to feel the strength of his body, his muscles hardened by work, his silence instilled by the mountains.

"I did not see the face of Christ," Iliana confessed.

"Nor I," Onofre said.

"What then?" Iliana asked.

"A dream," Onofre said, unsure of what she meant.

"Have I done wrong by dreaming?" Iliana asked.

Onofre shook his head. "I remember the old people saying, Life is a dream—"

"—and dreams are dreams," Iliana finished. "There is a meaning in my dreams, but I don't understand it. Do you understand your dreams, Onofre?"

"No," he said.

Holding her in the dark in the middle of the field, the desire he felt was new; it was desire rising from the trembling earth, through his legs, into his thoughts and sex, and into the pounding of his heart.

"Sometimes at night I awaken and go to the open door," he said. "I look at the beauty of the night. I look at you lying so peaceful in the bed. You make soft sounds of contentment. I wish I could be the one who draws those sounds from you. Then you awaken, and I step into the shadows, so I won't frighten you. I watch as you go to the door to look at the garden. I know you have awakened from a beautiful dream because you are alive with beauty. At those times, you are what I desire."

"We need to share our dreams," Iliana said. Onofre nodded.

"It is time to go home," Iliana said.

Yes, it was time to go home, to sleep, to unravel dreams. Arm in arm they walked across the field of alfalfa, walking together with much pleasure, stirring the purple blossoms of the night.

Devil Deer

At night frost settled like glass dust on the peaks of the Jemez Mountains, but when the sun came up, the cold dissolved. The falling leaves of the aspen were showers of gold coins. Deer sniffed the air and moved silently along the edges of the meadows in the high country. Clean and sharp and well defined, autumn had come to the mountain.

In the pueblo the red chile ristras hung against brown adobe walls, and large ears of corn filled kitchen corners. The harvest of the valley had been brought in, and the people rested. A haze of piñon smoke clung like a veil over the valley.

Late at night the men polished their rifles and told hunting stories. Neighbors on the way to work met in front of the post office or in the pueblo center to talk. It was deer season, a ritual shared by the entire pueblo. Friends made plans to go together, to stay maybe three or four days. The women kidded the men: "You better bring me a good one this time, a big buck who maybe got a lot of does pregnant in his life. Bring a good one."

Cruz heard the sound of laughter as neighbors talked. In the night, he made love to his wife with renewed energy. "That was good," his young wife whispered in the dark, under the covers, as she too dreamed of the buck her husband would bring—deer meat to make jerky, to cook with red chile in the winter.

These were the dreams and planning that made the pueblo happy when deer season came. The men were excited. The old men talked of hunts long ago, told stories of the deer they had seen in the high country, sometimes meeting deer with special powers, of an accident that happened long ago. Maybe a friend or brother had been shot. There were many stories to tell, and the old men talked far into the night.

The young men grew eager. They didn't want stories; they wanted the first day of deer season to come quickly so that they could get up there and bag a buck. Maybe they had already scouted an area, and they knew some good meadows where a herd of does came down to browse in the evening. Or maybe they had hunted there the year before, and they had seen deer signs.

Everyone knew the deer population was growing scarce. It was harder and harder to get a buck. Too many hunters, maybe. Over the years, there were fewer bucks. You had to go deeper into the forest, higher, maybe find new places, maybe have strong medicine.

Cruz thought of this as he planned. This time he and his friend Joe were going up to a place they called Black Ridge. They called it Black Ridge because there the pine trees were thick and dark. Part of the ridge was fenced in by the Los Alamos Laboratory, and few hunters wandered near the chain-link fence.

The place was difficult to get to, hard to hunt, and there were rumors that the fence carried electricity. Or there were electronic sensors, and if they went off, maybe a helicopter would swoop down and the lab guards would arrest you. The ridge lay silent and ominous on the side of the mountain.

All month Cruz and Joe planned, but a few days before the season started, Joe was unloading lumber at work and the pile slipped, crashed down, and broke his leg.

"Don't go alone," Joe told Cruz. "You don't want to be up there alone. Go with your cousin. They're going up to the brown bear area—"

"There's no deer there," Cruz complained. "Too many hunters." He wanted to go high, up to Black Ridge, where few hunters went. Something was telling him that he was going to get a big buck this year.

So on the night before the season opened, he drove his truck up to Black Ridge. He found an old road that had been cut when the Los Alamos fence had been put in, and he followed it as high as it went. That night he slept in his truck, not bothering to make a fire or to set up camp. He was going to get a buck early, he was sure, maybe be back at the pueblo by afternoon.

Cruz awoke from a dream and clutched the leather bag tied at his belt. The fetish of stone, a black bear, was in the bag. He had talked to the bear before he fell asleep, and the bear had come in his dreams, standing upright like a man, walking toward Cruz, words in its mouth as if it was about to speak.

Cruz stood frozen. The bear was deformed. One paw was twisted like an old tree root, and the other was missing. The legs were gnarled, and the huge animal walked like an old man with arthritis. The face was deformed, the mouth dripping with saliva. Only the eyes were clear as it looked at Cruz. Go away, it said, go away from this place. Not even the medicine of your grandfathers can help you here.

Cruz awakened and rolled down the truck window. What the hell did the dream mean? The thick forest around him was dark. A sound came from the trees and receded, like the moaning of wind, like a restless spirit breathing, just beyond the tech area fence of the laboratories. There was a blue glow in the dark forest, but it was too early for it to be the glow of dawn.

Cruz listened intently. Someone or something was dying in the forest, and breathing in agony. The breath of life was going out of the mountain; the mountain was dying. The eerie blue glow filled the night. In the old stories, when time was new, the earth had opened and bled its red, hot blood. But that was the coming to life of the mountain; now the glow was the emanation of death. The earth was dying, and the black bear had come to warn him.

Cruz slumped against the steering wheel. His body ached; he stretched. It isn't good to hunt alone, he thought, then instantly tried to erase the thought. He stepped out to urinate, then he turned to pray as the dawn came over the east rim of the ridge. He held the medicine bag that contained his bear. Give me strength, he thought, to take a deer to my family. Let me not be afraid.

It was the first time that he had even thought of being afraid on the mountain, and he found the thought disturbing.

He ate the beef sandwich his wife had packed for him, and drank coffee from the thermos. Then he checked his rifle and began to walk, following the old ruts of the road along the fence, looking for deer sign, looking for movement in the thick forest. When the sun came over the volcanic peaks of the Jemez, the frost disappeared. There were no clouds to the west, no sign of a storm.

Cruz had walked a short distance when a shadow in the pine trees made him freeze. Something was moving off to his right. He listened intently and heard the wheezing sound he had heard earlier. The sound was a slow inhaling and exhaling of breath. It's a buck, Cruz thought and drew up his rifle.

As he stood looking for the outline of the buck in the trees, he felt a vibration of the earth, as if the entire ridge were moving. The sound and the movement frightened him. He knew the mountain, he had hunted its peaks since he was a boy, and he had never felt anything like this. He saw movement again and turned to see the huge rack of the deer, dark antlers moving through the trees.

The buck was inside the fence, about fifty yards away. Cruz would have to go in for the deer. The dark pines were too thick to get a clear shot. He walked quietly along the fence. At any moment he expected the buck to startle and run; instead it seemed to follow him.

When Cruz stopped, the buck stopped, and it blended into the trees so that Cruz wasn't sure if it was a deer or if he was only imagining it. He knew excitement sometimes made the hunter see things. Tree branches became antlers, and hunters sometimes fired at movement in the brush. That's how accidents happened.

Cruz moved again, and the shadow of the buck moved with him, still partially hidden by the thick trees. Cruz stopped and lifted his rifle, but the form of the deer was gone. The deer is stalking me, Cruz thought. Well, this happened. A hunter would be following a deer, and the buck would circle around and follow the hunter. There were lots of stories. A buck would appear between two hunting parties, and the hunters would fire at each other while the buck slipped away.

Cruz sat on a log and looked into the forest. There it was, the outline of the buck in the shadows. Cruz opened his leather bag and took out the small stone bear. What he saw made him shudder. There was a crack along the length of the bear. A crack in his medicine. He looked up, and the blank eyes of the buck in the trees were staring at him.

Cruz fired from the hip, cursing the buck as he did. The report of the rifle echoed down the ridge. Nearby a black crow cried in surprise and rose into the air. The wind moaned in the treetops. The chill in the air made Cruz shiver. Why did I do that? he thought. He looked for the buck; it was still there. It had not moved.

Cruz rose and walked until he came to a place where someone had ripped a large hole in the fence. He stepped through the opening, knowing he shouldn't enter the area, but he wasn't going to lose the buck. The big bucks had been thinned out of the mountain; there weren't many left. This one had probably escaped by living inside the fenced area.

I'm going to get me a pampered Los Alamos buck, Cruz thought. Sonofabitch is not going to get away from me. The buck moved and Cruz followed. He knew that he had come a long way from the truck. If he got the buck, he would have to quarter it, and it would take two days to get it back. I'll find a way, he thought, not wanting to give up the buck, which led him forward. I can drive the truck up close to the fence.

But why didn't the buck spook when he fired at it? And why did he continue to hear the sound in the forest? And the vibration beneath his feet? What kind of devil machines were they running over in the labs that made the earth tremble? Accelerators. Plutonium. Atom smashers. What do I know? Cruz thought. I only know I want my brother to return to the pueblo with me. Feed my family. Venison steaks with fried potatoes and onions.

As he followed the buck, Cruz began to feel better. They had gone up to the top of the ridge and started back down. The buck was heading toward the truck. Good, Cruz thought.

Now the buck stopped, and Cruz could clearly see the large antlers for the first time. They were thick with velvet and lichen.

A pine branch clung to the antlers, Cruz thought, or patches of old velvet. But when he looked closely he saw it was patches of hair that grew on the antlers.

"God almighty," Cruz mumbled. He had never seen anything like that. He said a prayer and fired. The buck gave a grunt; Cruz fired again. The buck fell to its knees.

"Fall you sonofabitch!" Cruz cursed and fired again. He knew he had placed three bullets right in the heart.

The buck toppled on its side, and Cruz rushed forward to cut its throat and drain its blood. When he knelt down to lift the animal's head, he stopped. The deer was deformed. The hide was torn and bleeding in places, and green bile seeped from the holes the bullets had made. The hair on the antlers looked like mangy human hair, and the eyes were two white stones mottled with blood. The buck was blind.

Cruz felt his stomach heave. He turned and vomited, the sandwich and coffee of the morning meal splashing at his feet. He turned and looked at the buck again. Its legs were bent and gnarled. That's why it didn't bound away. The tail was long, like a donkey tail.

Cruz stood and looked at the deer, and he looked into the dark pine forest. On the other side of the ridge lay Los Alamos, the laboratories, and nobody knew what in hell went on there. But whatever it was, it was seeping into the earth, seeping into the animals of the forest. To live within the fence was deadly, and now there were holes in the fence.

Cruz felt no celebration in taking the life of the buck. He could not raise the buck's head and offer the breath of life to his people. He couldn't offer the corn meal. He was afraid to touch the buck, but something told him he couldn't leave the deer on the mountainside. He had to get it back to the pueblo; he had to let the old men see it.

He gathered his resolve and began dragging the buck down the ridge toward the truck. Patches of skin caught in the branches of fallen trees and ripped away. Cruz sweated and cursed. Why did this deer come to haunt me? he thought. The bear in the dream had warned him, and he had not paid attention to the vision. It was not a good sign, but he had to get the deformed deer to the old men.

It was dark when he drove into the pueblo. When he came over the hill and saw the lighted windows, his spirits rose. This was home, a safe circle. But in his soul, Cruz didn't feel well. Going into the fenced area for the deer had sapped his strength.

He turned down the dirt road to his home. Dogs came out to bark, and people peered from windows. They knew his truck. He parked in front of his home, but he remained in the truck. His wife came out, and sensing his mood, she said nothing. Joe appeared in the dark, hobbling, a flashlight in his hand.

"What happened?" Joe asked. Cruz motioned to the back of the truck. Joe flashed the light on the buck. It was an ugly sight, which made him recoil. "Oh God," he whispered. He whistled, and other shadows appeared in the dark, neighbors who had seen Cruz's truck drive in. The men looked at the buck and shook their heads.

"I got him inside the fence," Cruz said.

"Take Cruz into the house," one of the men told Joe. They would get rid of the animal.

"Come inside," Joe said. His friend had been up on the mountain all day, and he had killed this devil deer. Cruz's voice and vacant stare told the rest.

Cruz followed his wife and Joe into the house. He sat at the kitchen table and his wife poured him a cup of coffee. Cruz drank, thankful that the rich taste washed away the bitterness he felt in his mouth.

Joe said nothing. Outside the men were taking the deformed buck away. Probably will burn it, he thought. How in the hell did something like that happen? We've never seen a deer like this, the old men would say later. A new story would grow up around Cruz, the man who had killed the devil deer. Even his grandchildren would hear the story in the future.

And Cruz? What was to become of Cruz? He had gone into the forbidden land, into the mountain area surrounded by the laboratory fence, there where the forest glowed at night and the earth vibrated to the hum of atom smashers, lasers, and radioactivity.

The medicine men would perform a cleansing ceremony; they would pray for Cruz. But did they have enough good medicine to wash away the evil the young man had touched?

The Man Who Found a Pistol

"This is the man who found the pistol," Procopio said as he pushed the newspaper across the bar for me to read. Procopio has worked in the village cantina many years; he knows the stories of the village. Thoughtfully, he wiped the bar and placed my drink in front of me. When he begins a story, I listen. He doesn't embellish the story; he just tells it. If you listen, fine; if you don't, there's always another customer at the bar.

The story of the man who found the pistol reminded me of something that had happened to me years ago. My wife and I were driving up in the Jemez Mountains when we came to a stream. We stopped to eat lunch and enjoy the beauty. While my wife spread our picnic lunch, I walked along the bank of the stream, enjoying the beauty of the forest. I came to a place on the stream bank where I felt a presence.

There were no footprints, but I knew someone had been there. I looked around the clearing, but there was no one. Then I looked into the water. Submerged in the water lay a handsome double-bladed axe. Someone had left it there. Again I looked around, but there was no one in sight. Maybe one of the locals had forgotten it.

Why had he left it in the water? Perhaps he wanted the water to swell the wood so that the axe head would not slip. But there was no camp nearby, and no logging in the area. There was no sign of life.

I took the axe out of the water and felt its weight. It was a well-used axe, and it fitted snugly in my hands. I admired it, for I did not have such an axe. But as I held it, a strange feeling came over me. I felt I was being watched. Around me the forest grew very quiet. The mountain stream gurgled, and a few birds cried, but the forest grew still and sullen. I thought of taking the axe, but I didn't. I put it back in the cold water where I had found it, and I hurried back and told my wife what had happened. I felt I had come upon a mystery that was not for me. Many years later I still remembered the axe I found in the stream.

"The man who found the pistol lived in the village of Corrales. He taught at the university," Procopio told me. In the afternoons he came to the cantina to drink a beer after his walk. "He was a loner," Procopio continued. "Nobody in the village knew him well. He wasn't a talker."

The man's wife had told Procopio's wife that her husband grew up on a ranch in Texas. When he was a boy, her husband had been hunting rabbits with his brother when there had been an accident. That's all she said.

"What happened?" I wondered. Procopio shrugged and shook his head.

Procopio never told a story all at once; he told it piece by piece. He would be relating the events in his quiet way, then new customers would come in, and he would lumber off to serve them. I had to return to the bar from time to time to listen to the story.

I learned that the man who found the pistol used to go walking along the irrigation ditch in the afternoons. Tall grass covers the banks of the ditch. The fields and orchards in that part of the village are isolated. During his walk the man could have enjoyed the silence of the pastoral valley. That's why he had moved to Corrales, to be away from the city where he worked.

In the fields of the valley he could have been alone with his thoughts. I began to understand that the man was much like me. I, too, enjoy being alone; I like the silence of mountains. One has to be alone to know oneself. I also realize that one must return to the circle of the family to stay in balance. But the way Procopio told it, the man spent most of his time alone. His wife did all the chores and took care of the house; the man only taught his classes, then returned to walk alone in the fields.

Hearing Procopio talk about the man who found the pistol made me curious. I drove by his home, with the old, weathered barns. The place looked deserted and haunted in the sharp January wind. Dark curtains covered the windows, and the banging of a loose tin on the barn roof made a lonely sound. Later, when I told Procopio this, he looked at me strangely. "Let it go," he said.

I couldn't let it go. The story of the man who found the pistol became an obsession.

One day I walked along the irrigation ditch where the man had walked, and standing in the open fields, I could see what he had seen. He could look east and see the stately face of Sandia Mountain. The mountain reminds me of a giant turtle. When I was a boy, I had killed a turtle, and when I look at the mountain, I am sometimes reminded of that incident. This is the way of life: Remembering one incident kindles another memory, and one doesn't know where the stampede of thoughts may lead.

Around him he would have seen the fields, winter bare now, but in the summer they would have been green and buzzing with life, meadow larks calling, black birds flying to the horse corrals, pheasants laying their eggs in the tall grass, and an occasional roadrunner scuttling in front of him. How could a man who'd had so much beauty around him do what he did?

Maybe Procopio knew more than he was telling. I found excuses to ask questions of other people in the village, but no one had known the man well. They knew he had been a teacher; most said he'd kept to himself. He was always alone. The man who dug wells for a living had dug a well for the teacher. The well digger told me something horrible had happened back in Texas. There was a hunting accident, that's all the teacher had said, and he'd grown melancholy.

I stood in the field alone and thought about the man. Walking here, he would have met no one. Here he could have been at peace with himself. In the winter he could feel the earth sleeping, in the spring he could breathe the fresh scent of apple blossoms from the orchards, and in summer he could see the green of the alfalfa fields.

Was he not happy in that silence of the valley? Had it become like the silence in his heart, a haunting silence? When one is alone, the hum of the earth becomes a mantra whose vibration works its way into the soul. Maybe the man was sucked deeper and deeper into that loneliness until there was no escape.

"The day he found the pistol," Procopio said, "he came to the bar and he didn't order his usual beer, he drank a whiskey. His hands were trembling. 'I found a pistol,' he told us. There was only me and Primo in the bar, and Primo's nephew, the boy with the harelip. We looked at him. 'What should I do?' he asked. 'Don't give it to the sheriff,' Primo said. 'He will only keep it for himself.' The boy with the harelip said, 'You can shoot rabbits with it.' I said, 'Keep the pistol. You found it; it's yours.'

"I have thought often of the man finding the pistol in the grass by the side of the ditch," Procopio said. "Maybe it belonged to a criminal who threw it there to get rid of it. Maybe he had killed someone with it. There is a curse on things you find. They can never be yours."

There it was, I imagined, like a snake concealed in the grass, ready to strike, perhaps glistening in the sun. There was mud on it, perhaps the stain of blood. The man trembled when he stooped to pick it up. The hair along his neck stood on edge, he felt a shiver. It isn't every day a man finds a pistol. Should he dare to pick it up? Yes, he did, as I had picked up the axe. It fitted into his hand.

Should I take it? the man thought. He weighed it in his hand and then looked around. He was alone; the fields were quiet. A cool breeze hissed as it swept across the grass. The man shivered. Many thoughts must have gone through his mind, memories of the past, things he knew he had to resolve. Aren't we all like that, haunted by memories of the past, the sights and sounds that come to overwhelm us? Maybe he knew that, and that's why he sighed when he slipped the pistol into his pocket.

"After that he came to drink every day," Procopio said. "He would drink whiskey, always alone. Once he asked me if anyone had reported the pistol as lost or stolen. No one in the village had mentioned the pistol. His hand was always in his pocket, as if he were making sure the pistol was still there.

"He had cleaned the pistol until it was shiny," Procopio added. "He bought bullets for it, but I think he was afraid to fire it."

I listened intently. Something in the man's story seemed to be my story. A word, a fragrance, the time of day can transport me into that depth of memory I know so well. The man's story was doing that to me, allowing me no rest.

I began to go into the bar every day, and when Procopio had time, the conversation would get around to the story of the man who found the pistol. My own work began to suffer; I became even more obsessed with the story. Why did this man find the pistol? Was it his destiny? His destino, as we say in Spanish. Our tragic sense of life allied so closely to the emotions of memory.

"No one can escape el destino," Procopio said, as if reading my thoughts. "When your time comes, it comes." "Karma," I said, and we argued about the meaning of words.

That night I dreamed of the axe I had found in the mountain stream. I saw it submerged in the cold water of the stream, the steel as blue as the sky. I saw myself picking it up, and I heard a voice in the dream saying no. The next day I drove to the mountain to look for the place, but it had been years, and I no longer recognized the road that led to the stream. I wondered how many times the man who had found the pistol returned to the spot where he'd found it. Why didn't he throw it away and break the chain of events that was his destino?

"Why are you so nervous?" my wife asked me. I could not answer. I needed to be alone, and so every day I drove, up to the mountains or along the back roads of the silent mesas. When I was alone, I felt the presence I had felt in the forest the day I found the axe. I was sure the man had felt the same, but he had decided to take the pistol anyway. Troubled by my thoughts, I found myself returning to Procopio's cantina to listen to the story of the man who found the pistol.

"Late in the summer, his wife left him," Procopio said. "He had grown more moody and introverted. He didn't clean his place all summer; the weeds took over his fields. His cow got loose, and the people of the village complained, but he paid no attention. Perhaps they grew afraid of him. Maybe his wife became afraid also, and that's why she left."

Listening to Procopio, I thought I understood the man who had found the pistol. He was like me, or like any other man who wonders how the past has shaped his destiny. He was a scholar, a sensitive man who thought of these questions. All those days alone in the fields, brooding over what he could tell no one. It was bound to catch up.

"He tried to get rid of the pistol," Procopio said. "He was drunk one night, and he tried to give it to Primo, but Primo wouldn't take it. He begged Primo to take it, saying he was afraid something bad was going to happen. By then we knew there was a curse on the man. He always kept the pistol in his pocket, perhaps he slept with it. Now there was no peace for him in the silence of the valley. Even the mountain wore a stern, gray look as winter came."

Why? I asked myself, as late at night I thought of the man who had found the pistol. Why did finding the pistol change the man's life? He had committed no crime. He was a good man, a teacher. Was it because he had taken the pistol, or was there a greater design, a destiny he had to fulfill? Was the pistol like the axe, something that came to sever the cord of life?

The past haunts us, and only the person who carries the sack knows how much it weighs, as the saying goes.

"Do you remember the day we found the axe in the stream?" I asked my wife. But she had forgotten. To me the time and place and the texture of the day and the stream were so clear I would never forget. But she had forgotten. It was that way with the man who found the pistol; he would never forget that time and place. Maybe he knew that by taking the pistol, he would have to settle a score with the past.

Ghosts of the past come to haunt our lives. What ghost came to haunt this man? I felt I knew what the man had thought when he sat up late at night and stared at the pistol at his bedside, or when he walked through the village with the pistol in his pocket. He knew why the people let him pass in silence.

"Then they found the man dead," Procopio said softly. "Shot."

"Shot himself," I nodded. This is what I had assumed all along, but there was a new twist Procopio had not yet shared with me.

"No," Procopio shook his head. "That's what the paper said, but what do they know! I will tell you," he whispered. "You remember the boy with the harelip? He used to do odd jobs around the village?" I nodded.

"He was staying with the man, because the man had grown fearful of living alone. The boy slept in a small room near the front door. Late one night he heard someone knocking at the door. He got up and was going to open the door, but the man told him no. 'It is a ghost,' the man shouted. 'Don't open the door!'

"The man went to the door and listened. He shouted at the ghost to go away. The boy saw the man was terrified, and the boy, too, was full of fear. Both felt it was no ordinary person who came to knock at night.

"For weeks they were haunted by the knocking on the door. It was the feast of the Epiphany, and the night was cold. You remember, so cold it cracked some of the apple trees. Late at night the knocking came; the man went to the door. This time he held the pistol in his hand. This time he opened the door."

Procopio paused. I waited, my hands trembling. He poured me another shot, which I drank to calm myself.

"What?" I asked.

Procopio shrugged. "This is the strange part," he said. "The boy with the harelip swears that when the man opened the door, he saw the man's double standing there. The man raised the pistol and fired at his image. A cold wind shook the house, and the boy with the harelip rushed forward to shut the door. The man who had found the pistol was dead. The pistol was at his side. I don't know what made the boy grab the pistol and run away. Later he told me he had thrown it away. Somewhere in the fields."

Procopio wiped the glasses he was drying. He was sad, sad for the man who had found the pistol and for the boy who saw the death. "What was it?" I asked.

"Who knows," Procopio said. "A ghost from the past. Maybe just the boy's imagination."

I nodded. So he had made his peace. I shivered. There are certain stories that touch us close to the heart. We listen to the tale and secretly whisper, "There but for the grace of God go I." Procopio had told me only sketches of the man, but I felt I knew the man as if he were my brother.

I rose and walked outside. The night was cold, but the feel of spring was already in the air. What is the future, I thought, but a time that comes to swallow what we make of life.

Message from the Inca

He prayed and drank the coca tea, preparing himself for the run. He concentrated only on the task ahead of him, blocking out the sound of the fire sticks that sounded outside in the streets. The city of Cuzco, the capital city of the Incas, was under siege. The barbarians, speaking a strange tongue, had come, casting fire and death from their pointed sticks.

Even now the runner could hear the cries and screams of the people, and the terrifying curses of the barbarians. These bearded sorcerers were too powerful to stop; they rode huge beasts that trampled the people in their path. The runner had caught a glimpse of the carnage before the priest pulled him into the secret rooms beneath the Inca's temple. But even these sacred rooms would soon be discovered, and the barbarian's wrath would destroy everything.

Through the small window cut into the stone wall, he could see the glare of the holy city as it burned. The sight saddened the runner. All the Inca's warriors were powerless to stop the calamity. If Cuzco fell, the empire of the Inca would be lost.

Outside the cell, the runner heard the footsteps of the priest as he approached. The priest opened the door and looked at the young man, who had been taken from his parents when he was a child and trained to be a runner in the service of the Inca. He had run up and down the Mountains of the Gods, even to the sea coast. Now he was the only runner left in Cuzco. The others had been sent in all directions, carrying messages to the people, and none had returned. One, as he had tried to escape from the city, had been attacked by the dogs of the barbarians. He had died in the arms of the priests, crying that there was no way out.

The message this runner would carry to Machu Picchu would be the last communication to leave Cuzco before it fell. The salvation of the people of Vilcampa depended on the runner.

"Are you ready, my son?" the priest asked.

"Yes," the runner replied.

"Cuzco cannot be saved," the priest said. There was no fear in his voice, only finality. "Come," he said, and the runner stood and followed the priest down a dark corridor.

The runner could hear the faint reports of the fire sticks outside, and the cries of women. For a moment he thought of the woman he had known as a mother, then he shook the thought away.

He shivered. A horrifying time had come to the land of the Inca. The priests had warned the people that the bearded barbarians would destroy everything in their search for gold, but it was worse than they could have imagined. Time itself was ending.

The young man and the priest entered the room of the Inca, the room of gold. Here the torches reflected the glitter of the precious metal, this metal used to create the art of the Inca. This gift from the Sun God, used as decorations to please those one loved, was the obsession of the barbarians.

The runner bowed, low to the ground, not daring to look into the face of the Inca. Even so, he had caught a glimpse of the noble family, huddling in the shadows of the room. Only the Inca remained unperturbed. He sat on his throne like the god he was.

"My house is about to fall," the great king spoke to those gathered. The runner shivered. He had never before heard words from the Inca.

"My time is ending," the Inca continued. "I accept my destiny, but we must keep the Sun God crossing the heavens and giving warmth to the earth. Otherwise the earth will die. Send the runner to Vilcampa. Send him to the mountain of Machu Picchu, there where the virgins tie the Sun God to the post on the mountain. Let him warn them of the barbarians; let them guard our secrets."

The runner felt the eyes of the Inca upon him and heard the words entrusting him with the last message from the Inca.

"Leave no trail, cut the bridges behind you. Here we accept death at the hands of the barbarians, but we must save Vilcampa. We have been told, even time dies, but a new time must be born. Our knowledge is also for the time that is being born" were the Inca's last words.

The priest pulled the runner away from the presence of the Inca. In the corridor he handed him an intricately knotted cord, the quipu, which contained the message from the ruler.

"This is the message for the virgins of Vilcampa," the priest said. "It tells the chief priestess how long they must remain hidden from the world if they are to escape the wrath of the barbarians. The city of the virgins must be sealed; no one must pass through the portals of Machu Picchu. The city clothed in mountain mists will now be clothed in secrecy for all time. There the virgins will guard the knowledge of the Inca. Perhaps in a future time someone will read the message in the quipu and shed tears for the Inca."

Outside the thunder of the fire sticks grew louder, the murderous shouts of the barbarians closer.

"Go now." The priest hurried the runner down the corridor and to the secret door. "Take the message to the priestess of Vilcampa. Do not fail us."

The priest opened the door, and the screams and thunder grew louder. In the air floated a strange, acrid smoke. He pressed a pouch of dried coca leaves into the runner's hands. The runner would chew the leaves, and they would deaden the pain during the long run to Vilcampa. Many of the tambos, the rest houses along the trails in the Mountains of the Gods, had been destroyed. Now there were no runners to help relay the message; this runner would run a full day and a full night.

Without incident, he climbed out of the mountain bowl that was the Valley of Cuzco. The Inca had thrown all of his warriors into one last stand against the barbarians, a distraction to allow the runner to slip out of the palace. Now as the runner stood on the edge of the cliff, looking down on the burning city, a great sadness filled him.

The people of the Inca were being destroyed, there was no family left. Frightening sounds filled the air, sounds that echoed across the centuries of time. Cuzco was dying; now there was only the hope of Vilcampa in Machu Picchu.

Panting from the climb, the runner opened the pouch and took out the coca leaves. Now he would run continually, stopping only to cut the bridges that spanned the mountain ravines. These bridges, constructed of lianas, the vines from the Amazon, were the most valued possession of the Inca. The runner's instructions were to cut all the bridges on the trail to Vilcampa. He would not take time to rest.

He touched the quipu. There at the end, the priest had tied a piece of metal, perhaps a piece taken from one of the breastplates the barbarians wore. This hard and cold object was the symbol of the new age. The virgins of Vilcampa would shiver when they touched the metal.

Into the evening he ran, climbing higher and higher, following the hidden foot trail above the river valley. Behind him plumes of smoke rose into the orange sky, the fires of Cuzco burning. In the sky the runner saw a strange omen, a silver bird flying over the mountain. Below him he saw a giant snake made of metal, twisting its way along the Urubamba Valley. He shivered. These were the strange omens of the new time the Inca had predicted.

He entered the dusk, knowing his world had come to an end. Who would read the quipu when the children of the Inca were dead? Who would know the glory of Vilcampa and the virgins who tethered the Sun God at the Post of the Sun? Who would keep the calendars of the Inca, and the memory of the people?

He ran along the plain of the Urubamba, and all around him the terraced fields of the people were deserted. The people had fled into the mountains. He had tied the quipu to his belt, and as he ran, the corded string bounced on his thigh. The piece of metal at the end of the cord beat against his leg, bruising and then cutting open his flesh.

He ascended the mountains, pausing only to cut the foot bridges, sealing off the road to Vilcampa. He did not rest. The tambos on the trail were deserted, the ashes in the fireplaces cold. All runners and warriors had been called to defend the Inca. He was the only runner on the trail to Vilcampa.

He ran to the rhythm taught to the runners of the Inca, and still his lungs began to burn. He chewed the coca leaves, swallowing the bitter juice. The rhythm he kept and the deadening effect of the coca produced a new rhythm, a new awareness. He sang the songs of the Inca as he ran; his heart grew happy, and he knew he could run forever.

He could fly, yes, this is what the runners of the Inca could do. They had been taught by the shamans to fly. The runners are birds circling the Mountains of the Gods, the priests of the Inca had said, the runners are the sons of the Inca, sons of the Sun.

Below him the mighty waters of the Urubamba raged and rumbled as they surged down the mountain. The runner heard the rush of the river, and he heard another sound. It was the hiss of the iron serpent winding its way along the valley. A dark plume of smoke trailed the roaring viper.

Very well, the runner thought, I will run faster than the serpent of the barbarians. Let the new time come to the land of the Inca; I will deliver my message.

All night he ran, and visions came to him. He moved out of the time of the Inca into a new time. The old priests had taught him to run, and they had taught him that visions would come as he ran. He spoke to his father as if he were running by his side, remembering the stories his father had taught him. He moved back into the navel of time and spoke to runners of the past, runners who had run from the ocean to Cuzco, bearing fresh fish for the Inca's dinner. He moved so far back in time that he saw the first people arriving to settle the mountains, the first Incas in their thrones of gold. He saw the first stones laid to construct Vilcampa, the city guarded by Machu Picchu. Then the ultimate vision came, and he saw the virgins of Vilcampa tie the Sun God to its post. With perfect clarity he saw the golden disc tethered for a moment on the solstice day of rest, and peace filled him.

For a moment he saw the harmony, the earth and sun as one, the prayers of the virgins answered. Then visions of the future came, and he saw the devastation of his people. The people were enslaved; the old calendars of the sun were broken. The runner felt fatigue spreading in his muscles, and the visions became a clutter of people swarming around him, people from another time and place.

The light of dawn glowed around him, and still he had not stopped to rest. Into the new day he ran until there before him was the gate of Vilcampa. He had broken the stream of time to arrive with the message. He did not feel the exhaustion, even though the muscles of his legs quivered. He thanked the sun for his swiftness and safety; he had brought the message to Vilcampa.

He slowed to a walk as he passed through the stone gate. Just below, an alert sentry waved him forward. He paused to look at the city of the votaries of the sun, the virgins who cared for Vilcampa. The Urubamba River cut a wide curve around the promontory on which stood the city; the city was a fortress of the sun, protected by the mountains Machu and Picchu. The barbarians could follow the river, but from below they could not see the city. And he had cut the bridges and obliterated the signs on the trail. Now Vilcampa could be sealed off and exist in its own time.

Just below the sentry hut was the entry door. There in the middle of the city was the meadow where the dances were held. To the left stood the houses of the virgins, and nearby, the temple. And there was the sundial! Here was the center of the universe, the ombligo of time. He gazed upon the sundial and felt he was returning home, as others would come in future times. Vilcampa would stand for all time and belong to all people. That is what the Inca meant, that the message was also for the time being born.

Here, it was known, the virgins could tie the Sun God to the Post of the Sun. Only for a moment, only to renew its energy. Here the sun gazed on the altar of sacrifice, the smooth monolith where prayers and penance were done. Here the sun had intercourse with the virgins, penetrating their flesh, blessing the fields they cultivated, renewing time. This was the navel of the world where time converged.

The runner stood transfixed, feeling the luminous moment. The quality of light was so pure it was like the light of the first dawn on earth. The air was clear and scintillating. The green mountains of the Urubamba rose around him, clouds drifted across the peaks, dappling Vilcampa with bright sun, then shadow. An immense peace filled the runner's heart. Below him he could see the stone masons working at the quarry, and on the terraces, those who tended the maíz and potatoes. It was a serene image, and he wished he could sit and rest, but he had to deliver the message from the Inca.

He descended and was met at the sentry hut by a young woman. She greeted him. They had been expecting him.

"You are hurt," she said and looked at his thigh where the piece of metal on the tip of the quipu had drawn blood.

"It is nothing," he answered. "I bring a message from the Inca."

"Follow me," she said. At the gate she called to the others, and many stepped forward to help push the large stone into place. The city was now sealed.

"Our chief priestess had a vision," the young woman said as they walked toward the temple. "Strangers have come to burn Cuzco. We hear strange sounds in the valley."

She paused and looked at him.

"Behind me, everything is destroyed," he said sadly. "The time of the Inca is no more."

"And Vilcampa?" she asked.

He saw the fright in her eyes, and he wished he could say that Vilcampa was forever. But nothing was forever, only the path of the sun and the knowledge of the virgins. A weariness filled his body.

"For now, Vilcampa is safe. I will live here," he said.

He wanted to tell her that while he ran he'd had a vision of others trudging up the slopes of the mountain to the secret city, new generations who came seeking the knowledge of the Incas.

"The quipu carries the message," he said. "It will be passed on."

She led him through the narrow streets of the city, turning left toward the altar. There she invited him to sit. She left him for a moment and returned with water. She cleansed his wound, washing the blood away, and she washed his body. He closed his eyes while she washed him, enjoying the softness of her hands. Around him gathered other women, the virgins who kept Vilcampa, eager to know what message he had brought.

"Now you may deliver your message," the young woman said and led him toward the temple. They passed the sundial, the Post of the Sun, which was carved from one piece of stone.

She led him to the temple where the chief priestess waited. She was surrounded by other women, priestesses of the sun and workers from the fields and the quarry.

"Welcome, runner of the Inca," the priestess spoke and stepped forward. "Welcome to our home. We have been waiting for you."

The runner undid the quipu from the leather thong at his waist and handed it to her. She received it tremulously.

She read the message in a loud voice, and the wind of the mountain carried her sad words down the canyon of the Urubamba. She read the date the barbarians had come to destroy Cuzco, and of the many warriors of the Inca who had been killed. In the words of the Inca, time had come to an end; now a new time had to be born. Vilcampa was to keep the calendars of the sun and the knowledge of the Inca.

A deep silence filled the air. Only the moan of the wind could be heard. Then she showed them the piece of metal tied to the tip of the quipu, and she told them this was the cause of all the destruction.

"Did you cut the bridges on the mountain passes?" she asked the runner.

"Yes," he answered.

"The Inca has commanded," she said to all gathered, "no one is to leave Vilcampa. No one can enter. Our fate is sealed. We are the last city of the Inca; we will praise and renew the sun as always."

All nodded in assent. The time of the Inca had died, and now Vilcampa was a capsule anchored to the mountains of Machu Picchu. How long they would survive was not for them to say, for time on earth was short and the visions of the priests forever. They knew the secret of Vilcampa, and in the future others would come to know it. Of that they were sure.

The priestess returned the quipu to the runner. "It is yours," she said. "A message to be passed down through the centuries. Many people will come here seeking the knowledge of the Inca. They will want to know how we were attentive to the Sun God. They will seek knowledge of the harmony of our world. We will share that message," she said.

The runner nodded. The message of catastrophe and chaos had been received with courage. These women, these votaries of the sun, were all women of courage. They accepted the end of time because they knew a new time would be born. In their wombs they carried the rays of the sun, the penetrating light of the Giver of Life.

"Take the runner to the eating area," the priestess said to the young woman. "See that he is fed. See that he has a place to rest. He is one of us now. This is his home."

The young woman bowed and took the runner's hand. She led him through the open meadow, past a flock of alpacas and the houses of the workers.

"There," she said, "is the place to eat. The women will serve you. I will return for you."

He turned to look at the terrace where people were eating. They were clothed in garments he had never seen; they spoke a strange language. For a moment he was afraid. Was he, too, slipping away from the time of the Inca? Was there no spot of earth that was fixed forever? Had he died in Cuzco or in the mountain ravines? Was this his ghost moving across time to come to sit with the strangers?

"Do not be afraid," he heard the voice of the young woman. "You are one of us."

The runner's hand tightened on the quipu, as if by holding tight to the cord, he could hold on to reality. His body ached with fatigue; the effect of the coca had worn away. He felt hunger. He walked to the eating area. There was an empty chair, and the man next to it motioned to the runner.

"Sit here," the man said. He spoke the language of the barbarians, but his smile was kind. "I have come a long way to listen to the memories of Vilcampa," he said. He had been writing on the notebook that lay on the table.

A woman served the runner food and drink. The drink was cold and bitter. It was served in a marvelous glass bottle. The food was cold and tasteless; he couldn't eat. A swarm of people moved around him. Who are these strangers? he wondered. What has happened to the Vilcampa I knew? He looked for the young woman and spotted her near workers who stood by the large metal huts. Smoke poured from these cabins even as people stepped out of them.

"Too many tourists, too many buses," the man sitting by the runner whispered. He pointed to the long line of people disembarking. "We come looking for the magic, and we find only each other." He smiled.

It is a kind smile, the runner thought. This stranger from another country had dark curly hair and a dark face, but he was not a child of the Inca. The children of the Inca were the workers who spoke Quechua as they ate their lunches by the side of the road.

The runner looked at the quipu. He understood now what had happened during his run, and that it was time to pass on the message. This man, too, was a messenger; he wrote his stories in the notebook. The runner pushed the quipu across the table to the man, and the man took it. Their eyes met for a moment, and in that instant each knew the message from the Inca would never die. It would be passed on, generation to generation.

The runner nodded and rose. He bowed, and the man responded. Then the runner walked away from the eating place to join the workers. These were his people, men of strong backs and honest brown faces. They talked and joked in a language he could understand. They were cleaning the road that led down to the valley, but they had paused to eat their noonday meal. They accepted the runner easily into their company.

The young woman he had met when he entered the gate of Vilcampa handed him Quechua food, and he ate. Here he felt at ease. These men had been in the Mountains of the Gods a long time. They were the new workers in the city of Vilcampa. They ate and talked in the shadow of Machu Picchu. They will be here forever, the runner thought.

He relaxed, looked at the young woman, and smiled. He had delivered the message from the Inca; now it was in the hands of the man who sat at the table. That man would read the secret of the quipu, record it in his language, and pass it on. Each new time had its runners, those whose work carried them into new visions of reality.

Absalom

After her divorce she moved to the Negev, south of Be'er Sheva. There in the Israeli desert, she found the solitude she sought. She would awaken early in the morning to greet the sun, to smell the fresh air, which held the scent of fruit blossoms. Later, the breeze would smell of sand, rocks, desert heat, and the faint body sweat she thought must be of the sheepherders.

Around the desert settlement, there were small groups of Bedouin, dark men who tended goats and sheep and camels. She sometimes saw them when she drove to Be'er Sheva to teach her classes. She never spoke to them; it was not allowed. They kept to their world, she to hers.

But the smell of the desert tribes was the smell of the desert. For her there was something pleasing in it, something real. At night, when the breeze blew in from the desert, a trace of the acrid odor made her restless, disturbed her dreams.

In the morning it was the sweet fragrance she craved, the sweetness of the blossoming trees of the settlement. Trees of her people. Her Jews.

No, not her Jews, because she felt apart from them. She felt apart from everyone. Alone. She had always felt alone, even in New York she had been alone. It was there she had lost her soul, or the passion that is the fire of the soul.

Her husband had pursued ambition, the making of money, the goal of profit. She lived with him for years, but she never knew him. He never knew her. How strange, she thought, as she stood watching the blinding sun rise at the eastern horizon, to live with a man for so long and never know him.

To share a bed. Breakfast. Dinner. Parties. Year after year. He provided, but of his soul he gave nothing. And she who was so full of yearning learned to give nothing in return. She did not blame him, but she began to believe that men were essentially passionless. Even the lovers she took pleased her only for the moment; they did not give her whatever emotions they guarded within.

So she had left the sterility of the city and sought a new life in Israel. She taught, and in her teaching she found some satisfaction, which helped move her from one day to the next. Zionism, the commitment to the land and the nation, did not move her. The burden of her people's history did not move her.

She met men, men busy with politics or history or religion. They awakened her body, but none seemed able to drink from that stream of passion that ran beneath the flesh, deep in the soul. The surface of life, she believed, was the domain of men.

There were moments of fulfillment in the desert sun, in the early morning sweetness, in the green color of the trees, in the sight of the Bedouin who were like dark shadows on the rim of her life—dark men of passion she did not know, a dream that could not be shared.

The sudden warmth of the sun made her shiver. She tasted the sweetness of water on her tongue. Someone was watering the trees: The water soaked the sand and turned it dark, the trees grew green, the blossoms bright. For a moment the sun gave reassurance; then the moment was gone, and her loneliness returned.

She remembered lovers, the dullness of hurry, the quick sense of excitement. She could not remember their faces. There was never a sense of completeness, never fulfillment. New York had swept around her, and in the streets, other women shared her sadness, the common frustration of passion denied.

I have learned to please men, she thought. The instinct is in my blood. But never has one shared his true desire with me; never has one opened his heart.

One had come close. The priest. He gave a love that seemed sacred. Holy. He was handsome, strong, with a touch so delicate she had begun to feel the fire beyond the boundary of her dark curves. He kissed as if in prayer. Had it been only the sense of danger, the excitement? For a while they had loved as close as touching is to love.

She felt herself become woman, not mystery. From deep within, a perfume began to flow, and for a time she caught a wisp of it, the deep, rich woman smell released by his touch. Then it was gone; he held back. Did he save himself for God, as the others saved themselves for fame or power or greed or wife at home?

She remembered him with kindness as she stepped back into the kitchen to drink her coffee. Arabian coffee. The brick floor was cool to her feet. The stone walls were cool, white, immaculate. Only the books in the bookcase and the Bedouin wool rug near the door were warm.

Then Absalom came. That was not his name, of course, that's what she called him. Just as we might say her name is Tamar, a seductive, intriguing biblical name.

He was a North African with long black hair, and she called him Absalom because she had met him the day she had walked alone up the Qidron Valley to the tomb of Absalom. The Hassidim had closed the path to traffic, so now only the Arab children played there in the afternoon, rode their burros, carried stingy piles of firewood home. She walked beside the Arab houses, which clung to the hillside, daring the dark presence of eyes that knew she was a daughter of David.

At the tomb, at that dark monolith set against the hillside, by the cave, she stood alone. The western sun began to set on Jerusalem. At the Western Wall the faithful prayed; in the blue mosque on the Temple Mount, the prayers left their resonant silence on arabesque walls, prayers engraved into the silence of the rock, prayers for Mecca. Jerusalem was alive with fire, a white, burning city in the sunlight. Down the valley the prayer of the muezzin called from the minaret. The city was alive with prayer, alive and glowing with vibrant, living fire.

In that holy silence of the day's end, in that light that suffused everything, she heard a voice. From within the Pillar of Absalom, she heard a voice, a voice calling like the clear, quick water that ran beneath the valley to Gihon Spring. It was the voice of life, the dark water of the desert, a passion filling her as light and prayer filled the city. Fulfillment, the voice whispered, fulfillment.

The North African had watched her as she'd stood before the pillar. She smiled when she turned, and he led her away. He bought her coffee, the rich, dark Arabian coffee that stilled her trembling. He drove with her, south into the Negev, to her home. They made love, a dark, physical love that broke the bonds of separation, long into the night, fulfillment, a love fulfilling intense need.

Her woman's fragrance was released into his strong North African man smell. The desert scents of the night grew complete, her sweat and love dissolved into the flow of time. She cried out with joy. "Absalom! Absalom!"

The sound was a ripple across the dark of the night, disturbing dreams in the Bedouin camp, where the night fire died in orange embers.

Thereafter, he came from time to time, over the hills from Be'er Sheva, a man sometimes at war, exhausted, once wounded. She asked no questions, she became his woman. I will be happy, she thought. He draws ecstasy from my soul; his love is like fresh water in the desert. But he was a demanding man, a jealous man. They quarreled.

Manhood was his creed, his vision of life. That was what he offered. Her own rich and complex creed flooded over her, and suddenly the world was old, and as bone dry as the desert. She rose against him, and he sped away, full of anger.

"Absalom!" she cried, but it was too late. The desert of Be'er Sheva is filled with ghosts, as are most places on earth.

There are stories told in the Bedouin camps, stories as old as the desert itself. All revolve around the spirit of God or the spirit of love. The desert people know truth is reflected in the ecstasy of the soul and in the ecstasy of the flesh.

The old men whisper, "The hand of God seemed to reach down and grab the North African by the hair. His car, faster than any horse, went out from under him."

Over the cliff, down the ravine, he died in the mangled heap of metal, pierced by the shaft of the steering wheel. The night was full of stars.

What is the stream of life beneath the flesh of woman? Is it like the waters of the Qidron Valley, surging deep beneath the earth, gurgling in darkness until it rises at the Pool of Shiloah to refresh the gardens of the City of David? Or is it a stream of deception, drawing the man to drowning?

Every day Tamar must ask this question as she sees the mangled wreck when she drives to teach her classes. Absalom's tomb. Her Absalom. The desert begins to rust it, the wind grieves around the twisted wreck, and the Bedouins who move across the desert do not come near. They circle, keeping their distance, as always.

The Captain

The morning after we arrived, I went for a walk in the forest that surrounded the chalet. There had been a light drizzle in the night, but now the sun shown brightly and the droplets of water glistened as they clung to the trees. I had listened to the rain for a while, and the fatigue of the war had drained away and I had fallen asleep. It was the first soft, warm bed I had slept in since my last visit home over a year ago. I slept well, but I awakened early. I was accustomed to getting up early, because on the front, the artillery barrages always come at dawn, presaging the movement of troops or attack. But this morning there was nothing, only silence. Outside my window the birds chirped in the trees. The aroma of freshly brewed coffee tinged the cool, fresh air.

I decided to walk alone before breakfast. I put on an old pair of tweed trousers and a heavy wool sweater my wife had knitted for my birthday, then I made my way down a dark hallway toward the rear of the chalet. The führer's suite also occupied the rear wing of the chalet, and as I passed by an open door, I glanced in and saw him sitting at a small table by the window. He wore a dressing gown, and he was having his morning coffee as he read a newspaper. He looked up, smiled, and nodded. I drew myself up to salute, but he had already returned to his paper.

He had appeared shortly after we had arrived the night before. He had made a short talk, toasted us, and told us to enjoy ourselves. There would be no meetings. We would take our dinners together, but that was all; the rest of the time was ours to do with as we pleased. There was a spa, he said, a large game room adjoining the dining room, a comfortable den with plenty of recent newspapers, and of course there was the forest. He made a point of encouraging us to walk in the forest. There were good trails for walking and beautiful meadows full of spring flowers.

We were warriors, he said, and we had fought hard for our common goal, so now it was time to rest and enjoy this island of peace away from the war. The Eagle's Nest, he called it. He made a toast, smiled, thanked us for our adherence to his cause, then he disappeared. A tall blonde woman who had stood quietly in the background accompanied him.

"He is looking well," someone commented.

We nodded in agreement. We had heard rumors about his health, but those were dispelled when we saw him. He seemed in good spirits. His hair and moustache were neatly trimmed, and his uniform was impeccable.

As I passed the open door, I noticed a huge mirror, which covered almost one complete wall and reflected the rest of his suite: a wide bed, a valet polishing his boots, a fireplace at the far end of the room, and at another table near the fireplace, the same blonde woman whom I had seen the night before. She glanced up, saw my reflection in the mirror, and I thought she frowned. I proceeded and found my way to the rear exit, where a door opened onto a large terrace. There were tables and chairs, and at the edge of the retaining wall, a telescope. I walked to the edge of the terrace and looked down at the dense green forest that surrounded us. In the distance I could see the smoke of the village, where we had arrived by train the night before. Below me, along the slight grade that dropped into the valley, but within the fenced compound, there were many small meadows. They were bright with the flowers of spring. I could not remember a more beautiful sight. At that moment, the war seemed so far away. The only reminder was the sight of the guards stationed around the perimeter of the compound.

I lighted my pipe and wandered into the forest. Underneath the canopy of trees, patches of sunlight glistened and dazzled in the drops of water that clung to the leaves and in the mist that rose from the ground. Squirrels chattered in the trees. Blue jays and blackbirds hopped from branch to branch, calling shrilly to the stranger who had intruded in their sanctuary. Up ahead I saw a red fox disappear into the dense undergrowth, a female hunting, because it was followed by two cubs.

It could not be more beautiful, I thought as I walked aimlessly toward the meadows I had seen from the terrace, then turned at the fence and worked my way toward the road that led from the gate to the chalet. Even the guards at the gate had been pleasant last night. They had not asked for papers, merely saluted and waved us through when the driver said we were the führer's guests for the weekend. We were received with open arms by the servants. The cooks were waiting for us with a late dinner. They were jovial and served the meal in good spirits. The wine flowed freely, good French wine, which none of us had tasted since before the war.

I did not personally know most of the officers. We were all positioned along the eastern front and we knew each other through the war reports, but we were not staff or generals, so there was no reason for us to know each other. As a matter of fact, there was only one general in the group. "Fat Lips," I'll call him. He was the one who toasted the führer the loudest and longest. Long after I went to bed, he was still drinking. And there was Frank. We had been at the military academy together. It was good to see him again. We had talked briefly about old times, showed each other photographs of our families: He had two girls, I had one.

But why were we here? Frank had questioned me. Why had we been chosen? We were not part of the führer's group, we weren't politicians, and except for Fat Lips, we weren't generals. We did have good records as officers. During the early days of the eastern offensive, my men had proved themselves to be brave, capable soldiers. We had taken the northern flank, capturing thousands of prisoners, and I had been made a hero of sorts. But the days of heroes quickly passed. The cold had come, and the movement had bogged down. The war grew dismal.

I pushed those thoughts from my mind, sniffed the fresh spring air, and paused to light my pipe again. I had found the road that led to the chalet. I recalled the fragrance of the coffee, a luxury we rarely had on the northern flank. I was hungry. I looked forward to sitting down and eating a hearty breakfast. "Why be concerned about why we were invited," I thought aloud. "We are here; let's enjoy it." For me it was the first break from the front in over a year. As I walked toward the chalet, I thought of my wife and wished that she could be with me. Even for the officers, the letters were few and far between. The enemy was bombing the cities now, and I worried, for her and for my young daughter.

As I approached the chalet, an army bus rumbled up the road. I stepped aside to let it pass. I thought perhaps more officers were arriving and was surprised to see women in the bus. One of them was the führer's woman. The other women, evidently from the village, smiled and waved, and I waved back. For the most part they were handsome women, village peasants with round, pleasant faces. One in particular caught my eye. She was a young woman, perhaps eighteen. She smiled and looked directly at me as the bus drove past. When the bus stopped in front of the chalet, the other officers came out to greet the passengers. I joined them. The meeting was pleasant, with a great deal of laughter.

Fat Lips helped a heavy-set woman off the bus, and she responded by giving him a hug. Everyone laughed. My friend Frank reached out to assist a woman who reminded me vaguely of my wife. When the young woman who had caught my eye stepped down, she looked directly at me. She held out a small valise; I took it and offered my arm. At the door the servants took the bags; everyone was happy. Inside the cooks, seemingly delighted with the arrival of the women, were waiting to lead us into the dining room.

The only woman who did not come with us was the führer's woman. I paused at the door and looked back. She was still standing by the side of the bus. The führer had joined her. He stood by her side, seemed to lean slightly toward her to ask her something, then he smiled and looked toward us as we entered the chalet. He hooked his hands in his belt and seemed to rock back and forth, looking very pleased.

Breakfast was a delight. There were fresh eggs and bread from the village, lots of coffee, and of course the company of women. They were typical peasant women, broad shouldered and heavy bosomed. They had plain but warm faces, and they seemed pleased to be with us. The usual reservation and aloofness of the German woman was missing. They were the first female companionship most of us had known in a long time. They listened to our stories and jokes and laughed. We all laughed, even at the old jokes we had heard before.

The women told us their names but very little else about themselves. They insisted on hearing about us. We were the saviors of the homeland who had come to rest in their forest. They were there to serve us, they said. Of course it was what we needed, to talk to women—warm, clean women who leaned forward and listened intently as we unburdened ourselves.

Someone, Fat Lips I think, ordered brandy after breakfast. We drank it with our coffee, and the talk became more lighthearted and animated. Toasts were made. The women of the village were praised for their beauty. The war was praised. The führer was praised. He was the magnanimous person to have us at this Shangri-la, the colonel said. With him as a leader, we would conquer all our enemies. The lull in the war was only temporary. Everybody cheered. The women drank with us. Their faces grew ruddy and pleasant with the brandy and excitement.

Else, the woman who seemed to have chosen me, sat with me at breakfast. Now as the colonel stood to propose a new toast, she drew closer to me and took my hand beneath the table. I trembled and looked at her. Her hand was warm. She leaned closer to whisper that she would like to leave the party. Her breath was sweet on my face. When I looked into her eyes, she returned a look of admiration and invitation.

I was surprised at first, then tremulous. I had not felt my blood pulse to the closeness of a woman for a long time. In war a soldier learns to harden himself against loneliness. He learns that the heart must be cold and immune to the death around him. But when she held my hand, I felt like a young man again, like a lover who walks hand in hand with his girlfriend in the park in time of peace. Maybe that is why we had come here, to be rewarded for our soldiering with an interlude of peace. Still, I could not help but remember my wife, my young daughter, all my comrades who couldn't be with us on this island of peace, my men who had died on the bloody fields of war. I thought of all the times I had told them to go out and die for the Fatherland. I saw the frozen bodies that had fallen along the road as we pushed eastward, and now it was spring, spring in the forest, a moment of peace.

I looked into Else's eyes and she encouraged me. I felt a need for her, the need to take her in my arms. I was hungry for companionship, eager to tell this young woman the events that had become part of my life since the war began; I wanted to free myself of the death and suffering I had seen, and she as a woman could provide that freedom and release. They were the same things I would tell my wife.

"I know a place in the forest," she said as if she had read my thoughts, "a meadow where we can take a picnic lunch. If you would like to go?"

"Yes," I answered.

She smiled and slipped into the kitchen, and when she returned, she was carrying a picnic basket. She handed it to me, then she picked up a blanket from a couch and led me out of the chalet and into the forest. The others were also wandering into the forest to enjoy the bright, sunny day.

"There are beautiful meadows just below the chalet," Else said. "Come, I know one that will be dry after last night's rain. It is a beautiful spot."

I followed her, and she led me down toward the meadows I had seen earlier that morning. We came to a sunlit meadow, where she spread the blanket. We were alone. The others had found their own quiet places in the forest. The only visible sign of life was the sprawling chalet at the top of the promontory. When I looked up, I thought I could see the führer and his woman on the terrace, but it was too far for me to be sure.

"Come, sit down." Else beckoned. She opened the wine and we sipped. She uncovered the basket, and there were delicious cold cuts of cheese and liverwurst, a loaf of bread, and winter apples, which I hadn't tasted since the war had begun. We ate and laughed. The wine grew warm as the day grew warm, but we didn't care. We were happy. Else teased me and hand fed me small pieces of cheese and apples.

When I could eat no more, I stretched on my back and enjoyed the sun. "Come," Else coaxed me, "you said you were hungry. Now eat." She held a thin slice of apple in her lips, leaned over me, and placed it to my mouth. I took it, nibbled at it, our lips brushed, then I pulled her down and kissed her. She responded, covering my mouth with her warm lips. At that moment I needed her more than I needed anything. "The sun is warm," she said. In the bright sunlight, her white body was flushed. For a moment I could only look at her and admire her beauty. Then she smiled and reached out to touch me, and I pulled her close.

She laughed softly when I lay quietly by her side. "Why are you in such a hurry?" she asked in her teasing way.

"Because I was afraid you would vanish . . . I was afraid that this is a dream that will fade," I answered. "And because I haven't been with a woman in over a year. My wife—"

"I know," she said as she caressed me. She ran her hand up and down my naked body, letting her fingers wander softly and aimlessly, needing no words to arouse me again. Then she laughed as I kissed her and ran my fingers through her long, silky hair. She held my face in her hands and looked up at me with her bright blue eyes.

"You are a tender lover," she said and smiled.

"And you are a beautiful woman," I answered, but the thought came that it was my wife I had yearned for this past year, and it was she I seemed to hold when I made love to Else.

Maybe she saw or sensed my mood in my eyes, because she said softly, "Let today and tomorrow be ours. Let them be special to us." She kissed me, and I returned her kisses. Yes, I thought, let these two days be ours. We dissolved into each other, like innocent children exploring the beauty of our warm bodies, pausing to sip wine and nibble the fresh cheese and apples. We came together again and again in the warm, spring sunlight.

In the late afternoon, when we lay quietly, side by side, enjoying the sun, the reality of the war came back to me. Even on this island of quiet and peace, I thought I could feel a quake in the earth as I sensed the rumble of heavy artillery far in the distance.

"Tell me about your wife," she said to draw me out of my silence, and I told her about my wife and young daughter.

When the sun began to set and the afternoon grew cool, we walked back to the chalet. At dinner I spoke briefly to Frank. He seemed very happy. He said that he and his woman had also spent the day in the forest. There was only one ominous note at the end of the day. The führer dined with us, but he sat at the far end of the table. He didn't speak to us as he had the night before. There was a distracted look in his eyes, a frown on his forehead. From time to time he would look up at us and shake his head. His woman, who was dressed in a striking gown, touched his arm, and when he looked at her he smiled briefly, then the frown crossed his face again.

The next day Else and I didn't stay for breakfast. With basket and blanket in hand, we headed early in the morning for our meadow. We had been blessed by another warm day, and we were happy. We ate and sunned and made love. At one point during the day, I asked her who the woman with the führer was, and she simply replied that it was the führer's woman.

"What does she do?" I asked.

"Her job is to please the führer," Else answered.

I asked her if she had noticed the führer's countenance the night before at dinner, but she said that was something not to be talked about. When I pressed her for the reason, she said it was because it was rumored that the führer could not make love to women as other men could, and that is what caused his distress.

It was then that I looked up at the chalet and knew it was he on the terrace. I remembered the telescope and the view of the meadows from the terrace. I took the blanket and pulled it over

Else, and when she asked why, I said it was because I felt a chill in the air. The rest of the day my thoughts were troubled. I wondered again why we had been invited to the führer's, and I could not help but look up at the chalet from time to time and see the small, nervous figure of the führer pacing back and forth on the terrace.

Later in the afternoon a wind came up, and we were forced to return sooner than we wanted. Rain clouds darkened the rooms of the chalet, and a strange silence permeated everything. Else disappeared, and when I went to dinner, neither she nor the other women appeared. I asked why they had not joined us, and Fat Lips said, "It has to do with the führer's health."

"We won't see them until we leave in the morning," the colonel added. We ate in silence, enveloped in a gloom that even the French wine could not dispel. I had looked forward to my last night with Else. I had ordered wine and flowers for my room, and I had planned to give her a gift, one of my medals that she had admired. It was a decoration for valor, and I wanted her to have it.

The others drifted into the game room, and I could hear the sound of billiard balls as they struck each other. I remained at the table, trying to understand the disquietude that kept nagging me. I missed Else, I knew that, but there was that other thing: the führer on the terrace, the telescope, and now the women had disappeared. We had all heard rumors about the führer's strange sexual needs, but those of us who were loyal to him discounted them. Great men have their detractors, we had told ourselves, and after enjoying the pleasant stay for two days, I was convinced the stories were lies.

I got up and wandered aimlessly toward my room. I didn't want to be with the others. Perhaps it is just as well the women were occupied with something else, I thought, perhaps I needed the time to be alone. I wanted to write to my wife, I wanted to tell her about the führer's haven and to tell her that the führer was a good man, and now I was sure that with time we would be victorious over our enemies.

As my apartment lay in the same direction as the führer's, the two guards at the door saluted and let me pass. But instead of turning toward my room, I turned toward the exit I had used my first morning at the chalet. A walk would do me good, I thought, and clear away the uneasy feeling that crowded my mind. It wasn't until I was in front of his door that I remembered the hallway would take me past the führer's room. The door to the room was ajar. I started to walk quickly, but the sounds of the women made me stop. At first I thought they were having a party. They were whispering and laughing lightly, and I heard the clinking of glasses. I turned and looked at the mirror on the wall, and what I saw made me gasp. I felt the evening meal and wine sour in my stomach and a bitter taste fill my mouth as the image in the mirror swirled before me. He was there, on the bed, and they seemed to dance around him, naked, whispering, teasing . . . .

I shook my head and stepped back, not wanting to believe what I was seeing in the mirror. I suddenly knew why we were here. Stunned and angry, I turned away, and as I turned, I came face to face with the führer's mistress and Else. Both were dressed in sheer gowns. Else looked beautiful. Her long blonde hair fell like silk over her naked shoulders. Her cheeks were red with rouge and her lips bright with lipstick. The sweet fragrance of perfume filled the dimly lighted hallway.

"What are you doing here?" the führer's woman asked sharply. She tightened her grip on Else's arm.

"I was on my way outside," I answered and looked at Else. I knew where she was going, I knew what she was going to do, and yet there was no shame in her eyes. She looked at me as if she didn't recognize me.

"The girl!" I heard the führer call. "Bring the girl!"

"On your way," the führer's mistress snapped as she led Else past me and into the führer's room. The door closed sharply in front of me.

I felt my legs tremble as I leaned against the wall for support. I felt a nausea in my stomach, the same sick feeling I had felt when I killed my first enemy. I wanted to reach out and pull her out of the room, to protest in some way, but there was nothing I could do. He was the führer; his word was law. He had brought the war, and he had brought us to his hideaway. Now I knew why.

I don't remember what I did the rest of that night. I know I walked in the trails of the forest. In the dark I felt better. I didn't want to be seen. I walked and wished there were some way to forget the scene in the führer's room, forget Else's love, the way she had looked as she stood next to the führer's mistress, and I wished I could spit away the bitter taste that kept rising into my mouth. It helped if I concentrated on the war, if I thought about my responsibilities in the field. It helped if I went over the logistics of the war and of my job until I was thinking only of the minutest details, which had to do with moving men and supplies and reading charts and plotting movements of troops.

I walked until early morning, then I went to my room, showered and shaved, and put on my dress uniform. When I looked in the mirror I had to turn away, and I knew then it would always be difficult for me to see reflections without remembering the scene of the night before. I walked briskly to breakfast, because I was now in a hurry to leave the place. My fellow officers were there, all in dress uniforms, gathered around the table along with the women and the führer and his mistress. The führer looked to be in good spirits; he was talking and joking with the men.

"It has been a most pleasant stay," Fat Lips was saying. "I feel rested enough now to fight this war until doomsday!"

"Ach, let us hope we don't have to fight that long," the führer answered. Everybody laughed.

I looked at Else. She looked drawn and tired. All the women looked tired. They smiled and laughed and tried to keep up the pretense, but beneath the makeup, their faces were hard and bitter.

"For such a leader we will fight forever!" the colonel said as he stood, and everyone raised his glass and toasted the führer and his health.

The men ate heartily, the women only played with their food as they listened to the talk of war. From time to time I looked at Else, but when her eyes met mine, she looked away.

After breakfast the führer thanked us again. He hoped our stay had been a pleasant one. He assured us that a turning point in the war was coming. We were a master race, which would not be denied its destiny. We would be victorious. We would rule the world. The officers cheered and stood and saluted as he marched out. "Long live the führer!" they shouted. "Long live the Fatherland!"

Then we boarded the bus for the ride back to the village. The women rode with us. The men were in good spirits, still praising the führer, but the women were silent. I looked closely at them, trying to decipher what they felt, what they were thinking, but their eyes turned away from me.

The führer's car was at the railroad station when we arrived. He was standing in the bright sunlight, talking to a man I assumed was the mayor of the village. When we descended from the bus, a small orchestra struck up the national anthem. The women moved away from us quickly. There were no partings. They hurried to their families, who stood behind the line of troopers that separated us from the villagers. I looked at the villagers, rural broad-shouldered men who stood silent and stiff, awaiting the return of their daughters. They said nothing as the women were met by their mothers or sisters, but in their eyes was a gleam of contempt I had begun to recognize.

"It has been a good stay," the führer said to the mayor.

"We are pleased, Your Excellency." The old man bowed. He held his hat in his hands and twisted it nervously.

"Yes, it has been excellent," the führer said, loudly enough for the villagers to hear. Then he leaned and whispered as he pointed to Else. Because I was close, I heard him whisper, "The girl. Does she have any sisters?"

The mayor nodded. "Yes, Your Excellency. She comes from a big family. She has two younger sisters. See, they are standing by her."

I looked to where Else stood with her family. The two younger girls that stood by her side were very pretty, but they were very young. I turned and saw the führer smile.

"Ah, yes, beautiful girls," he said and rubbed his hands. The mayor bowed. "Well, until the next time," the führer finished, saluted us, then turned and walked briskly to his car. He and his mistress boarded it and sped away.

I felt a shudder through my body; my knees grew weak. At the same time, the conductor called for us to board the train. My fellow officers waved at the women, but they did not respond. A silence had come over the villagers. The faces of the men were cold and set, as if they had been chiseled from the granite of the nearby hills. I looked at Else, and she turned to look at me. She did not smile. Frank touched my shoulder. I was holding up the line. I opened my clenched fist, and the medal, which had cut my palm, dropped to the black, oily gravel at my feet. We boarded the train quickly, and it moved away from the small station, returning us to the war we had left for that bitter interlude.

In Search of Epifano

She drove into the desert of Sonora in search of Epifano. For years, when summer came and she had finished her classes, she would load her old Jeep with supplies and drive south into Mexico.

Now she was almost eighty and, she thought, ready for death, not afraid of death. The pain of the bone-jarring journey was her reality, not thoughts of death. But that did not diminish the urgency she felt as she drove south, across the desert. She was following the north rim of el Cañon de Cobre, toward the land of the Tarahumaras. In the Indian villages, there was always a welcome and fresh water.

The battered Jeep kicked up a cloud of chalky dust, which rose into the empty and searing sky of summer. Around her, nothing moved in the heat. Dry mirages rose and shimmered, without content, without form. Her bright, clear eyes remained fixed on the rocky, rutted road in front. Around her, there was only the vast and empty space of the desert. The dry heat.

The Jeep wrenched sideways, the low gear groaning and complaining. It had broken down once, and it had cost her many days' delay in Mexicali. The mechanic at the garage had told her not to worry. In one day the parts would be in Calexico, and she would be on her way.

But she knew the way of the Mexican, so she rented a room in a hotel nearby. Yes, she knew the Mexican. Part of her blood was Mexican, wasn't it? Her great-grandfather Epifano had come north to Chihuahua to ranch and to mine. She knew the stories whispered about the man, how he had built a great ranch in the desert.

His picture was preserved in the family album, his wife, a dark-haired woman, at his side. Around them, their sons.

The dry desert air burned her nostrils. The scent of the green ocotillo reminded her of other times, other years. She knew how to live in the sun, how to travel and how to survive, and she knew how to be alone under the stars. Night was her time in the desert. She liked to lie in her bedroll and look up at the swirling dance of the stars. In the cool of evening her pulse would quicken. The sure path of the stars was her map, drawing her south.

Sweat streaked her wrinkled skin. Sweat and dust, the scent commingling. She felt alive. "At least I'm not dry and dead," she said aloud. Sweat and pleasure, they came together.

The Jeep worried her now. A sound somewhere in the gearbox was not right. "It has trouble," the mechanic had said, wiping his oily hands on a dirty rag. What he meant was that he did not trust his work. It was best to return home, he suggested with a shrug. He had seen her musing over the old and tattered map, and he was concerned about the old woman going south. Alone. It was not good.

"We all have trouble," she mumbled. We live too long, and the bones get brittle, and the blood dries up. Why can't I taste the desert in my mouth? Have I grown so old? Epifano? How does it feel to become a spirit of the desert?

Her back and arms ached from driving; she was covered with the dust of the desert. Deep inside, in her liver or in her spleen, in one of those organs the ancients called the seat of life, there was an ache, a dull, persistent pain. In her heart there was a tightness. Would she die and never reach the land of Epifano?

She slept while she waited for the Jeep to be repaired. Slept and dreamed under the shade of the laurel in the patio of the small hotel. Around her, Mexican sounds and colors permeated her dream. What did she dream? That it was too late in her life to go once again into the desert? That she was an old woman and her life was lived, and the only evidence she would leave of her existence would be her sketches and paintings? Even now as weariness filled her, the dreams came, and she slipped in and out of past and present. In her dreams she heard the voice of the old man, Epifano.

She saw his eyes, blue and bright like hers, piercing, but soft. The eyes of a kind man. He had died. Of course he had died. He belonged to the past. But she had not forgotten him. In the family album she carried with her, his gaze was the one that looked out at her and drew her into the desert. She was the artist of the family. She had taken up painting. She heard voices. The voice of her great-grandfather. The rest of her family had forgotten the past, forgotten Mexico and the old man Epifano.

The groaning of the Jeep shattered the silence of the desert. She tasted dust in her mouth, and she yearned for a drink of water. She smiled. A thirst to be satisfied. Always there was one more desire to be satisfied. Her paintings were like that, a need from within to be satisfied, a call to do one more sketch of the desert in the molten light before night came. And always the voice of Epifano drawing her to her trek into the past.

The immense solitude of the desert swallowed her. She was only a moving shadow in the burning day. Overhead, vultures circled in the sky; the heat grew intense. She was alone on a dirt road she barely remembered, taking her bearings only by instinct, roughly following the north rim of el Cañon de Cobre, drawn by the thin line of the horizon, where the dull peaks of las montañas met the dull blue of the sky. Whirlwinds danced in her eyes; memories flooded her soul.

She had married young. She had thought she was in love; he was a man of ambition. It took her years to learn that he had little desire or passion. He could not, or would not, fulfill her. What was the fulfillment she sought? It had to do with something that lay beneath the moments of love or children carried in the womb. Of that she was sure.

She turned to painting, she took classes, she traveled alone. She came to understand that she and the man were not meant for each other.

A strange thing had happened in the chapel where the family had gathered to attend her wedding. An Indian had entered and stood at the back of the room. She had turned and looked at him. Then he was gone, and later she was not sure if the appearance had been real or imagined.

But she did not forget. She had looked into his eyes. His features were those of a Tarahumara. Was he Epifano's messenger? Had he brought a warning? For a moment she hesitated, then she had turned and said yes to the preacher's question. Yes to the man who could never understand her longing. She did what was expected of her there in the land of ocean and sun. She bore him a daughter and a son. But in all those years the man never understood the desire in her; he never explored her depth of passion. She turned to her dreams, and there she heard the voice of Epifano, a resonant voice imparting seductive images of the past.

Years later she left her husband, left everything, left the dream of southern California, where there was no love in the arms of the man, no sweet juices in the nights of love pretended. She left the circle of pretend. She needed a meaning; she needed desperately to understand the voices that spoke in her soul. She drove south, alone, in search of Epifano. The desert dried her by day but replenished her at night. She learned that the mystery of the stars at night was like the mystery in her soul.

She sketched, she painted, and each year in springtime, she drove farther south. On her map she marked her goal, the place where Epifano's hacienda had once stood.

In the desert the voices were clear. She followed the road into Tarahumara country, and she dreamed of the old man Epifano. She was his blood, the only one who remembered him.

At the end of day she stood at the side of a pool of water, a small desert spring surrounded by desert trees. The smell of the air was cool, wet. At her feet, tracks of deer, a desert cat. Ocelot. She stooped to drink, like a cautious animal.

"Thank the gods for this water, which quenches our thirst," she said, splashing the precious water on her face, knowing there is no life in the desert without the water that flows from deep within the earth. Around her, the first stars of dusk began to appear.

She had come at last to the ranch of Epifano. There, below the spring where she stood, on the flat ground, was the hacienda. Now could be seen only the outlines of the foundation and the shape of the old corrals. From here his family had spread, northwest, up into Mexicali, and finally into southern California. Seeds. Desert seeds seeking precious water. The water of desire. And only she had returned.

She sat and gazed at the desert, the peaceful quiet, the mauve of the setting sun. She felt a deep sadness within. An old woman, sitting alone in the wide desert, her dream done.

A noise caused her to turn, perhaps an animal come to drink at the spring, the same spring where Epifano had once wet his lips. She waited, and in the shadows of the palo verde and the desert willows, she saw the Indian appear. She smiled.

She was dressed in white, the color of desire not consummated. Shadows moved around her. She had come home, home to the arms of Epifano. The Indian was a tall, splendid man. Silent. He wore paint, as they had in the old days when they ran the game of the pelota up and down las montañas of el Cañon de Cobre.

"Epifano," she said. "I came in search of Epifano." He understood the name. Epifano. He held his hand to his chest. His eyes were bright and blue, not Tarahumara eyes, but the eyes of Epifano. He had known she would come. Around her, other shadows moved, the women. Indian women of the desert. They moved silently around her, a circle of women, an old ceremony about to begin.

The sadness left her. She struggled to rise, and in the dying light of the sun, a blinding flash filled her body. Like desire, or like an arrow from the bow of the Indian, the light filled her and she quivered.

The moan of love is like the moan of life. She was dressed in white.

Dead End

Maria hurried down the noisy, crowded hallway to her locker. She was on her way to calculus class, and she had forgotten her notebook with yesterday's notes.

She paused when she saw Frankie Galvan and his friends standing in front of her locker. Maria's heart skipped a beat. He was handsome, and lately he had been watching her.

"Hi, Maria," he said and moved away.

"Hi," Maria replied and fumbled as she opened her locker.

The other girls waited until Frankie was gone, then they teased Maria.

"Hi, Maria," Sandra said, imitating Frankie. "My you look nice today." The girls laughed. They were sharp dressers, while Maria wore only plain skirts and blouses.

"If you want Frankie to notice you, put on some lipstick," Denise said. She finished doing her lips and held out the stick.

Maria shook her head. "Gotta go to class."

"The cholos like lips red as wine." Ana laughed.

"And get out of those rags," Sandra remarked sarcastically. She was dressed in skin-tight jeans and a low-cut tank top that revealed her full breasts. Her lips were bright red, her eyelids purple with eye shadow.

As Maria walked away, she secretly wished she could be like those girls. They didn't spend time with homework. Each day after school, they cruised around the barrio. On weekends they went to parties, drank, smoked dope, and climbed in the back seats of cars with the homeboys.

Each morning they arrived late to school, sauntered into the bathroom to smoke, then, when they were good and ready, they dragged to class and sat. They did their nails and discussed the prior night's adventure. They were tough, and they were always getting suspended for one thing or another.

Maria wished she could belong to their gang. She wished she could be free and easy like them, but since Maria could remember, her mother had impressed on her the importance of an education.

"I never had the chance," her mother said, "because an education was only for boys. A girl was supposed to get married, raise kids, take care of her family. But you're smart, Maria. You must study and become educated."

Two years ago, at her mother's deathbed, Maria had promised she would not give up her dream of getting a good education. Her mother's life had been hard, and the promise had brought a smile to her lips. Her daughter would be someone important, a teacher or a doctor. She would help people, and her life would have meaning.

Now the promise weighed heavily on Maria. She had very little idea of what getting a good education entailed, even though she tried hard at school. There was no one to talk to; her father was seldom home after the death of her mother. Once a week he gave her enough money to buy food for her and her younger brother and sister; otherwise he returned only late at night. On weekends he was always gone.

There had been love in the family; now there was only bitterness in her father's face, a sense of loss.

She sent her brother and sister to school each morning and prepared supper at night. In the evenings she helped them with their homework. She was a senior in high school; she had too much to do. She had to be like a mother to them and still keep up her studies.

Many nights when she couldn't sleep, she got up and stood looking out the window. Things seemed hopeless, and she wondered how she could keep going. Then she would remember the promise she had made her mother and she would feel better.

That night as Maria was helping her little sister with her homework, the gang from school parked in front of Maria's home. They honked the horn; their car radio blasted the latest rap.

"Hey, Maria! Let's cruise!" Denise shouted.

"Let's have fun!" Ana yelled.

Maria looked through the window at the car outside. The kids were drinking beer and laughing wildly. The girls were dressed in low-cut blouses, shorts, and summer sandals. They snuggled against the boys and teased them.

Eduardo was driving, and Sandra had her arms wrapped around him. Next to them, Frankie Galvan sat alone. He looked out the open window at Maria.

Maria's heart melted. Frankie Galvan was about the most handsome guy in school. For the past few weeks, he had been hanging around her locker, and the girls began to whisper that he had a crush on Maria. They wondered why Frankie was interested in Maria when he could have any girl.

"Who is it?" Maria's sister asked behind her.

"Frankie Galvan," her brother said, peering through the parted curtains. "He's the baddest vato in the barrio."

Maria looked out again.

Yes, he was sitting alone; his black hair was slicked back, his dark eyes staring ahead. A gold chain glittered around his neck. The kids said he took dope. A year ago his girlfriend had died in a car accident, and it had really affected Frankie. Sometimes he hung around with the gang, but usually he was alone.

He's lonely, Maria thought. Her heart went out to him. When she saw him at school, he smiled and she felt goose bumps. She daydreamed of being held in his arms. She had never had a boyfriend or made love in the back seat of a car. She was too busy trying to keep the family together.

"Don't go," her little sister whimpered. "Don't leave us alone," she said, her eyes full of tears.

Her sister still hadn't accepted their mother's death. Sometimes she had nightmares at night, and Maria had to sleep with her to calm her fears.

Her brother was only thirteen, but already he was a leader in his own gang. "I wanna be like Frankie someday. Nobody messes with him," he said, then he turned away and ran out the back door.

Maria started after him, because she knew that the barrio streets at night could be dangerous for a thirteen-year-old. Some of the boys smoked marijuana, some sniffed spray paint, and the door of the crack house on Delmar Street was always open.

She could hear the kids yelling and singing outside. "Hasta la vista, baby!" Denise called.

Maria looked through the window and saw Frankie turn to look at her; his eyes were inviting. Then the kids were gone.

Maria slumped into the sofa. She felt anger inside, a terrible anger at the unfairness of it all. Why couldn't she be out there? Why couldn't she dress like the other girls and cruise at night? Why couldn't she sit in the back seat of Frankie's car and feel his strong arms around her, and his warm kisses?

Tears wet her cheeks. Her sister stood beside her and stroked Maria's long black hair. Maria smiled at her. "Come on," she said, "let's finish your homework."

The next day, the gang hung out around the entrance to the school, taking last-minute drags of their cigarettes before they went in. Maria and her friend Sue Yonemoto were hurrying to calculus class.

Ana stopped Maria as she passed by,

"Hey, Mary, why didn't you come with us last night?"

Maria looked at her but didn't answer.

"Frankie was lonely," Sandra said. The girls around her made swooning sounds and laughed.

"She don't have a chance with Frankie," Denise said.

Just then Frankie came around the corner.

Suddenly there was a silence in the air, a chill. Everyone knew nobody messed with Frankie.

Frankie scowled at Denise. She turned away in embarrassment. Then he smiled at Maria. He knew she read books, that she was smart. She answered the teacher's questions in class. She wasn't like the other girls. She was different, and he wanted her.

That night Frankie drove up in front of Maria's house. He was alone. He parked and waited. Maria finally went out and walked slowly to the car. She could smell the fresh air of the spring night, and a faint fragrance of blossoms. School was almost out, and Frankie had come to park in front of her house.

She felt like she was floating in air. That morning as he had passed by her, he had whispered, "Hey, I'll come by tonight." The way he'd looked at her told her he was serious.

"Hi," she said, smiling.

"Hey," Frankie answered. "Want to cruise?"

She looked back at the house where her sister and brother stood at the window.

"I can go for a while," she said and waved at her brother and sister. "Be back in an hour!" she called and got into the car.

Frankie drove off slowly. In the dark, his handsome features were outlined against the lights of the street. The car smelled of sweet smoke mixed with the fragrance of hair dressing. He offered her a cigarette.

"I don't smoke," Maria said.

"What do you do?" Frankie asked, a strange laughter in his voice.

Frankie headed toward the bridge. There he parked and finished his cigarette. The sounds of the city seemed distant and remote.

When he finished smoking, he took Maria in his arms and kissed her. The warmth of his kiss excited her. She had never been kissed like this. She kissed him back, but when his hands begin to explore her body, she resisted.

"Why not?" he asked.

She didn't know why not. Making out was what most of the girls talked about in the school bathroom. Going all the way was expected; it just depended on who you did it with. And how high you got.

"I'm just not ready," Maria answered, and she thought of the promise she had made her mother. She knew the kids who cruised every night didn't keep up with their schoolwork.

Couldn't she do both? For a moment she thought the promise she had made was a foolish thing. Even if she got into a university, even if she got grants and loans, she still needed more money on top of that. And where was it going to come from? Who was going to take care of her brother and sister? It was a crazy dream, and she might as well forget it.

"Maybe this will help," Frankie whispered, and he lit a joint. He inhaled deeply and passed it to Maria. "Go on, take a hit. Make you mellow."

Maria hesitated. She had heard the story a thousand times, especially from the girls:

"A little weed puts you in a loving mood."

"Mellow, mellow for your fellow."

A lot of those girls had dropped out, and some had gone on to be regulars at the crack house on Delmar.

"Go on," Frankie whispered in the dark. The glowing ember of the joint was bright in the dark, and the thin feather of smoke was like a snake that swayed as it rose.

Suck me in and hold me, the smoke said, and watch the problems slip away.

Maria reached out and took the joint. She had tried smoking once, in the privacy of her bathroom. It had made her sick. But she had wondered what marijuana was like, why it was so widely used by the kids. She had thought of trying it. Now was her chance.

She paused. Was she doing it for herself, or for Frankie? Was she doing it just to belong?

Outside, near the looming shadow of the dark bridge, a shadow moved. She heard a moaning sound, like a woman crying.

"Look!"

Frankie looked as the shadow disappeared into the dark.

"Bag lady," he said. "Go on, take a hit."

"She was crying," Maria said.

"You're not afraid, are you? Miss Wonder Woman who gets A's in all her tests, scared?" Frankie chuckled.

"Did you ever hear the story of la Llorona?" Maria asked.

"Yeah, the crazy woman who cries at night?" Frankie laughed. "Yeah, my mom used to tell it to me. It's just a story to scare kids."

"Maybe," Maria replied. "My mother told me that the story really happened. The young woman fell in love with a man. He was a sharp dresser, always had women around him. He made his living playing cards. He promised to love her, got her pregnant, then he wouldn't help her."

"Smart dude," Frankie said. "I figure if a woman wants to get pregnant, that's her problem."

Maria continued. "The girl's father said the family's honor had been soiled, so he kicked her out of the house. She had nowhere to go, no one to turn to. When the baby was born, she drowned it."

Frankie sat up straight. "It's not a real story, is it?"

Maria nodded. "She drowned the child here, beneath the bridge."

"You're kidding," Frankie said.

"She had no help," Maria continued. "She went crazy and drowned the baby. Now she cries at night, looking for her child."

"Damn," Frankie whispered. He looked out into the darkness. The night had grown cool. There was only silence in the night, except for strange sounds, the distant wail of a siren.

"I'm going to be different," Maria said softly. Frankie looked puzzled.

She handed the marijuana cigarette back to him.

He took it. "Why not?"

"I don't want to drown my children," Maria answered.

Frankie didn't understand what she meant. He touched saliva to his fingertips and put out the joint. "What's the matter with you? You don't smoke, you don't dress like the other girls. You think you're too good?"

Maria shuddered. She had heard that accusation before. The girls whispered behind her back. "She thinks she's too good for us. Runs around with the Japanese girl. Calculus Club. Just too damn good!"

First, Maria had tried to explain. No, she didn't think she was too good for them. But she couldn't explain to them about the promise to her mother. She couldn't tell them she wanted to go to college, because few of the girls from that school had ever dared try. Most of them drifted off, got married, or just disappeared. Maria didn't want to just disappear. She wanted her life to have meaning, and that meant keeping to her mother's dream.

"Take me home," Maria said. She knew that saying "take me home" meant she was saying goodbye to Frankie Galvan. It also meant not belonging to the gang.

"Yeah, okay," Frankie answered. He started the car and they drove slowly back to Maria's. As they drove, Maria felt the anguish of her choice. Why, she asked herself, oh why couldn't I just let go? Let go of my dream. Follow Frankie. He was the only young man who had ever invited her out, held her in his arms, kissed her. She wanted to reach out and touch him and tell him she would stay with him.

She felt a real longing for him, and she knew that she would always remember this night. But seeing the figure of the woman in the night had reminded her that life was a struggle, and that she had to take care of herself. Frankie's life was headed toward a dead end. She just didn't want to wind up with him on that street.

He parked and looked at her. "Hey, I like you. I'm sorry for what I said. So, you're different. That's why I like you. Maybe I can call you later."

"School's almost over, and all the exams are coming up," Maria said.

"School isn't everything." Frankie smiled in the dark. "You gotta have some fun."

Yes, she thought. School isn't everything. When he had kissed her, she had felt she really cared for him. Maybe she had put too much of her time and energy into schoolwork.

"Maybe after exams are over," she said.

"Yeah, maybe," he replied.

"Goodbye," she whispered and leaned toward him. "Thank you." She kissed Frankie on the cheek.

She quickly got out of the car and ran into the house.

The Man Who Could Fly

One evening in the village of Agua Bendita, the neighbors of don Necio and doña Catarina gathered in their patio. The villagers had worked hard in their fields all day, and the cool of the evening was a welcome respite.

A small fire was lighted in the center of the patio to provide light and a center for the storytelling. Don Necio burned dry cow chips in the hot coals. The smoke would keep the mosquitoes away.

That morning don Necio had put two large watermelons in the cold water of his well. Now the cold watermelons were sliced and eaten, a perfect end to the day.

Tonight the conversation drifted to the topic of flight. When they worked in their fields, the villagers would hear the roar of airplanes overhead. They would lift their gazes skyward and see the tiny specks in the blue sky. There was a war going on, and the airplanes were on their way to join the fighting.

The people discussed these things in their quiet way, and they formed opinions of the world beyond their isolated village.

During a lull in the conversation, don Sarco leaned forward. The light from the flames made his face appear mysterious.

"What about those people who can fly without the aid of machines," he whispered.

"No such thing!" Don Necio countered. He and don Sarco loved to argue.

"Witches!" Doña Catarina shivered.

Suddenly the night grew cool, and those gathered around the dying fire drew closer. There were things in the night they knew little about, and there were many stories of witches who roamed the countryside.

In the hills a coyote yelped, and along the river an owl hooted an answer.

"I heard of a man over in Llano Seco who could fly," don Sarco said. "Yes, they claimed the old man could fly."

The neighbors smiled uneasily and stole glances at don Volo, the man who sat alone in the dark corner of the patio. He was from Llano Seco, and he had appeared in the valley a few years ago.

The villagers knew very little about his past, for he kept to himself. He had come to live in Agua Bendita, and he farmed the poorest land along the valley, but he made it prosper. There was something in his quiet dignity the people respected.

"I heard that story," don Necio said, "but I don't believe it. Flight is for the birds. Or for angels. But a man who can fly, no señor."

"If the Lord had intended for us to fly, he would have given us wings," his compadre agreed, hoping to put an end to the discussion.

"We would be half bird, half human," someone joked.

"At least we could eat corn," another said.

"But which half of us would be bird and which half human?" someone asked.

"If the front half is bird, then we can eat corn, but we couldn't plant corn," don Necio said. "What good are wings if you can't plant corn?"

Yes, the neighbors agreed with the hawk-nosed don Necio.

"And if the back half is a bird, we would have bird legs," doña Catarina said. "I couldn't pick the ripe vegetables to take to market."

The neighbors smiled in agreement. Don Necio and doña Catarina were respected for their wisdom. The story of the man who could fly was just that, a story.

Only don Volo seemed to disagree. He rose to speak. All turned to look at him across the dying flames.

In the starry summer night, the ripe scent of the cornfields wafted into the patio. The fragrance of the ripening apples in the orchards also lent a perfume to the night air. Overhead the swirl of the Milky Way was a river of starlight.

"Forgive me," don Volo said. "But I must say I disagree with you. The story of the man who could fly is real."

Don Necio scoffed. "I think we have proven how difficult it would be to be half bird and half man."

"He was not half man and half bird," don Volo answered. "He was a man like you and me. Plain, hardworking, but he lived in a world of magic we do not understand."

"Ah," the neighbors intoned. So this was a story about magic. They loved stories of ghosts and witches. Such stories had been handed down for generations in the valley, and they knew most by heart. But they didn't know the real story of the man who could fly.

"Allow me to tell you the story," don Volo said.

Don Necio glanced at the stars. He felt the cool breeze rising from the river. It was late, and tomorrow they had to hoe the fields. But they could not resist a good story.

"Fine, but make it short. Farmers must rise early to work."

"This happened not far from here," don Volo began. "On the open grass plain called Llano Seco. Some young vaqueros and the owner of the ranch had been rounding up cattle. After many days of hard work, they had the large herd together.

"The young vaqueros knew that a dance was taking place in the village of Las Animas, ten miles away, and they were eager to go. They put on their clean clothes and saddled fresh horses. Only the old man who was the cook did not hurry."

"Aren't you going to the dance?" the ranch owner asked.

"Yes," the old man replied. "But first I will wash the dishes and clean the camp."

"Do that tomorrow," the young vaqueros replied. "By the time you clean up we will have danced half the night."

"Oh no," the old man answered. "You go ahead. I'll clean everything and be at the dance before you."

The vaqueros laughed. "But you have only your old burro to ride," they said. "How can you be there before us?"

"I'll be there before you," the old man answered, slowly going about his business.

The owner of the herd grew irritated. "If you get there before us, my entire herd is yours. If we are there before you, then you must work for me without pay for the rest of your life."

"My life of work for your herd is not an even bet," the old man said. "Why not add all the land you own?"

The ranch owner looked at the old man and his burro. There was no way he could beat the vaqueros on fast horses to the dance. "Very well," he said, "my land and herds are yours if you win."

Here don Volo paused in his story. He cocked his head when an owl hooted nearby. A breeze fanned the dying embers, then the patio grew dark.

"They shook hands, and when the ranch owner felt the hand of the old man, he felt a surge of energy he had never felt before."

Don Necio leaned forward. "What happened?" he asked.

Don Volo's voice was hushed as he answered.

"The vaqueros rode hard. They had fresh horses, and yet when they arrived at the dance hall, the cook from the camp was waiting for them by the door."

Everyone gasped. They had heard stories of the man who could fly. Some people believed such stories, others didn't.

"Impossible," don Necio whispered.

"No, it is true," don Volo replied.

"Who told you this story? Why should we believe it?" Don Necio asked.

Don Volo paused. "I was the rancher who bet his land and herds that night," he replied.

The villagers stared in astonishment. Don Volo was the man who had made a bet with the man who could fly. For many years the story of the old man who could fly had been whispered, but nobody knew of the rancher who bet his wealth.

He had lost the wager, but he had learned a great lesson, for he had been there at that moment of magic.

"Man can fly," don Volo whispered, and as the last embers of the fire died, a rustling of owl wings filled the dark patio, and he stepped into the dark and was gone.

Acknowledgments

"Absalom" was originally published in *Imagine: International Chicano Poetry Journal* (vol. 2, no. 2, 1998), 10–13.

"The Apple Orchard" was previously published in *Hispanics in the United States, An Anthology of Creative Literature* (Gary D. Keller and Francisco Jiménez, eds., Tempe, Ariz.: Bilingual Review Press, 1980), 129–36; *The Silence of the Llano* (Berkeley, Calif.: Tonatiuh-Quinto Sol, 1982), 67–83 (first printing), 65–81 (second printing); and *Growing Up Latino: Memoirs and Stories* (Harold Augenbraum and Ilan Stavans, eds., Boston: Houghton Mifflin, 1993), 292–304.

"B. Traven is Alive and Well in Cuernavaca" was previously published in *Escolios* (vol. 4, no. 1-2, May–November, 1979), 1–12; *The Silence of the Llano* (Berkeley, Calif.: Tonatiuh-Quinto Sol, 1982), 127–46 (first printing), 129–49 (second printing); *Cuentos Chicanos: A Short Story Anthology* (Rudolfo A. Anaya and Antonio Márquez, eds., Albuquerque: University of New Mexico Press, 1984), 1–13; *Harper American Literature* (vol. 2, Donald McQuade et al., ed., New York: Harper and Row, 1987), 2644–54; *The Winchester Reader* (Donald McQuade and Robert Atwan, eds., Boston: St. Martin's Press, 1991); *Fictions* (4th ed., Joseph F. Trimmer and C. Wade Jennings, eds., Fort Worth, Tex.: Harcourt Brace College Publishers, 1998); and *The Literary West: An Anthology of Western American Literature* (Thomas J. Lyon, ed., New York: Oxford University Press, 1999) 291–303.

"The Captain" was previously published in *A Decade of Hispanic Literature: An Anniversary Anthology* (Nicolas Kanellos, ed., Houston, Tex.: Revista Chicano-Riquena, 1982), 151–60; and *The Floating Borderlands: Twenty-five Years of U.S. Hispanic Literature* (Lauro Flores, ed., Seattle: University of Washington Press, 1998), 15–23.

"Children of the Desert" was published as "Figli del Deserto" in *L'umana Avventura* (Milan, Italy, Spring/Summer 1989), 108–110, and as "Children of the Desert" in *The Seattle Review* (Donna Gerstenberger, ed., vol. XIII, no. 1, Seattle: University of Washington, 1990), 130–37, and in *The Best of the West 4: New Stories From the Wide Side of the Missouri* (James Thomas and Denise Thomas, eds., New York: W.W. Norton and Company, 1991), 87–95.

"Dead End" was previously published in *Join In: Multiethnic Short Stories* (Donald R. Gallo, ed., New York: Delacorte Press, 1993), 101–109. Reprinted with permission.

"Devil Deer" was previously published in *Arellano* (Juan Estevan Arellano, ed., vol. 1, no. 2, March\April, 1992), 10–11; *Literature and Environment* (Scott Anderson and Scott Slovic, eds., High Bridge, N.J.: Fred Courtright, 1997); and *Getting over the Color Green: Contemporary Environmental Literature of the Southwest* (Scott Slovic, ed., Tucson: University of Arizona Press, 2001), 275–81.

"Iliana of the Pleasure Dreams" was previously published in *ZYZZYVA* (vol. 1, no. 4, 1985), 50–61; *Tierra: Contemporary Short Fiction of New Mexico* (Rudolfo A. Anaya, ed., El Paso, Tex.: Cinco Puntos Press, 1989), 255–65; and *Dreams and Desperados: Contemporary Short Fiction of the American West* (Craig Lesley, ed., New York: Dell Publishing, 1993), 23–33.

"In Search of Epifano" was previously published in *Voces: An Anthology of Nuevo Mexicano Writers* (Rudolfo Anaya, ed., Albuquerque: University of New Mexico Press, 1987), 222–26; *Wind Row* (vol. 5, no. 2, Pullman, Wash.: Washington State University, Department of English, 1987), 1–3; *Iguana Dreams: New Latino Fiction* (Delia Poey and Virgil Suarez, ed., New York: Harper Collins, 1992), 17–23; *Literature, Race, and Ethnicity: Contesting American Identities* (Joseph Skerrett, ed., Niles, Ill.: Longman Publishers, 2001), 373–75; *Da Costa a Costa* (Mario Materassi, ed., Bari, Italy: Palomar, 2004), 69–75; and *American Love Stories* (Reingard M. Nischik, ed., Stuttgart, Germany: Reclam, 2003), 148–57.

"Jerónimo's Journey" was originally published as "The Gift" in *2Plus2: A Collection of International Writing* (James Gill, ed., Lausanne, Switzerland: Mylabris Press, 1986), 38–49.

"The Man Who Could Fly" was previously unpublished.

"The Man Who Found a Pistol" was previously published in *Mirrors Beneath the Earth: Short Fiction by Chicano Writers* (Ray González, ed., Willimantic, Conn.: Curbstone Press, 1992), 280–87; and *LC Literary Cavalcade* (vol. 48, no. 2, 1995), 9–11.

"Message From the Inca" was previously published in *RSA Journal, Rivista Annuale della Associazione di Studi Nord-Americani* (Mario Materassi, ed., no. 4, October Florence, Italy, 1994), 87–96.

"The Place of the Swallows" was previously published in *Voices from the Rio Grande: Selections From the First Rio Grande Writers Conference* (Albuquerque, N.Mex.: Rio Grande Writers Associated Press, 1976), 98–106; *The Silence of the Llano* (Berkeley, Calif.: Tonatiuh-Quinto Sol, 1982), 45–54 (first printing), 43–51 (second printing); *Nuestro* (vol. 7, no. 3, 1983), 18–19; and *Fiction Monthly* (vol. 1, no. 3, 1984), 1–2, 7.

"The Road to Platero" was previously published in *Anuario de Letras Chicanas* (Editorial Justa, 1979); *Rocky Mountain Magazine* (April 1982), 61–62, 84; and *The Silence of the Llano* (Berkeley, Calif.: Tonatiuh-Quinto Sol, 1982), 33–42 (first printing), 31–39 (second printing).

"The Silence of the Llano" was previously published in *The Silence of the Llano* (Berkeley, Calif.: Tonatiuh-Quinto Sol, 1982), 7–31 (first printing), 3–28 (second printing); *The Grito Del Sol Collection* (Octavio I. Romano, ed., Berkeley, Calif.: Tonatiuh-Quinto Sol, Winter 1984), 109–133; and *Mexican-American Short Stories* (Marga Munkelt, ed., Reclam Educational, Stuttgart, Germany: Reclam, 2004), 5–37.

"A Story" was previously published in *Grito del Sol* (vol. 3, no. 4, 1978), 45–46; *The Silence of the Llano* (Berkeley, Calif.: Tonatiuh-Quinto Sol, 1982), 111–25; *Understanding Fiction* (Judith Roof, ed., Boston: Houghton Mifflin, 2004), 514–21; and *Understanding Literature: An Introduction to Reading and Writing* (Walter Kalaidjian, Judith Roof, and Stephen Watt, eds., Boston: Houghton Mifflin, 2004), 514–21.

"The Village That the Gods Painted Yellow" was originally published as "The Village Which the Gods Painted Yellow" in *The Silence of the Llano* (Berkeley, Calif.: Tonatiuh-Quinto Sol, 1982), 149–71 (first printing), 153–74 (second printing).

Rudolfo Anaya, born in 1937, is a leading contemporary writer and a central figure in the rise of Chicano literature in the 1970s and in its later development. He has received many awards and distinctions worldwide, including the National Medal of Arts, the Premio Quinto Sol, and the Pen Center USA West Award. A professor emeritus of English at the University of New Mexico, he has been a major presence in Chicano and American literature and culture for almost forty years. He has also been a constant source of encouragement and support for young writers and scholars. He and his wife, Patricia, live in Albuquerque, New Mexico.